Life's little stage

by

Agnes Giberne

Double9
BOOKS

Life's little stage
by Agnes Giberne

Copyright © 2024

All Rights reserved.

ISBN: 978-93-64283-60-1

Published by

DOUBLE 9 BOOKS

2/13-B, Ansari Road
Daryaganj, New Delhi – 110002
info@double9books.com
www.double9books.com
Tel. 011-40042856

ABOUT THE AUTHOR

The British author Agnes Giberne lived from November 19, 1845, to August 20, 1939. She wrote a lot of novels and science papers. Her stories were typical of Victorian Christian stories for kids that had religious or moral themes. For kids, she wrote science books, and she also wrote a few historical stories and a well-known biography. Giberne was born in Belgaum, Karnataka, India. Her parents were Captain Charles Giberne (16 June 1808 – 21 December 1902) of the Bengal Native Infantry and Lydia Mary Wilson (c. 1816 – 20 May 1890). The Huguenots in her family tree came from Languedoc in France. The "de Gibernes" lived in Chateau de Gibertain. Charles Giberne came from a big family. Besides his brother, he had eight sisters. It was also where three of his brothers served. The wedding took place at St. Mary the Virgin, Walthamstow, on December 11, 1838, and Giberne was born. There is some doubt about how many brothers Giberne had. The India Family History and Families in British India Society records at the British Library show. By the 1851 census, Lydia Mary was living with the Rector of Eyam in Derbyshire and his family at Beach in Weston-super-Mare with her four children who were still alive.

CONTENTS

"Who can over-estimate the value of these little Opportunities?
How angels must weep to see us throw them away!
. . . And how can we ever expect to meet the great trials
worthily, unless we learn discipline by those which to others
may seem but trifles?" —ANON.

FOREWORD

THERE are many girls who, on leaving School for Home-life, find the year or two following rather "difficult." They seem often not quite to know what to do with themselves, with their time, with their gifts; and they are apt to fall into some needless mistakes for want of a guiding hand. My wish, in writing this tale, has been to give such girls a little help. It may be that one here or there, in reading it, will find out how to avoid such mistakes from the struggles, the defeats, and the non-defeats of Magda Royston.

AGNES GIBERNE.

EASTBOURNE.

CHAPTER I
GOOD-BYE TO SCHOOL

"SOME girls would be glad in your place."

"It's just the other way with me."

"Not that you have not been happy here. I know you have. Still—home is home."

"This is my other home."

Miss Mordaunt smiled. It was hardly in human nature not to be gratified.

"If only I could have stayed two years longer! Or even one year! Father might let me. It's such a horrid bore to have to leave now."

"But since no choice is left, you must make the best of things."

The two stood facing one another in the bow-window of Miss Mordaunt's pretty drawing-room; tears in the eyes of the elder woman, for hers was a sympathetic nature; no tears in the eyes of the girl, but a sharp ache at her heart. Till the arrival of this morning's post she never quite lost hope, though notice of her removal was given months before. A final appeal, vehemently worded, after the writer's fashion, had lately gone; and the reply was decisive.

Many a tussle of wills had taken place during the last four years between these two; and a time was when the pupil indulged in hard thoughts of the kind Principal. But Miss Mordaunt possessed power to win love; and though she found in Magda Royston a difficult subject, she conquered in the end. Out of battling grew strong affection—how strong on the side of Magda perhaps neither quite knew until this hour.

"There isn't any 'best.' It's just simply horrid."

"Still, if you are wanted at home, your duty lies there."

"I'm not. That's the thing. Nobody wants me. Mother has Penrose; and father has Merryl; and Frip—I mean, Francie—is the family pet. And I come in nowhere. I'm a sort of extraneous atom that can't coalesce with any other atom." A tinge of self-satisfaction crept into the tone. "It's not my fault.

Nobody at home needs me—not one least little bit. And there isn't a person in all the town that I care for—not one blessed individual!"

Miss Mordaunt seated herself on the sofa, drawing the speaker to her side, with a protesting touch.

"There isn't. Pen snaps them all up. And if she didn't, it would come to the same thing. I'm not chummy with girls—never was. I had a real friend once; but he was a boy; and boys are so different. Ned Fairfax and I were immense chums; but he was years and years older than me; and he went right away when I was only eleven. I've never set eyes on him since, and I don't even know now what has become of him. Only I know we should be friends again—directly—if ever we met! The girls and I get on well enough here, but we're not friends."

"Except Beatrice."

"Bee is a little dear, and I dote on her; and she worships the ground I tread on. But after all—though she is more than a year older, she always seems the younger. And I'm much more to her than she is to me. Don't you see? I wouldn't say that to everybody, but it's true. I want something more than that, if it is to satisfy! Bee looks up to me. I want some one that I can look up to."

"There is much more in Bee than appears on the surface."

"I dare say. She pegs away, and gets on. She'll be awfully useful at home. And in a sort of way she is taking."

"People find her extremely taking. She is a friend worth having and worth keeping. But I hope you are going to have friends in Burwood."

"There's nobody. Oh well, yes, there is one—but she doesn't live there. She only comes down to a place near for a week or ten days at a time. Her name is Patricia, and she is a picture! I've seen her just three times, and I fell in love straight off. But I haven't a ghost of a chance. Everybody runs after her. Oh, I shall get on all right. There's Rob, you know. He and I have always been cronies; and it's quite settled that I shall keep house for him some day. Not till he gets a living; and that won't be yet. He was only ordained two years ago."

"I should advise you not to build too much on that notion. Your brother may marry."

Magda's eyes blazed. They were singular golden-brown eyes, with a reddish tinge in the iris, matching her hair.

"You don't know Rob! He always says he never comes across any girls to be compared with his sisters. And I always was his special! He promised—years ago—that I should live with him by-and-by. At least—if he didn't exactly promise, he said it. Father jeers at the idea, but Rob means what he says."

Miss Mordaunt hesitated to throw further cold water. Life itself would bring the chill splash soon enough.

"Well—perhaps," she admitted. "Only, it is always wiser not to look forward too confidently. Things turn out so unlike what one expects beforehand. Have you not found it so?"

"I'm sure this won't. It will all come right, I know. But just imagine father talking about my having 'finished my education.' Oh dear me, if he would but understand! He says his own sisters finished theirs at seventeen, and he doesn't see any need for new-fangled ways. You may read it!" Magda held out the sheet with an indignant thrust. "As if it mattered what they used to do in the Dark Ages."

Miss Mordaunt could not quite suppress another smile. She read the letter and gave it back.

"That settles the matter, I am afraid. I see that your father wants his daughter."

"He doesn't!" bluntly. "He wants nobody except Merryl. 'Finished my education' indeed! Why, I'm not seventeen till next month; and I'm only just beginning to know what real work means."

Miss Mordaunt could have endorsed this; but an interruption came. She was called away; and Magda wandered to one of the class-rooms, where, as she expected, she found a girl alone bending over a desk, hard at work—a girl nearly as tall as herself, but so slight in make that people often spoke of her as "little;" the more so, perhaps, from her gentle retiring manner, and from the look of wistful appeal in her brown eyes. It was a pale face, even-featured, with rather marked dark brows and brown hair full of natural waves. As Magda entered she jumped up.

"I've been wanting to see you, Magda. Only think—"

"I went to tell Miss Mordaunt—father has written at last."

"Has he? And he says—?"

"I'm to go home for good at the end of the term."

"Then we leave together, after all."

"It's right enough for you. You've had an extra year. But I do hate it—just as I am getting to love work—to have to stop."

"You won't stop. You are so clever. You will keep on with everything."

"It can't be the same—working all alone."

Beatrice looked sympathetic, but only remarked—"I have heard from my mother too. And only think! We are to leave town. Not now, but some time next year; when the lease of our house is up. Guess where we may perhaps live!"

"Not—Burwood!" dubiously.

Bee clapped joyous hands.

"What can have made your mother think of such a thing?"

"Why, Magda! Wouldn't you be glad to have us?"

"Of course. But I mean—how did it come into her head?"

"I put the notion there. Wouldn't you have done it in my place? London never has suited her; and our doctor advises the country. And I said something in my last about Burwood—not really thinking that anything would come of it. But mother has quite taken to the idea. She used to stay near, sometimes, when she was a child; and she remembers well how pretty the walks and drives were. It would make all the difference to me if we were near to you. I should not mind so very much then having to leave Amy."

Magda was not especially fond of hearing about this other great friend—Amy Smith. Whatever her estimate might be, in the abstract, of the value of Bee, she liked to have the whole of her; not to share her with somebody else. Certainly not with a "Miss Smith!"

"You see, I've been near Amy all my life; and she is so good to me—too good! She's years older, but we are just like sisters, and I don't know how I shall get on without her. But if it is to come near you, dear, saying good-bye won't be quite so hard."

"It will be frightfully nice if you do. We can do no end of things together. I suppose it's not settled yet."

"No; only, if mother once takes to a plan, she doesn't soon give it up. So I'm very hopeful. Just think! If I were always near you! And you were always coming in and out!"

"It would be frightfully nice!" repeated Magda, throwing into her voice what Bee would expect to hear. But when she strolled away, she questioned within herself—was she glad? Would she be more disappointed or more relieved if the scheme fell through?

The notion of introducing Beatrice Major to her home-circle did not quite appeal to her. The Roystons held their heads high, and moved in county circles, and were extremely particular as to whom they deigned to know. Bee herself was the dearest little creature—pretty and lovable, sweet and kind; but she had been only two years in the school, and Magda had met none of Bee's people. They might very easily fail to suit her people.

Beatrice, it was true, never seemed to mind being questioned about her home and connections; but it was equally true that she never appeared to have very much to say—at least of any such particulars as would impress the Royston imagination; and this was suggestive. Magda had heard so much all her life about people's antecedents, that she might be excused for feeling nervous. She had seen a photo of Bee's mother, and thought her a very unattractive person; also a photo of Amy Smith, which was worse still. She knew that Mrs. Major could not be too well off, for Bee's command of pocket-money was by no means plentiful, and her wardrobe was limited.

They would probably live in some poky little house. And though Magda could talk grandly about not caring what other people thought, and though personally she would not perhaps mind about the said house, yet she would mind extremely if her own particular friend were looked down upon by her home-folks. The very idea of Pen's air of mild disdain stung sharply.

So altogether she felt that, if the plan failed, she would not be very sorry. But Bee might on no account guess this.

Several weeks later came the day of parting; and once more Magda stood before Miss Mordaunt with a lump in her throat.

"You will have to work steadily, if you do not mean to lose all you have gained, Magda."

"I know. I shall make a plan for every day, and stick to it."

"Except when home duties come between."

"I've no home duties. Pen goes everywhere with mother, and Merryl does all the little useful fidgets. There's nothing left for me. Nobody will care what I'm after."

Miss Mordaunt studied the impressionable face. Some eager thought was at work below the surface.

"What is it, my dear?"

"You always know when I've something on my mind. I've been thinking a lot lately. Miss Mordaunt, I want to do something with my life. Not just to drift along anyhow, as so many girls do. I want to make something of it. Something great, you know!"—and her eyes glowed. "Do you think I shall ever be able? Does the chance come to everybody some time or other? I've heard it said that it does."

"It may. Many miss the 'chance,' as you call it, when it does come. I should rather call it 'the opportunity.' What do you mean by 'something great'?"

"Oh—Why!—You know! Something above the common run. Like Grace Darling, or Miss Florence Nightingale, or that Duchess who stayed behind in the French bazaar to be burnt to death, so that others might escape. It was noblesse oblige with her, wasn't it? I think it would be grand to do something of that sort,—that would be always remembered and talked about."

"Perhaps so. But don't forget that what one is in the little things of life, one is also in the great things. More than one rehearsal is generally given to us before the 'great opportunity' is sent. And if we fail in the rehearsals, we fail then also."

"Yes—I know. And I do mean to work at my studies. But all the same, I should like to do something, some day, really and truly great."

Miss Mordaunt looked wistfully at the girl. "Dear Magda—real greatness does not mean being talked about. It means—doing the Will of God in our lives—doing our duty, and doing it for Him."

CHAPTER II
WHAT WAS THE USE?

MANY months later that parting interview with Miss Mordaunt recurred vividly to Magda.

"What's the good of it all, I wonder?" she had been asking aloud.

And suddenly, as if called up from a far distance, she saw again Miss Mordaunt's face, and heard again her own confident utterances.

It was a bitterly cold March afternoon. She stood alone under the great walnut tree in the back garden—which was divided by a tall hedge from the kitchen garden. Over her head was a network of bare boughs; and upon the grass at her feet lay a pure white carpet. Some lilac bushes near had begun to show promise of coming buds; but they looked doleful enough now, weighed down by snow.

She had with such readiness promised steady work in the future! And she had meant it too.

The thing seemed so easy beforehand. And for a time she really had tried. But she had not kept it up. She had not worked persistently. She had not "stuck" to her plans. The contrast between intention and non-fulfilment came upon her now with force.

Six months had gone by of home-life, of emancipation from school control. Six months of aimless drifting—the very thing she had resolved sturdily against.

"Oh, bother! What's the use of worrying? Why can't I take things as Pen does? Pen never seems to mind." But she was in the grip of a cogitative mood, and thinking would not be stayed.

She had begun well enough—had planned daily two hours of music, an hour of history, an hour of literature, an hour alternately of French and German. It had all looked fair and promising. And the whole had ended in smoke.

Something always seemed to come in the way. The children wanted a ramble. Or she was sent on an errand. Or a caller came in. Or there was an invitation. Or—oftener and worse!—disinclination had her by the throat.

Disinclination which, no doubt, might have been, and ought to have been, grappled with and overcome. Only, she had not grappled with it. She had not overcome. She had yielded, time after time.

It was so difficult to work alone; so dull to sit and read in her own room; so stupid to write a translation that nobody would see; so tiresome to practice when there was none to praise or blame. Not that she liked blame; and not that she was not expected to practice; but no marked interest was shown in her advance; and she wanted sympathy and craved an object. And it was so fatally easy to put off, to let things slide, to get out of the way of regular plans. The fact that any time would do equally well soon meant no time.

This had been a typical day; and she reviewed it ruefully. A morning of aimless nothings; the mending of clothes idly deferred; hours spent in the reading of a foolish novel; jars with Penrose; friction with her mother; a sharp set-down from her father; then forgetfulness of wrongs and resentment during a romp in the snow with Merryl and Frip—till the younger girls were summoned indoors, leaving her to descend at a plunge from gaiety to disquiet. Magda's variations were many.

She stood pondering the subject—a long-limbed well-grown girl, young in look for her years, with a curly mass of red-brown hair, seldom tidy, and a pair of expressive eyes. They could look gentle and loving, though that phase was not common; they could sparkle with joy or blaze with anger; they could be dull as a November fog; they could, as at this moment, turn their regards inwards with uneasy self-condemnation.

But it was a condemnation of self which she would not have liked anybody else to echo. No one quicker, you may be sure, than Magda Royston in self-defence! Even now words of excuse sprang readily, as she stood at the bar of her own judgment.

"After all, I don't see that it is my fault. I can't help things being as they are. And suppose I had worked all these months at music and history and languages—what then? What would be the good? It would be all for myself. I should be just as useless to other people."

A vision arose of the great things she had wished to do, and she stamped the snow flat.

"It's no good. I've no chance. There's nothing to be done that I can see. If I had heaps of money to give away! Or if I had a special gift—if I could write books, or could paint pictures! Or even if my people were poor, and I could work hard to get money for them! Anything like that would make all the difference. As it is—well, I know I have brains of a sort; better brains than Pen! But I don't see what I can do with them. I don't see that I can do anything out of the common, or better than hundreds of other people do. And that is so stupid. Not worth the trouble!"

"Mag-da!" sounded in Pen's clear voice.

"She never can leave me in peace! I'm not going indoors yet."

"Mag-da!" Three times repeated, was followed by—"Where are you? Mother says you are to come."

This could not be disregarded. "Coming," she called carelessly, and in a slow saunter she followed the boundary of the kitchen garden hedge, trailed through the back yard, stopped to exchange a greeting with the house-dog as he sprang to the extent of his chain, stroked the stately Persian cat on the door-step, and finally presented herself in the inner hall.

It was one of the oldest houses in the country town of Burwood; rather small, but antique. Once upon a time it had stood alone, surrounded by its own broad acres; but things were changed, and the acres had shrunk—through the extravagance of former Roystons—to only a fair-sized garden. The rest of the land had been sold for building; and other houses in gardens stood near. In the opinion of old residents, this was no longer real country; and with new-comers, the Roystons no longer ranked as quite the most important people in the near neighbourhood. Their means were limited enough to make it no easy matter for them to remain on in the house, and they could do little in the way of entertaining. But they prided themselves still on their exclusiveness.

Penrose stood waiting; a contrast to Magda, who was five years her junior. Not nearly so tall and much more slim, she had rather pretty blue eyes and a neat figure, which comprised her all in the way of good looks. Her manner towards Magda was superior and mildly positive, though with people in general she knew how to be agreeable. Magda's air in response was combative.

"Did you not hear me calling?"

"If not, I shouldn't be here now."

"I think you need not have kept me so long."

Magda vouchsafed no excuse. "What's up?" she demanded.

"Mother wants you in the drawing-room."

"What for?"

"She found your drawers untidy."

"Of course you sent her to look at them."

"I don't 'send' mother about. And I have not been in your room to-day."

"I understand!" Magda spoke pointedly.

Penrose glanced up and down her sister with critical eyes. A word of warning would be kind. Magda seemed blissfully unconscious of her outward condition; and Pen had this moment heard a ring at the front door, which might mean callers.

"You've done the business now, so I hope you're satisfied," Magda went on. "Mother would never have thought of looking in my drawers, if you had not said something. I know! I did make hay in them yesterday, when I couldn't find my gloves, but I meant to put them straight to-night. It's too bad of you."

Pen's lips, parted for speech, closed again. If Magda chose to fling untrue accusations, she might manage for herself. And indeed small chance was given her to say more. Magda marched off, just as she was, straight for the drawing-room—her skirts pinned abnormally high for the snow-frolic; her shoes encased in snow; her tam-o'-shanter half-covering a mass of wild hair; her bare hands soiled and red with cold and scratched with brambles.

"Yes, mother. Pen says you want me."

She sent the words in advance with no gentle voice, as she whisked open the drawing-room door. Then she stopped.

Mrs. Royston, a graceful woman, looked in displeasure towards the figure in the doorway; for she was not alone.

Callers had arrived, as Pen conjectured; and through the front window might be seen two thoroughbreds champing their bits, and a footman standing stolidly. Why had Pen given no hint? How unkind! Then she recalled her own curt turning away, and knew that she was to blame.

"Really!" with a faint laugh protested Mrs. Royston.

"So I thought we would look in for five minutes on our way back from Sir John's," the elder caller was remarking in a manly voice.

She was a large woman, more in breadth and portliness than in height, and her magnificent furs made her look like a big brown bear sitting on end. Her face too was large and strongly outlined.

Magda guessed in a moment what her mother felt; for the Honourable Mrs. Framley was a county magnate; the weightiest personality in more senses than one to be found for many a mile around. A call from her was reckoned by some people as second only to a call from Royalty. The girl's first impulse was to flee; but a solid outstretched hand commanded her approach.

"Now, which of your young folks is this?" demanded Mrs. Framley, examining Magda through an eye-glass. "Let me see—you've got—how many daughters? Penrose—Magda—Merryl—Frances. I've not forgotten their names, though it's—how long?—since I was here last. Months, I'm afraid. But this is not your neat Penrose; and my jolly little friend Merryl can't have shot up to that height since I saw her; and Magda is out. Came out in the autumn, didn't she? So who is this? A niece?"

"I'm Magda," the girl said in shamefaced confession, for Mrs. Royston seemed voiceless.

Mrs. Framley leant back in her chair, and laughed till she was exhausted.

"So that's a specimen of the modern young woman, eh?"—when she could regain her voice. "My dear—" to Mrs. Royston—"pray don't apologise. It's I who should apologise. But really—really—it's irresistible." She went into another fit, and emerged from it, wheezing. "The child doesn't look a day over fifteen." The speaker wiped her eyes. "Don't send her away. Unadulterated Nature is always worth seeing—eh, Patricia?"

Magda turned startled eyes in the direction of the second caller, a girl three or four years older than herself, and the last person whom she expected to see. The last person, perhaps, whom at that moment she wished to see. For despite Magda's boasted non-chumminess with girls, this was the one girl whom she did, honestly and heartily, though not hopefully, desire for a friend. She had fallen in love at first sight with Mrs. Framley's niece, and had cherished her image ever since in the most secret recess of her heart.

"She'll think me just a silly idiotic school-girl!" flashed through Magda's mind, as she made an involuntary movement forward with extended hand—a soiled hand, as already said, scratched and slightly bleeding.

Patricia Vincent, standing thus far with amused eyes in the background, hesitated. She was immaculately dressed in grey, with a grey-feathered hat, relieved by touches of salmon-pink, and the daintiest of pale grey kid gloves. Contact with that hand did not quite suit her fastidious sense. A mere fraction of a second—and then she would have responded; but Magda, with crimsoning cheeks, had snatched the offending member away.

"I think you had better go and send Pen," interposed Mrs. Royston. Under the quiet words lay a command, "Do not come back."

Magda fled, without a good-bye, and went to the school-room, where she flung herself into an old armchair. The gas was low, but a good fire gave light; and she sat there in a dishevelled heap, weighing her grievances.

It was too bad of Pen, quite too bad, not to have warned her! And now the mischief was done. Patricia Vincent would never forget. Pen would go in and win; while she, as usual, would be nowhere in the race.

And all because she had not first rushed upstairs, to smooth her hair and wash her hands! Such nonsense!

As if Pen had not friends enough already! Just the single girl that she wanted for herself! If she might have Patricia, Pen was welcome to the rest of the world. But that was always the way! If one cared for a thing particularly, that thing was certain to be out of reach.

She was smarting still over the thought of that refused handshake; but her anger all went in the direction of Pen, not of Patricia. Pen alone was to blame!

Presently the front door was opened and shut; and then Mrs. Royston came in, moving with her usual graceful deliberation.

"What could have made you behave so, Magda?" she asked. "To come before callers in such a state!"

Magda was instantly up in arms. "Pen never told me there were callers."

"She did not know it. She would have reminded you how untidy you were—certainly in no condition to come into the drawing-room, even if I had been alone! But you show so much annoyance if she speaks."

"Pen is always in the right, of course."

"That is not the way to speak to me. I would rather have had this happen before anybody than before Mrs. Framley."

Magda shut her lips.

"Why did you not send Pen, as I told you?"

"I forgot."

"You always do forget. There is more dependence to be put upon Francie than upon you. You think of nothing, and care for nothing, except your own concerns. I am disappointed in you. It seems sometimes as if you had no sense of duty. And you ought to leave off giving way to temper as you do. It is so unlike your sisters. Nothing ever seems right with you."

"I can't help it. It isn't my fault."

"Then you ought to help it. You are not a little child any longer."

Mrs. Royston hesitated, as if about to say more; but Magda held up her head with an air of indifference, though invisible tears were scorching the backs of her eyes; and with a sigh she left the room. Magda would let no tear fall. She was angry, as well as unhappy.

Why should she be always the one in disgrace—and never Pen? True, Pen was careful, and neat, and sensible. All through girlhood Pen had been in the right. She had done her lessons, not indeed brilliantly, but with punctuality and exactness. Her hair was always neat; her stockings were always darned; her room was always in order; she never forgot what she undertook to do; she never gave a message upside-down or wrong end before. While Magda—but it is enough to say that in all these items she was the exact reverse of Penrose.

This week she in her turn had charge of the school-room, which was also the play-room. And the result, but for thoughtful Merryl, would have been "confusion worse confounded." Mr. Royston was wont to declare that when his second daughter passed through a room, she left such traces as are commonly left by a tropical cyclone. There was some truth in the remark, if Magda happened to be in a tumultuous mood.

Penrose had her faults, as well as Magda, though somehow she was seldom blamed for them. She had a knack of being always in the right, at least to outward appearance. No doubt her faults were exaggerated by Magda; but they did exist. She wanted the best of everything for herself; she alone must be popular; she could not endure that Magda should do anything better than she did; she was not always strictly true. Magda saw and felt these defects; but nobody else seemed to be aware of them; and she could prove nothing. If she tried, she only managed to get into hot water, while Pen was sure to come off with flying colours.

"And it will be just the same with Patricia Vincent," was the outcome of this soliloquy. "The moment Pen guesses that I like her, she'll step in and oust me. I know she will."

CHAPTER III
ROBERT

WITH a creak, the door was cautiously opened. Somebody put in his head.

"All alone, Magda!"

Depression vanished, and the transformation in Magda's face was like an instantaneous leap from November to June. In a moment her eyes were alight, her limbs alert.

"Rob!" she cried.

"Well, old girl! How are you?"

"You dear old fellow—I am glad."

The new-comer was about her own height, which though fairly tall for a girl could not be so counted for a man. He was slim in make, like Pen; also, like Pen, scrupulously neat in dress. Her eager welcome met with a quiet kiss; after which he seated himself; and his eyes travelled over her, with a rather dubious expression.

"It's awfully jolly to have you here again. You never told us you were coming."

"I happened not to know it myself till this morning. What have you been after?"

"Just now? Playing in the snow."

Rob's gaze reached her shoes, and she laughed.

"Yes, I know! Of course, I ought to have changed them. But it didn't seem worth while. I shall have to dress for dinner soon."

"And, meantime, you are anxious to start early rheumatism!"

"My dear Rob! I never had a twinge of it in my life—I don't know what it means."

"So much the better. It would be more sensible to continue in ignorance."

"Oh, all right. I'll be sensible, and change—presently. I really can't just now. I must have you while I can. When the others know you are here, I shall not have a chance. Are you going to stay?"

"One night. I must be off the first thing to-morrow morning."

"And I've oceans to say! Things that can't by any possibility be written."

"Fire away then. There's no time like the present."

"We shall be interrupted in two minutes. It's always the way! Why do things always go contrary, I wonder? At least, they do with me. If I could only come and live with you, Rob!—now!"

"That is to be your future life—is it?"

"Why, you know! Haven't we always said so? And whenever I am miserable, I always comfort myself by looking forward to a home with you."

"What are you miserable about?"

"All sorts of things. Some days everything goes wrong and I can't get on with people. It's not my fault. They don't understand me."

"I wonder whether you understand them?" murmured Rob.

"And there's nothing in life that's worth doing. Nothing in my life, I mean."

"Or rather—you have not found it yet."

"No, I don't mean that. I mean that there isn't anything. Really and truly!"

Rob said only, "H'm!"

"Yes, I dare say! But just think what I have to do. Tennis and hockey; cycling and walking; mending my clothes and making blouses—not that I'm much good at that! Going to tea with people I don't care a fig for; and having people here that I shouldn't mind never setting eyes on again! Smothering down all I think and feel, because nobody cares. Worrying and being worried, and all to no good. Nothing to show for the half-year that is gone, and nothing to look to in the year that's begun. The months are just simply frittered away, and no human being is the better for my being alive. It's not what I call Life. It is just getting through time. Don't you see? It suits Peñ well enough. So long as she gets a decent amount of attention, she's happy. But I'm not made that way; and I can't see what life is given us for, if it means nothing better."

When she stopped, pleased with her own eloquence, Rob merely remarked—

"Don't you think that bit of hard judgment might have been left out? It wasn't a needful peroration."

Magda blushed; and Robert pondered.

"But, Rob—would you like to live such a life?"

Rob's gesture was sufficient answer.

"And yet you think I oughtn't to mind?"

"I beg your pardon. You are wrong to live it."

"But what can I do?"

"Find work. Take care that somebody is the better for your existence."

"I've tried. I can't. It's no good."

"There are always people to be helped—people you can be kind to—people you can cheer up, when they feel dull."

"Pick up old ladies' stitches, I suppose. Interesting!"

"I did not know you wished to be interested. I thought you wanted to be of use."

"Well—of course! But that's so commonplace. I want to do something out of the ordinary beat."

"You want some agreeable duty, manufactured to suit your especial taste!"

"Oh, bother! Somebody is coming. What a plague! And I have heaps more to say. Won't you give me another talk?"

"I'll manage it."

He stood up to greet his mother, as she came in, followed by the two younger girls. The news of his unexpected arrival seemed all at once to pervade the household.

Penrose entered next; and behind her Mr. Royston, a thick-set grey-haired man, of impulsive manners, sometimes more kindly than judicious.

He was devoted to his family; not much given to books; ready to help anybody and everybody who might appeal to him; generally more or less in financial difficulties, partly from his inherited tendency to allow pounds and pence to slide too rapidly through his fingers. A pleasant and genial man, so long as he did not encounter opposition; but it was out of his power to understand why all the world should not agree with himself. His wife gave in to him ninety-nine times in a hundred; and if, the hundredth time, she set her foot down firmly, he gave in to her; for he was a most affectionate husband.

As for his daughters, he doted on them. Steady Penrose, useful Merryl, picturesque little Frip, were everything that he desired. Magda alone puzzled him. He could not make out what she wanted, or why she would not be content to fit in with others, to play games, to sit and work, to do anything or nothing with equal content. Dreams and aspirations, indeed! Nonsense! Humbug! What did girls want with such notions? They had to be good girls, to do as they were told, and to make themselves agreeable. A vexed face annoyed him beyond expression. He could not get over it. He could never ignore it. By his want of tact, though with the kindest intentions, he often managed to put a finishing stroke to Magda's uncomfortable moods.

"Why can't father leave me alone?" she sometimes complained.

Mr. Royston never did leave anybody alone, whether for weal or for woe. Nor did he ever learn wisdom through his own mistakes.

This afternoon, happily, there were no dismal faces. With Rob to the fore, even though he had not fallen in with her views, Magda was in the best of spirits.

She took pains with her toilette that evening—which she was not always at the trouble to do. Sometimes it did not seem "worth while." Yet she well repaid care in that direction. Though not strictly good-looking, she had a nice figure, and knew how to carry herself; and the mass of reddish-gold hair came out well, if properly dressed; and when she smiled and was pleased, her face would hardly have been recognised by one who had seen her only in one of her "November fogs." Rob looked her over, and signified approval by a quiet—"That's right." She expected no more. He never wasted unnecessary words.

Further confidential talk that day proved out of the question, for Rob was very much in request. But Magda waited patiently; for he had promised, and he always kept his promises. Bedtime arrived; and still she felt sure.

"I'm off early," he said, and he looked at her. "Seven-thirty train. Will you be down at seven, and walk to the station with me?"

"This weather!" demurred Mrs. Royston.

"It won't hurt her, mother. She's strong."

"I'm as strong as a horse. Of course it wont hurt me."

"Mayn't we come too?" begged Merryl.

"Only Magda." Rob's tone was final.

"She will never be down in time. Magda is always late," put in Penrose.

Magda's eyes flamed, but she had no need to speak.

"I don't think she will fail me," Rob said tranquilly.

CHAPTER IV
THE INEFFABLE PATRICIA

"THAT'S right," Robert remarked, finding Magda already in the breakfast-room, before a blazing fire. She had on a little round cap and motor-veil, and a heavy ulster lay at hand. "Awful morning. You'll have to let me go alone."

"No, indeed! You said I might."

"Well!" Rob shook his head dubiously. "Got thick boots on? We must hurry. I'm late, though you are not."

Breakfast claimed immediate attention, for only ten minutes remained. On leaving the front door, they found themselves in a smothering hail of small hard snow-pellets, driven by an icy gale, dead ahead. It took all their breath to bore through that opposing blast; and conversation by the way was a thing impossible. One or two gasping remarks were all that could be exchanged.

Umbrellas were out of the question; nor could they get along at the speed they wished. When two white-clad figures at length stumbled upon the platform, Rob's train, though not yet signalled, was three minutes over due.

"I might have missed it!" he said, trying to stamp himself free from a superabundant covering. They took refuge in a sheltered corner beside the closed bookstall, where the wind no longer reached them. "My plan has been a failure. I'm sorry. We must have our talk out next time I come."

"When will you?"

"Ah—that's the question."

Magda spoke abruptly. "Somebody said not long ago that my dream of living with you would never come true, because you were sure to marry."

Robert laughed. "I can't afford it. And my work leaves no leisure. And—I've never seen the girl. Three cogent reasons. So you may pretty well count upon me. I'm a non-marrying man."

Magda's sigh was one of relief. "I'm glad. I don't think I could endure all the home-worries, if I had not that to look forward to. I only wish I could come to you now!"

"Nobody is the worse for waiting. Don't let your life be empty meantime—that's all."

"I've been thinking since yesterday—but really and truly, I can't see what to take up. Father would never let me be trained as a nurse. And I do hate sick-rooms and sick people. And commonplace nursing is such awful drudgery."

"The cure for that is to put one's heart into it. No work is drudgery, if one loves it."

"I should love nursing soldiers in war-time. Or people in some great plague outbreak."

"If you were not trained beforehand, I rather pity the victims of war and plague."

"Of course I should have to learn. But, Rob—you needn't think I mind all drudgery. If I could see any use in hard work, I would work like a horse. But where's the good? Music and French and German are of no earthly use to any one except myself."

"You don't know how soon they may be of use. There are some nice girls who come every week to sing to our hospital patients. Suppose they had never learnt to sing! The other day I came across a poor German sailor, unable to speak a word of English. I would have given much for somebody good at German."

"But to work for years beforehand—just for the chance of things being needed—it seems so vague!"

"That's no matter. Make yourself ready, and there is small fear but that a use will some time be found for you. It is like preparing for an exam—not knowing what questions may be asked, and so having to study a variety of books."

Magda liked the idea, yet persisted—"I don't see, all the same, what I've got to do."

"You have to train yourself—your powers—your whole being—your character—your habits of body and mind. Don't you see? You have to get the upper hand over yourself—not to be a victim to moods—to be ready for whatever by-and-by you may be called to do."

"It isn't so easy!" she said resentfully.

"It's not easy at all. We are not put here to lounge in armchairs and to feel comfortable."

"I sometimes wonder what we are put here for."

"That is easily answered. To do the Will of God, whatever that Will may be. And one part of His loving Will for His children is that they must work—and fight—and conquer."

"If only everything wasn't so abominably humdrum! If there were any sort of a chance of doing anything worth doing!"

"There are hundreds of chances, Magda. They lie all round, in every direction. In ninety-nine cases out of a hundred, when lives are wasted, it is not the opportunity that is wanting, but the will."

"I'm sure I've got the will—if I could see what to do."

As she spoke the train came in. Rob opened a door, put in his bag, and turned for a last word.

"You harp on doing great things," he said. "But the very essence of greatness lies in simple duty and self-sacrifice. It is no question of what you like or don't like, but simply of what God has given you to do. Nothing short of the highest service is worth anything. Don't expect to find things easy. They are not meant to be easy. But we are meant to conquer; and in Christ our Lord, victory is certain. Life is a tremendous gift. See that you use it!"

The train had begun to move. He stepped in and was borne away, waving farewell. She stood motionless, forgetful of the piercing cold. "See that you use it!" rang still in her ears.

But how? Go home to chit-chat, to worries and vexations, to tiresome misunderstandings, to objectless study—which he said ought not to be objectless! Was that using the "tremendous gift" of life?

She was vexed with him for not taking her view of matters, and she was vexed with herself for being vexed; but also she was impressed by what he had said.

"How do you do? So glad to see you!" a pretty voice said. And she turned to meet no less a person than Patricia Vincent, in a fur-lined coat of dark silk, the grey "fox" of its high collar framing her delicate face, with its ivory and rose tinting, its smiling eyes, its fair hair clustering below a dainty fur cap. She might have come out of some old Gainsborough portrait.

"How do you do?" Magda rather shyly responded. Patricia alone had power to make her shy. She felt herself so inferior a creation in that fascinating presence.

"Cold—isn't it? I have been seeing off an old school friend; and she has to go all the way to Scotland. I don't envy her, in such weather. Why did you not come back yesterday? I wanted to see you again."

"I was in such a mess. I couldn't!"

"You had a lovely time in the snow, I dare say. I should have liked it too—only not in my quite new gloves!" The tactful little hint at an apology was perfect. "Is that your brother who is just gone?"

"Yes—Robert."

"I've not seen him before. Somebody was speaking about him yesterday."

"I'm desperately fond of Rob."

Patricia smiled her sympathy. "I'm sure you must be. I could not help noticing you two, though you were much too busy to see me. He looks like—somebody out of the common—if you don't mind my saying so."

"But he is just that. Rob never was the least scrap commonplace. I'm awfully proud of him. And they do like him so much in his parish—everybody does. Have you any brothers or sisters?"

"None at all. And I was left an orphan long ago. So you see I stand alone. Did you know that I had come to stay at Claughton—perhaps for months?"

"No. Oh, I'm glad! Then—I shall see you again!"

The glow of delight was not to be mistaken. Patricia at once recognised a new admirer. She was well used to adulation, and she had plenty, yet never too much, for she could not exist without it; and the earliest token of a fresh worshipper was always hailed with encouragement. Instinctively, she gazed into her companion's eyes, and her soft little hand squeezed Magda's.

"We shall meet very often, I hope. Why not? I think you and I will have to be friends."

"Oh!" Magda cried, breathless. "Oh, I've wanted it so much! I can't tell you how much! Ever since the very first time I saw you, I've longed to have you for a friend. There is nobody else here that I care for—in that way."

"And I have no friends here either. I shall miss all my London friends. But I am quite sure you and I will suit. I always know from the first."

"Oh, and so do I! But you couldn't have thought—yesterday—"

"Yes, I liked you yesterday. I wanted to see you again."

Magda devoured her in response with eager eyes; and Patricia smiled, well-pleased.

"I wonder whether you could come to tea with me to-morrow at four o'clock. My aunt will be out, and we could have a good chat. Can you manage the distance?"

"Oh, quite well. That's nothing. Only five miles. If I can't bicycle, I'll do it by train. There's one that reaches Claughton at ten minutes to four. I shall love to come. How good of you!"

"That will be charming. Now how are you going to get home? Walking! How plucky you are! I wish I could give you a lift, but I have to hurry back; and it is just the other way. So good-bye till to-morrow, Magda. Of course, if it is a 'blizzard,' I shall not expect you."

Magda privately resolved that, blizzard or no blizzard, she would not be deterred. She watched the brougham out of sight, then hurried home with the wind in her back, helping now instead of hindering. She trod upon air, so great was her exultation.

That Patricia should want her for a friend! Patricia, of all people! It was sublime! The impression made by Rob's words sank for a time into the background of her mind. She could think of nothing but this new delight.

After all—life was worth living—with such a prospect!

CHAPTER V
UNWELCOME NEWS

MAGDA, having removed her snowy garments, found the family round the breakfast-table; and she did not disdain a second course of tea and toast after her early outing.

She certainly looked no worse for the walk. Her face glowed with delight.

"Letters—letters!" quoth Merryl, next in age to Magda, and a complete child still, despite her fifteen years—plump and rosy, unformed in feature, but with a look of beaming good-nature and pure happiness, which must have transformed the plainest face into pleasantness. She was busily engaged in buttering her father's toast. From early infancy she had been his especial pet; and her seat was always by his side. Mr. Royston without Merryl was like a ship without its rudder—a helpless object.

"Lots of letters for everybody except Magda," piped Francie's small treble.

"So much the better for me! I haven't the bother of answering them," Magda said joyously.

"Seem to have liked your walk," Mr. Royston remarked in puzzled accents. For Magda, after parting with Rob, was usually what he described as "in the dumps" for hours.

"I just love a fight with the snow. And I've seen Patricia Vincent. She was at the station too. And she has asked me to tea to-morrow."

There was a note of triumph in the tone, for Magda was aware that Pen had been counting on some such invitation for herself.

"How did you manage to bring that about?" asked Pen, obviously not pleased.

"I didn't manage at all. She simply asked me."

"You must have said something. It is not the Claughton Manor way to invite people informally."

"I suppose it's her way. Now she has come to live there—"

"She has not."

"Well, anyhow, to stay for a long while—"

Penrose demurred again, and Mrs. Royston put in a word.

"Yes, dear. Mrs. Framley told me, and I forgot to mention it. Miss Vincent has lived for years with some London cousins; but the eldest daughter was lately married; and things now are not so comfortable. I fancy she and the second daughter do not much care for one another. And Mr. and Mrs. Framley have proposed that she should make the Manor her headquarters. The plan is to be tried."

"She has plenty of money. Why doesn't she live in a house of her own?"

"Too young, Pen. She is only twenty-two."

"She is the very sweetest—" began Magda rapturously, and checked herself at the sound of Pen's little laugh. Magda crimsoned.

"Heigh-ho! What's wrong now?" Mr. Royston stopped in the act of turning his newspaper inside-out, and fixed inquiring eyes upon his second daughter.

"Pen is so disagreeable."

"Come, come! You needn't complain of other people. Pen is a good girl—always was! I wish other girls were as good."

Pen wore an air of pretty and appropriate meekness.

"I know! I'm always the one in the wrong."

"Then, if I were you, I wouldn't be—that's all. I would take care to be in the right."

Mrs. Royston wisely rose, and a general move followed. Magda fled upstairs, only to find her room in process of being "done;" so she caught up a rough-coat and a tam-o'-shanter, and escaped into the garden. Already the snow had ceased to fall, and the sky was clearing.

To and fro on a white carpet in the kitchen garden she paced, pitying herself at first for home grievances, but turning soon to the thought of Patricia, going over the past interview, seeing again the dainty flower-like face, hearing afresh the pretty voice, picturing the joys of coming intimacy.

Now at last she would have a real friend, the sort of friend she had always wanted, a satisfying friend, one who would meet her needs, one who would understand her feelings, one who would enter into her dreams and aspirations, one to whom she could look up with unbounded admiration—different altogether from good little Beatrice Major, who was well enough in her way, but totally unlike this!

That word—"aspirations"—pulled up the recollection of Rob and of all that he had said. She was to begin at once to make ready for her future life with him.

Yes, of course; and she meant to do it. She was not going to "drift" any longer. She would hunt out her neglected plan of study, and would start with it afresh. That was all right. If once she really made up her mind, of course she would do it. She was not one of those weak creatures who could not carry out a resolution.

Only—not this morning. There was so much to think about!—and Pen was so annoying!—and she felt so unsettled! To seat herself down to a French translation or a German exercise in her present condition was impossible.

"You've got to get the upper hand over yourself. Not to be a victim to moods!" So Rob had said.

Oh, bother! what did Rob know about moods? He never had any. He was always the same—always calm and composed and steady; the dearest old fellow, but without a notion of what it meant to be made up of all sorts of opposite characteristics, and never in the same state for two consecutive quarters of an hour. People could not help being what they were made! She meant to get the upper hand of herself—in time. But it was absurd to expect impossibilities.

So the hours drifted by; and another day was added to the waste pile.

After the next night came a rapid thaw. The world around streamed with water, while a wet fog hung overhead. It made no difference to Magda. Go she would, no matter what the elements might say.

Mrs. Royston tried remonstrance, but Magda's agony at the notion of giving up was too patent, and she desisted. Bicycling was out of the question; so the train had to be resorted to and twenty minutes' walk through the soaking grounds brought her to the Manor with boots clogged in mud.

What did that matter? After an abnormal amount of boot-rubbing, she was shown upstairs into Patricia's special sanctum, a "study in blue," as she was presently informed, carpet, curtains, cretonne covers, all partaking of the same hue. Patricia, also in blue, welcomed her sweetly, exclaimed at her condition, set her down before the fire to dry, gave her tea, and gradually unlocked a tongue, which at first seemed tied.

However, once it was untied, the young hostess had no further trouble. Magda could talk; none faster! She poured out the contents of her mind for Patricia's inspection; and Patricia listened, with always those sweetly smiling eyes, and little pearly teeth just showing themselves. Once or twice a close observer might have detected a puzzled look at some of Magda's flights; but she was invariably sympathetic—or she seemed so, which did as well under the circumstances.

Magda was used to sympathy from Bee, though hardly of the same kind. Bee would sometimes differ from Magda; never otherwise than gently, yet with decision. Patricia disagreed with nothing. She had that captivating habit, possessed by some agreeable people, of managing always to say exactly what her listener would have wished to hear. Though not by birth Irish, she really might have been so; for this is one of the Green Isle's characteristics.

So, whatever Magda chose to utter, she found herself in the right; and if aught had been needed to complete the enchaining process, this was sufficient. When she went home that afternoon, she was wildly happy. In Patricia she had found an ideal friend; the dearest, the sweetest, the loveliest, ever seen. She had now all she wanted!

The fascination grew. Magda never did anything by halves; and during the next few weeks she had eyes, ears, thoughts, for Patricia only. When they parted, she could not be content unless the time and place of their next meeting were named. If she could not see her idol for two or three days, she sent rapturous notes by post. Every spare shilling of her pocket-money went in gifts for Patricia. Half her time was spent upon the road between Burwood and Claughton.

"It is getting to be a perfect craze," Mrs. Royston one day remarked to Penrose. "I really don't know what to do. The Framleys will be bored to death, if it goes on."

"Patricia herself is having rather too much of it, I suspect. I noticed her face yesterday afternoon when Magda was hanging round and would not leave her for a moment. Naturally she wanted to be free for other people."

"I thought she was affectionate to Magda. Still, the thing may go too far. Magda has no balance. Some day I shall have to give her a word of warning."

"I would, mother!"

But Mrs. Royston delayed. Magda seemed aboundingly happy; and she rather shrank from putting a spoke in the wheel. Matters might right themselves.

One morning, after an especially rapturous afternoon of intercourse with Patricia, Magda found on the breakfast-table a letter from Bee. She had not given much thought to Bee lately—had not written to her for weeks. She felt a little ashamed, and began to read under a sense of compunction.

Then a startled—"Oh!"—all but escaped her.

"Anything wrong?" asked Pen.

"Why should anything be wrong?"

"You looked the reverse of pleased."

Magda retreated into herself, and refused to discuss the question. Breakfast ended, she escaped to her favourite quarter, the kitchen garden, now a blaze of spring sunshine, and there she went through the letter a second time.

"Bother! I hoped that was all given up!" she sighed.

"Think, how lovely!" wrote Bee in her pretty ladylike hand. "We really are coming to Burwood. Do you remember my telling you that it was spoken about? My mother heard of a little house which she went to see; and she liked it so much that she made up her mind quickly. She did not tell me this till I got home; and there were one or two hitches, so I would not say any more to you till everything was arranged."

"Now papers are all signed, and the house will be ours in the end of June. It has to be painted and papered, and I suppose we shall not get in before August. It is near the Post Office in High Street—standing back in a little garden—and it is all grown over with Virginia creeper—so pretty, mother says. It is called 'Virginia Villa.'"

"I cannot hope that you will be as glad as I am; still I do feel sure that it will be a pleasure to my darling Magda to have her 'little Bee' within such easy reach. Only think of it! I often sit and dream of what it will be to have you always in and out—every day, I hope, and as often in the day as you can manage it. You will know that you cannot come too often."

"I'm hoping for a most lovely treat this summer. Isn't it sweet of Amy? She has been saving and laying by money all the last year, and now she is bent on taking me to Switzerland for three weeks in July. I can hardly believe it to be true. I've always had such a longing for Swiss mountains!"

"To-morrow I am going into the country for three weeks with Aunt Belle and Aunt Emma—mother's sisters, you know. If you should write to me then, please address—'Wratt-Wrothesley, —shire.' I am longing to hear from you again."

Magda was half touched, half aggrieved. She hardly knew how to take it. She and Beatrice had been friends through two long years of school-life; and though she might make little of the tie to Miss Mordaunt, it had been a close one. Bee had loved her devotedly; and she had been really fond of Bee. Yet, somehow, she did not take to the idea of having Bee permanently in Burwood, for reasons earlier explained.

Things looked even worse to her now than when she was at school. Her mother and Pen were so awfully critical and particular. She minded Pen's little laugh of disdain almost more than she minded anything. It would be horrid if that laugh were called forth by a friend of hers.

And then the small creeper-grown house in High Street, where till now a successful dressmaker had lived—it really was too dreadful! To think of her especial friend living there—in Virginia Villa! She was certain that nothing would ever induce her mother to leave a card at that door. And if not—if Mrs. Royston declined to call—it would be quite as objectionable. To have a friend in a different stratum, so to speak, just allowed in their house on occasions, just tolerated perhaps, but looked upon as belonging to a lower level—how unbearable! And Bee's relatives might be—well, anything! They might tread upon the sensitive toes of her people at every turn. If only Bee had never thought of the plan!

Worse still—much worse!—there was this delightful new friendship with Patricia Vincent. Most certainly neither Patricia nor her aunt, Mrs. Framley, would deign to look at any human being who should live in

Virginia Villa. To them it would be an impossible locality. For a dressmaker, well enough—and nothing would exceed their gracious kindness to the said dressmaker. But—for a friend! Magda went hot and cold by turns. She had not haunted Patricia for weeks, without becoming pretty well acquainted with the Framley scales of measurement.

When the Majors should have settled in, she would have to keep her two friends absolutely apart—to segregate them in water-tight compartments, so to speak. But would this be possible? Suppose, some day, they should come together! Suppose that Patricia should find her chosen friend's other friend to be a mere nobody, living in that wretched little house! Why, it might squash altogether this new glorious friendship of hers!

And the more she considered, the more certain she felt that the two must sooner or later meet. Burwood was not a large town. Everybody there knew all about everybody else. To be sure, the Framleys lived apart, and held themselves very much aloof from the townsfolk generally. Still, accidental encounters do take place, even under such conditions, just when least desired.

And Bee was so simple; she would never understand. Nobody could call so gentle a creature "pushing;" but on the other hand it would never occur to her mind that anybody could object to know her, merely because she lived in an insignificant house. She had a pretty natural way of always expecting to find herself welcome. Magda had heard that way admired; but she felt at this moment that she could have dispensed with it.

She would have to make Bee understand—somehow. She would have to explain that not all her friends and acquaintances would be likely to call— in fact, that probably very few would. It would be very difficult and horrid; but since the Majors chose to come, they must take the consequences.

Always in and out! That was very fine; but neither her mother nor Pen would stand such a state of things—considering the position of Virginia Villa. Magda had a good deal of liberty, within limits; but those limits were clearly defined.

In this direction she did not want more liberty. She could not be perpetually going after Bee. Her time was already full—of Patricia.

True, Bee was the old friend, Patricia was the new. But she had always felt that Bee could not fully meet her needs, and Patricia could—which made all the difference. Patricia was more to her—oh, miles more!—than poor little Bee.

As she felt her way through this maze of difficulties, a thought suggested itself. Why need she say anything at present about the coming of the Majors to Burwood?

Nobody in the place knew them. It was nobody's business except her own. There was plenty of time. They would not arrive for weeks and weeks. And each week was of importance to her for the further cementing of her new friendship. She could at least—wait.

By-and-by, of course, it must be told; and her mother must be asked to call; and Pen's little laugh of disdain must be endured. But there was no hurry. For a while longer she might allow herself to revel in the Patricia sunshine, without fear of a rising cloud.

CHAPTER VI
SWISS ENCOUNTERS

TWO girls sat in a tiny verandah, outside the third storey of a Swiss hotel, facing a horseshoe group of dazzling peaks. Or rather, one of the two faced it, while the other faced her.

She who gazed upon the mountains, a slender maiden, pale, with brown eyes and wavy hair and rather heavy dark brows, did nothing else. It was enough to be there, enough to look, enough to study and absorb Nature's glories.

But the second—a girl only by courtesy, being many years the older—a short plump vigorous person, snub-nosed, with insignificant light eyes and tow-coloured hair—seemed to find an occasional glance at lofty peaks sufficient. For each glance sent in that direction, half-a-dozen glances went towards her companion; and in addition, she busily darned a dilapidated stocking.

Despite the difference in age, a difference amounting to over twelve years, those two were intimate friends. Yet it was a friendship of sorts; not alike on both sides. The younger girl's love for her senior was gentle and sincere. The elder's love for her junior amounted to an absorbing passion. Amy Smith would have done anything, given anything, endured anything, for the sake of Beatrice Major.

"Amy—if you could only know what a delight this trip has been to me!—has been and is!"

"My dear, one couldn't watch your face and not know."

"But to think that it is all you!—that you have saved and scraped and denied yourself—and just for my sake! And I never dreaming all those months, when you said you could not afford this and that and the other—never dreaming what you had in your mind!"

"It has been one long joy to me. You wouldn't wish to deprive me of it."

"But that you should have given up so much—for me!"

"Nobody minds giving up a shilling for the sake of a guinea."

"If I could feel that I deserved it—but I don't."

"I know, my dear!"

"You don't—and I can't make you."

She looked up to meet the steadfast gaze; a gaze which she understood. It meant that if Amy had her, there was no need for aught beside. And she could not return this devotion in kind or in degree. She did want something else.

"C'est toujours l'un qui aime, et l'autre qui se laisse aimé." Was it always so? Not altogether; for she did love dear kind Amy, truly and faithfully. But with the same love!—ah, no. And this seemed cruel for Amy.

"How I shall miss you in Burwood!" she said, with an earnest wish to give pleasure. And, indeed, it was true! She could not but miss the constant outpouring of affection which she had had from childhood, even though at times she might have felt its expression a trifle burdensome. But she would not miss as she would be missed.

"Will you—really?" Amy was generally blunt in speech and manner; yet she could be wistful. The plump plain face softened; the little snub nose flushed with the flushing of her freckled brow and tanned cheeks; and the pale grey eyes grew moist. "Bee—will you want me?"

"Of course I shall, at every turn. Think how long I have had you always."

"You will have Magda Royston now."

"Yes." Bee forgot to say more. She looked away at the lofty peaks opposite, where a ruby gleam lay athwart the snows. Yes, she would have Magda. She remembered in a flash her letter to Magda, telling her so eagerly of the settled plans; and her own hurt feeling at receiving no response.

In a month the response came; but before the close of that month another personality had entered her life. The three weeks at "Aunt Belle's" meant much to her. She had been in close touch with one whom she could never forget, who could never in the future be to her as a stranger. An impress had been made upon her life, transforming her at one touch into a woman. And if her love for Amy had paled a little before her warmer love for Magda, as starlight pales before moonlight, her love for Magda paled before this fresh experience, as moonlight pales before sunlight. Not that in either case her affection actually waned or altered, but that the lesser light became of necessity dim by comparison with the greater.

Nobody knew or suspected what had happened. Her gentle self-control prevented any betrayal of feeling on her part. The two had indeed been a great deal together, during those three weeks, but intercourse came about so simply and naturally, that she never could decide how far it was purely accidental, how far as a result of effort on his part. He seemed to enjoy being with her; and they seemed to suit; but whether he would remember her, whether he had any strong desire to meet her again, were questions which she had no power to decide. Their paths might lie permanently apart.

When the expected letter at last came from Magda, though she was a little grieved at the manifest lack of real delight in the prospect of having her at Burwood, it could not mean the same that it would have meant before that visit. For one who has been in strong sunshine, the brightest moonlight must seem pale.

"Bee, what are you cogitating about? I don't understand your face."

Bee smiled. "I was thinking over—varieties. These mountains make one think. Yes, I shall have Magda. But one friend does not fill another's place. You will always be you to me."

"And she will be she, I suppose."

"Yes; but she can never be you. Don't you see?"

Amy sighed profoundly. "All I know is that London will be a desert without you. And I'm torn in half—do you know that sensation?—between two longings. I long for you to be happy in Burwood; and if you weren't happy, I should be miserable. And yet I long for you to miss me so desperately that you can't be happy without me. There!—it's out! Horrid and mean of me! But it's true."

"Amy, you never could be mean. You are only too good—too unselfish."

"It's all selfishness. You don't understand. I love doing anything in the world for you, purely as a matter of self-gratification. Real unselfishness would only want you to be perfectly happy—apart from myself. And what I do want is that I should make you happy. Which means that, if I can't, I'd rather nobody else should. Isn't it disgusting?"

"But you have made me happy. I can't tell you half or a quarter of the joy this trip has been to me. I have so longed all my life to see Swiss mountains. And you have given me the joy! I do believe there is going to be an afterglow, and we shall miss it! Just time for table d'hôte."

Once before the glow had occurred when they were all engaged in what Amy disdainfully described as "gormandizing."

"We've got to be in bed early to-night, mind, Bee. I want you to get well rested for to-morrow's exertions. Sure you are fit for it?"

"I never was more fit in my life. It will be splendid."

"And to-morrow night we sleep at the Hut."

"Delightful! Such an experience! I don't believe I shall sleep a wink to-night, thinking about all we are going to see."

"You must, or you won't be up to the walking."

After two weeks of lesser practice, and divers small climbs, they were going on a real expedition—their first ascent, worthy of the name—under charge of Peter Steimathen, than whom they could have found no more dependable guide, and his son, Abraham. Both girls were of slight physique; both were by nature sure of foot; and both dearly loved climbing. Since both were Londoners, their opportunities hitherto had not been great in that line; but they had taken to it like ducklings to water. Peter Steimathen, after some consultation, pronounced that they might safely, under his guidance, make the attempt.

At table d'hôte Beatrice found a stranger by her side; a reticent young English clergyman, slim in make, with quiet observant eyes. She had never met him before; yet something once and again in his look seemed familiar, and she vainly tried to "locate" the resemblance. He and she fell easily into talk—strictly on the surface of things.

"Yes, we are going for a climb to-morrow," she said soon. "Nothing big, of course. We are only beginners. It is called the Rothstock—a lesser peak of the Blümlisalp group."

"You will want a guide for that, if you are beginners."

"We would not venture without Peter Steimathen."

"I know him. You couldn't do better."

"Are you going up somewhere too?"

"The Blümlisalphorn."

"Not alone! You have a guide."

"No, I have a friend. Not here—he has a room in a châlet close by. We are both well used to the mountains. No need for a guide."

"People say that is not safe."

"Depends!" And he smiled. "We've done a good deal together that way."

"Without guides?"

"Without guides."

"I hope you won't come to grief some day."

"I hope not!"

"You think it is wise?" dubiously.

"Extremely wise. But you must be careful—excuse me! There are traps for beginners that don't affect old hands."

"Peter Steimathen!" she suggested.

"He is excellent. But you must do as he tells you."

"Oh, I've learnt to obey," laughed Bee.

Then she saw that his attention was distracted; and her own became distracted also. Two new arrivals had just come in; a middle-aged lady, stout and handsomely dressed; and a girl, young, and quite lovely. She had one of those picture-faces which are seen two or three times in a half-century. Not Bee's gaze alone suffered distraction. The whole room gazed; and the object of all this attention received it calmly, without a change of colour or the flicker of an eyelid.

"She's used to it," Bee remarked to herself.

But it was impossible not to go on gazing. The face was one that nobody could glance at once and not glance again. Soft curly fair hair clustered about a fair brow; and the delicately tinted complexion made one think of snowflakes and rose-buds, or of early dawn in June. A slender figure, full of grace, shell-white arms and hands, features pretty enough not to detract from the exquisite colouring, helped to make up the tout-ensemble; and the forget-me-not blue eyes smiled graciously at the elder lady, at the waiters, at the table-cloth, at anything and everything that they happened to encounter.

Beatrice cast an involuntary side-glance towards her neighbour. He too was gazing; and in the quiet eyes she detected a subdued intensity, of which she would not have thought them capable.

"Isn't she sweet?" breathed Bee.

The remark was not even heard, and no reply came. Their broken talk was not renewed; and he disposed of eatables with the air of one who hardly knew what was before him. Dinner ended, the vision disappeared, and so did Bee's neighbour; but an hour later she was amused to see him at the further end of the saloon, in close talk with the pretty new arrival.

Meeting him still later in a passage, she paused and made some slight reference to the girl.

"I wonder who she is," Bee said.

"A friend of my sister's," he replied. "Singular, our meeting here. I have heard of her before."

Bee noted again a suppressed gleam in his eyes.

CHAPTER VII
A MOUNTAIN HUT BY NIGHT

THE Frauenbahn Hut, at last!

For eight hours and a half, including rests, they had been en route, with their guide and porter, making the steep ascent from Kandersteg, winding through pine-woods, pausing at the rough Oeschinen Hotel, skirting the deep-grey waters of the lake from which it took its name—then mounting again to the "Upper Alp," only to leave that also behind, as they yet more steeply zig-zagged onward over rough shale, with the glacier to their right and the Hut for their aim.

An experienced mountaineer would have covered in six hours the distance they had come; but, naturally, it took them a good deal longer, which meant arriving late.

Both were very tired and very happy, and in a state of mental exhilaration, which, despite fatigue, gave small promise of getting quickly to sleep amid such unwonted surroundings. Thus far, though the way had been steep, they had had a rugged path. On the morrow they would quit beaten tracks, and would do a "bit of the real thing," as Amy expressed it.

The guide, Peter Steimathen, had proved himself a pleasant companion all that day. Fortunately, since neither of the two was a practised German speaker, he had some command of English.

A rough little place was this Frauenbahn Hut, though better than most mountain refuges, for, in addition to the room on the ground-floor, it boasted a loft above, both being on occasions crammed with climbers. Nearly half the lower room consisted of a shelf, some three feet from the floor, covered with a bedding of straw; and on this the girls would spend their night, rolled up in rugs, provided for sleepers. High above their heads the guides would repose on another shelf, to reach which some agility was needed.

Beatrice and Amy counted themselves fortunate in finding the Hut empty. Apparently they would have the place to themselves. They looked round with interest at the wooden walls, the small window, and the stove at which the guide was preparing to boil water for their soup.

"But come—come outside," urged Amy. "Don't let us miss the sunset. It won't wait our pleasure. We can examine things inside by-and-by. Come!"

And they went, commandeering hut rugs for wraps, since it was "a nipping and an eager air" here, nine thousand feet above the sea-level.

"To think of it! Up in the very midst of the mountain amphitheatre!" murmured Amy.

When seated side by side on the bench, silence fell. They had chatted much in the early stage of their ascent; or rather, Amy had chatted and Bee had listened, which was a not unusual division of labour between them. Bee was a good listener. But more than once Amy had detected a wandering of attention, which was not common. At least, it had not been common till lately.

"Dreaming, Bee?" she had asked; and Bee blushed. Amy noted the blush, putting that down also as something new.

But Amy too for once became dumb, as they gazed from their Alpine Hut over the wide snowy expanse. It was hardly a scene to induce light chatter.

The track by which they had mounted from the Oeschinensee was already lost in darkness. But in front stood forth the roseate peaks of the Blümlisalp; notably the Weisse Frau, square-shouldered, and clothed in a mantle of ineffably delicate pink; and beyond her, almost bending over her like a devoted bridegroom, stood the yet loftier Blümlisalphorn, scarcely less pure, though broken by lines and ridges of rock which lay at too sharp an angle to retain snow. Nearer was the bare and rocky Blümlisalp-stock, cold and grim in the twilight, rising abruptly from the névé of the glacier.

Long lingered the mysterious radiance of the afterglow on the spurs and slopes of those great Gothic peaks, until the last filmy veil, sea-green in hue, faded before the onslaught of night. Then attendant stars began to twinkle in the vault over the Blümlisalphorn, forming a little crown above his head.

The two girls held their breath, clasping hands under the rugs.

"It's too lovely," murmured Amy. "What a splendid world ours is! Do you remember what Ruskin says—'Did you ever see one sunrise like another? Does not God vary His clouds for you every morning and every night?' Does He really—for us? Are you and I meant to enjoy this, Bee? And has nobody ever seen, and will nobody else ever see, just precisely what we are seeing now? Isn't it a perfectly extraordinary idea? Why, even a mile off—even half a mile off—it wouldn't be the same."

Bee did not answer at once. She could not so readily as Amy put her thoughts into words. After a pause she suggested—

"It makes one feel how small one's life is."

"Does it? No, no, Bee—just the other way. I always feel how terrifically full life is—absolutely brim-full! There's any amount, every day, of what one could do, and might do, and ought to do—and of what one doesn't do! Isn't that true?"

Then, with a change of tone—"Bee, do you ever look forward, and picture life in the future—think and dream of what may lie ahead!" Bee's imprisoned hand stirred, for did she not? Amy went on, unheeding the movement—"I do! I'm always and for ever dreaming of the time when you and I will live together; when we shall be just everything to each other. One knows that changes must come, as years pass on; and why shouldn't one think of the things that will lie beyond those changes? Do you remember my telling you last summer of this vision of mine?—Of the dear little home that is to be ours, and of how the days will fly, and of how I shall shelter and guard and pet my darling, and of how we shall want nothing and nobody except just our two selves! Think—how perfect it will be. You remember— don't you?"

Yes; Bee remembered, though, truth to tell, the said talk had made no very profound impression upon her mind. Amy had talked, and she had listened and had pleasantly assented, only to dismiss the subject later from her thoughts. Plainly, Amy had taken it much more seriously.

"When I'm vexed or worried, nothing comforts me like thinking about that sweet little future home of ours. Does it comfort you too?"

Bee hesitated, too truthful to say yes. "I don't know—" she murmured at length. "I haven't thought much about it."

"You haven't!"

"One can't look forward with any sort of certainty. Life is often so different—so unlike what one has fancied."

"That wasn't the way you took it last time."

"I'm older now."

"You're not twenty; and I'm over thirty."

"Yes, I know. But don't you think one learns to see things a little differently as time goes on?"

"Nothing could make me see that differently. I have always counted myself yours for life—and you mine. I have always felt sure that you did too."

"At all events—nothing can ever alter our friendship," remarked Bee cheerfully.

"It would be very much altered, if I believed that you didn't care for me as I care for you."

"I don't think it's a question of caring—but only—one never knows what life may be by-and-by."

Amy made an impatient movement. "Of course I see what all this means. I suppose you're thinking of marrying some day."

Another little pause, broken by Bee's soft tones.

"One can't shut one's eyes quite to possibilities," she said. "Either you or I might some day come across the right man. I dare say it isn't likely—but still—"

"So—that's it!" Amy drew a long breath. "Why didn't you tell me sooner? Who is the lucky person?"

"You are talking nonsense now, Amy. All I say is that the thing might some day happen for either of us. And then—I'm afraid the little house—"

"Would be tenantless! No doubt! And if this supposititious individual did turn up—you'd care for him, of course, a great deal more than you care for—"

Bee laughed a little. "I shouldn't think you could compare the two sorts of feeling. I shall always care for you, no matter what else happens. But I don't see the use of planning so far ahead."

Amy was busily thinking. "Somebody or other is at the bottom of this," she cogitated. "Who can it be? Let me think—Bee has not been her usual self since—since—that visit to her aunts! I know! There were two house-parties while she was there, and she saw no end of people. And—yes, she did mention one name several times—a great pet of the old ladies! I remember! He was there nearly as long as Bee. What was his name?"

"So you can't compare the two feelings!" she remarked aloud. "Which means that you know both, my dear! Ah, now you've given yourself away, you transparent person! Come—you may as well 'fess! Who is the objectionable individual?"

"You are talking nonsense again!"

"I'm not so sure! Let me think—whom have you been seeing lately? Wasn't there a very delightful person at your aunts' house—yes, you certainly spoke of somebody two or three times, and said he was nice. Which from you is high praise. What is the man's name?"

Bee was thankful for the darkness. She wished now that she had not been so foolish as to differ from Amy. Why had she not fallen in with her friend's mood, and allowed her to expatiate as long as she liked on that "sweet little home," which in Bee's eyes looked so far from attractive? It would have been wiser not to risk awakening her suspicions.

"A great many nice people were in the house. Amy, look at that gleam of light on the snow—just dying away."

"I'm more interested in the lights and shades of human beings. I suppose he didn't actually propose."

Bee stood up, and her tone held a touch of gentle dignity.

"Amy, you are talking in a very foolish way—in a way you have no right to talk. I am tired of listening, and I shall go inside."

Amy was in a perverse mood, at the root of which lay jealousy; and this offended her. She, too, jumped up.

"Just as you like! I'll come too. But you can't throw dust in my eyes, my dear. You never can hide things from me, you know. Much better confess that your poor little heart has been taken captive. I have it now! I remember his name! And I shall always owe a grudge to Wratt-Wrothesley after this. Of course—it's that Mr. Ivor! Wretched man, to rob me of my Bee!"

She slightly raised her voice that Bee might hear. And as the latter disappeared within the hut door, making no reply, a soft sound floated down from the loft, just over Amy's head—the unmistakable sound of a subdued masculine snore.

"Gracious!" uttered Amy under her breath. "Somebody must be up there! What a mercy he's asleep!"

She found Bee inside, looking pale, and disposed to hold coldly aloof. Amy, already ashamed of herself, was constrained to whisper—

"Never mind! I was only talking nonsense! I won't again! It's all right!"

CHAPTER VIII
IN AN AVALANCHE

THE Hut was not, as Amy and Beatrice had supposed, occupied only by themselves, their guide and their porter. Unknown to them all, two guideless climbers had arrived earlier—none other than the young English clergyman and his friend. They had retired to rest in the loft, purposing to ascend the Blümlisalphorn the next day. As they meant to start in the very small hours of the morning, they were glad to get to sleep without loss of time; and by thus retreating to the loft they hoped to secure an absence of interruptions.

Steimathen had quickly discovered, by the remains of a fire in the stove, that somebody had preceded them; but this fact he had not happened to name to the girls.

One of the two men, out of sight in the loft, was Robert Royston, now abroad for his short summer holiday. The other, strange to say, was actually Lancelot Dennis Ivor himself—with whom Bee had been thrown during her three weeks' visit to her aunts.

Bee had known, and had not forgotten, that he was an adept at mountaineering. Nay, it was he who had advised her to do a little scrambling in this very district, when she had mentioned her hope of a visit to Switzerland in the summer. She did not dream of coming across him, since he had said that Switzerland this year would be for him an impossibility, on account of certain engagements. Plans had changed, however; and here he was in company with his old college friend, Robert Royston.

At table d'hôte the evening before, though Robert alluded to his proposed ascent, he did not speak of the Hut; and she failed to deduce the fact that he and his friend were likely to sleep there. Neither did he utter his friend's name. Possibly, had Patricia not appeared just when she did, drawing off everybody's attention, he might have done either; in which case she and Amy would have been upon their guard. As things were, they had not the smallest suspicion that any human being was within earshot—the guide and his son being quite cut off by the solid wall of the Hut.

Voices under the open loft-window aroused Ivor from a light sleep. Not for some time fully. He lay in semi-consciousness—vaguely wishing that he had not been disturbed, envying the calm slumber of Rob, hearing partly as in a dream what was said, and regarding the same with the uncritical detachment and indifference of a dreamer.

The soft tones of one speaker sounded familiar; and though he was too far gone to attach a name, they transported him in imagination to Wratt-Wrothesley; and he saw himself again wandering through the lovely grounds with Bee.

A girlish argument of some sort seemed to be going on; and he took a drowsy dislike to Amy, as he rolled over and tried to forget himself once more.

Then the sounds grew clearer, more definite. That gentle-voiced girl was being pestered—worried—and he felt a touch of indignation. It dawned upon him that he was listening to something not meant for his ears; and he was rousing himself to give a loud cough of warning, when—

"Much better confess that your poor little heart has been taken captive," checked him abruptly, with a feeling that the listening girl must not know what he had heard. Then came the name of the place where he had met Bee Major, and his own name following.

In a moment he was wide awake. In a moment also he had the blankets over his ears, shutting out further sounds.

He recognised now well enough that soft voice. The only marvel was that he had not instantly known it. He had seen much of Bee during three weeks, had liked her much. If the impression made by him upon her was deep, the impression made by her upon him was not slight. He admired her; he enjoyed intercourse with her; he hoped some day before long to meet her again; he had even recognised as a possibility that he might by-and-bye find himself in love with her.

But he was not yet in love. He told himself so, almost angrily, as he clutched the blanket round his head. And of all wretched contretemps, what could be worse than this? That he and she should have come together, high in the mountains, away from the crowds, neither knowing of the other's presence, and that he should have overheard, without intending it, words which—whether truly or falsely—no doubt implied that he had somehow captured her heart! It was appalling!

Of course it might be all a mistake. Probably it was all a mistake. The girl was joking, teasing her companion, trying to get a rise out of her, as girls will; and Beatrice might never give the careless words another thought, if—it all hung upon that!—if she did not discover that he had been close at hand, and that he had or might have overheard. But if she did find this out—his whole being rose in revolt for Bee's sake. What would she not think? What would she not feel?

Small chance of sleep remained to him. He lay thinking the matter over, worrying himself, and planning how to escape in the early morning, before she should become aware of his presence.

An odd realisation crept over him, as he tossed and turned, that—if it were true—and no doubt it was not true, it was mere nonsense!—but if it were, then to be so loved would be a new and beautiful thing. Through his twenty-five years of life he had never yet known what it was to be first in a woman's heart. His mother had died in his infancy, and he had no sisters. He was well off, successful, and popular. Match-making mothers had courted him; and girls of a sort—the sort he would never dream of marrying, for he held a high ideal of what a woman should be—had flirted with him. But he knew Bee well enough to grasp that this would be altogether different. If Bee Major loved, hers would be a love worth having.

Of course it was all nonsense; a silly joke of that other unpleasant girl. Only—if it were—

He knew himself to be companionable and agreeable, liked by people in general, one who made and kept friends. But to be utterly and absolutely first with another—to be the one and only man to one only woman—that would put him on a new level, would give to life a fresh colouring.

No use dwelling on all that, he told himself impatiently. Bee Major had probably laughed at the silly words; and he himself was not in love. He was, however, very much concerned to prevent her from becoming aware of his presence in the Hut; and when one o'clock arrived, he wakened Robert, and impressed on him the need for abnormal caution, lest they should disturb two lady-climbers, sleeping on the ground-floor.

With exaggerated care, he set the example, creeping down the ladder like a mouse, and keeping as much as possible in shadow behind the stove, lest they also should have planned an early start, and should arouse themselves. Not likely, at one o'clock in the morning; but on such occasions nothing is impossible.

Besides, Beatrice might be awake, despite her stillness; and though she should catch no glimpse of his face, she might recognise his voice. So, in sombre silence, and not without some nervous glances towards the lower shelf, on which lay two dimly-outlined figures rolled in rugs, he drank his coffee. Rob kept equal silence.

It was a relief to Ivor to find himself safe outside the Hut. Quietly he and Rob started on their dark upward tramp, lighted only by stars, and by the glimmering lantern which swayed to and fro in the leader's hand. An hour later, as they were crossing the hard frozen neve, he received a fresh shock. Some words passed about their return route, and Rob remarked that he had entered a note as to their intentions in the Visitor's Book at the Hut.

"You didn't write our names!" Ivor involuntarily exclaimed.

"Yes, of course—why not?"

Why not, indeed? Ivor could offer no reason. He said only—

"I meant to do it on our way back."

"Always better to leave word of one's plans in case of an accident."

This was true enough; and Ivor made no further protest. He recalled that Rob had stayed behind for a minute or two, when he had made his way out of the Hut in readiness to start. He was very much annoyed—not with Rob for doing what was quite reasonable, but with the fact. Beatrice Major would undoubtedly look at the book, and she could not fail to see his name. She would at once surmise, not that he had actually heard her friend's foolish words, but that he might have done so. Too late now to do anything; but the day was more or less spoilt for him.

Such thoughts had to be put on one side, as the difficulties of the way increased. They were still there, lying as a weight at the back of his mind, though he had resolutely to ignore them and to bend all his energies to the task in hand. The ascent of the Blümlisalphorn is not exactly playwork, even for experienced climbers.

For a good while there was easy going over the frozen snow, and only for a few hundred yards was their route shadowed by the possibility—a slight one at such an early hour—of a falling avalanche. Breakfast on a pure white table-cloth followed; and after this began the exciting part of their ascent.

At first they mounted snow in good condition, lying on a foundation of rock, which here and there cropped through. Then it steepened and hardened, and the cutting of steps became necessary, till they reached the col or narrow neck, from which one looks down on the little Oeschinen Lake and the Valley of Kandersteg.

Thence the usual route is followed by the arête, now ice, now rock, not only narrow but steeply ascending. If the leader, as he cuts steps up the knife-edge of ice, should slip and fall, the instant duty of his companion on the rope is to fling himself over on the opposite side, where his weight would counterbalance that of his friend, and so prevent both from being dashed to pieces three thousand feet below. For such prompt action, in such a position, no little nerve is requisite; yet not to do it spells a double fatality. Both Ivor and Rob were men of calm nerve and quick decision.

While traversing the arête, no thinking about Beatrice could be allowed himself by Ivor; and he was hardly conscious of the scenery. Nothing but close and exclusive regard to each successive planting of the feet ensures safety, as, steadying himself with his ice-axe, a climber moves slowly upward and onward, till the summit is gained.

They stood there at length, side by side, triumphant,—just in time to revel in the magnificent sight of a cloudless panorama of peaks, each with its own wealth of golden light and azure shade, its morning glories and fleeting shadows, its crumpled and rifted glaciers, its uncountable revelations of beauty. Silent and entranced, they drank in the loveliness with supreme enjoyment; though perhaps neither could quite banish from his mind a recollection of that nerve-testing "knife-edge," which had soon to be descended.

Coming down such a mauvais pas is, as everybody knows, always far worse than going up it. Doubtless, it was as well that the Blümlisalphorn does not lend itself to a picnic or a lengthy rest upon the summit; for muscles are apt to stiffen with delay. A few minutes were all that could be safely spared.

As they gazed, neither of the two was thinking only and exclusively of the view.

In Rob's mind, together with the mountain glory, lay the picture of a girl's face, fair and smiling, which he could not banish. Patricia had laid her spell upon him; and even while his attention was most taken up with the perils of the way, that face remained. It sprang up now with a fresh insistence.

"If ever I marry—" he found himself saying, as his eyes roved from height to height, from glacier to glacier—"If ever I marry, she shall be my wife!" He was not conscious of haste in this decision—if a dream may be called a decision; and he did not even remember his words to Magda about not being a marrying man. He had not then "seen the girl." To-day he had seen her.

Ivor also, while his glance wandered hither and thither, was haunted by a presence. His chivalry had been troubled on behalf of Bee; and the thought of what she must go through, when she became aware of his nearness the evening before, pressed upon his mind. So soon as active exertion ceased, the burden made itself felt; and he began again to picture her state of mind.

If he did not really care for Bee, more than he was yet aware, it might seem singular that he should be so much disturbed. This view of the question did occur, and he had no answer ready—yet still he was disquieted. When, however, the moment arrived for starting; when the "knife-edge" had once more to be tackled—then he put her out of his thoughts; and then, too, Rob had for the time to forget Patricia. All their attention, all their nerve, were required.

Chip, chip, went the leader's axe, as he improved the steps made on their ascent; and when one was clean-cut, the nail-studded boot slid forward, and found good hold. Again the axe was at work; and the other boot crept to its place. So each in turn advanced; and never did the two climbers move together; and never was the rope that bound them in a bond of comradeship allowed to sag. Its tautness was their only insurance against the disaster which must otherwise have followed upon a slip. But, happily, no slip occurred.

They had come to a determination, on the preceding day, that if all went well they would return by another route from the col overlooking Kandersteg—a route rarely attempted, since the condition of an open couloir, a wide gully full of snow, which would have to be descended, was seldom tempting. In addition, there was always a possibility of the bergshrund below the couloir—a huge crevasse at the foot of the snow-slope—entirely stopping their further progress, and forcing them to re-ascend to the col, after half the descent had been done. But they hoped to find either a bridge of winter snow across the bergshrund, or else a place where they could turn it. And they were young and enthusiastic, and willing to run a certain amount of risk.

So they decided to venture on the attempt. And this was the scheme which Rob, the moment before they started, had scribbled in the Visitors' Book at the Hut, together with their two names.

The variation from the more ordinary route at first promised well; and the soft snow of the open couloir or gully allowed them, as they came down it, to kick for themselves deep and safe steps.

But gradually, almost imperceptibly, the character of the snow changed. It became powdery in substance; and each downward step started a miniature avalanche—so small as to discount precaution.

They were now hardly two hundred yards from the yawning bergshrund at the bottom of the slope; and to turn back without having examined it would be really too exasperating. Thus it was that the warning given by that shifting snow was allowed to pass almost unheeded. Rob, who was now the leader, did his best to pack it firmly, before trusting his weight to each foothold; and so far all seemed safe.

Ivor indeed felt so secure, as he plunged his foot into one deep step after another made by his friend, that he a little relaxed his watchful caution, and allowed his attention to wander, indulging in speculations whether he and Rob would find the two girls still at the Hut. But for that unfortunate remark overheard the evening before, he would have wished that it might be so. He would have liked nothing better than to see Bee Major again. He might never reach the point of actually falling in love with her; yet she was undoubtedly a very sweet and taking girl.

Such thoughts were travelling through his mind when something occurred, against which not all the acumen of the most experienced guides could have insured, had they ventured to trust themselves upon so treacherous a slope.

The sheet of snow which the two were descending began to stir! At first slightly—then more decisively.

Ivor, well behind Rob, the rope between them being nearly taut, was the first to awake to the awful fact that a wave had formed in front of him. Only too well he knew what that meant; and he instantaneously dug his ice-axe deep into the snow. This had small effect; for, as the snow-sheet slid downward, Rob was carried with it. For one second the rope tightened round Ivor; but, as the silent onrush of the avalanche fought for the mastery, he too felt himself gently yet irresistibly drawn into the white stream. Their eyes met, saying what their lips did not utter—"We are lost!"

Down and down, sliding, struggling, borne along by the moving mass, went both men; but Ivor was more in the actual stream than Rob, who happened to be swept to one side. It was a small avalanche, neither deep nor wide; and while Ivor remained near the centre, Rob was on the border. Though perforce moving with it, he was subject to less impetus; and as the white wave curled round a rib of rock outstanding from the snow, the rope caught firmly. On swirled the shallow snow, and he remained behind.

All might have been well with them both, had the rope held. But when Ivor's weight came on it with a heavy jerk, it severed on the sharp rock, as though cut by a knife.

Ivor was swept rapidly downwards; and without a sound, he disappeared over the edge, into the bergshrund. From that deep snow-prison, even if the hapless climber had not been at once killed by the fall, or smothered in the cataract of snow, Rob—barely escaping the same fate, and with only a short end of broken rope—was powerless to rescue him.

CHAPTER IX
FRIENDS IN PERIL

FOUR hours after the departure of the two men, the girls were up, starting for their smaller ascent of the little Rothstock. They had a delightful five-hours' scramble, at the end of which, they again reached the Hut.

No contretemps, no false step on the part of either, had marred the climb. Amy had, in the early hours, shown a slight tendency to moodiness; and Bee had been silent and grave. But as the charm of their expedition gripped them, the spirits of both girls improved. As yet Bee remained in complete ignorance of the presence of others in the loft through the night. She could not easily throw off her displeasure at Amy's conduct; but she did her best to hide it. After all Amy had not meant to be unkind. She had only been—silly! It was wiser on her part to treat the affair as nonsense. And as the day went on, the recollection sank out of mind.

They resolved to have an hour's rest, before tackling the easy descent to Kandersteg; and as Amy flung herself down outside the Hut, Bee went inside, returning with the Visitors' Book in her hands.

"We haven't taken a look at the list of climbers yet," she said.

Amy had hoped to avert this. The last thing she wished was for Bee to awake to the possibility of those imprudent words having been overheard by some chance tourist. Unknown to Bee, she had found out that, not one man only, but two men had slept in the loft; and all day she had been at pains to keep clear of the subject.

"Yes, of course. We must sign our own names as conquerors of the Rothstock," she said quickly. "I'll do that presently. You've got to rest now. Give me the book, and I'll read the list aloud."

"Thanks, but we can both look. I like to see." Bee turned to the latest page, and exclaimed in surprise—"Robert Royston!—Magda's brother—" and the last word remained only half-uttered, as her eyes fell upon the name following. A deep flush suffused her cheeks. Amy, glancing at the page and then, in dismay, at her face, knew in a moment that what she had half-jestingly surmised was true.

Bee's colour faded faster than it had arisen. She grew white to the lips as if on the verge of fainting.

"They were here—last night!" Her eyes met those of her companion. "Amy!—Did you know?"

"Of course I didn't know. How should I? We both felt sure there was nobody here except ourselves. I never dreamt of such a thing. But we talked so low—they couldn't have heard a word!"

"Oh, no—no! You called out—loudly!"

"Bee, I'm sure I didn't. It isn't my way. You are fancying. And the window would be shut—"

"They are English. It would be open."

"But they were sound asleep. Of course they were sound!" Amy was really grieved at Bee's pale distress. "Quite sound!"

"It is easy to say so! You do not know."

"But Peter told me they went to bed very early, on purpose to sleep. Yes, I asked him, because—just after you went in, I heard a snore. I didn't see any use in worrying you, but I did ask Peter, and he said there were two Herren in the loft, and they had gone off in the night. I wonder we didn't hear them go. But I heard the snore quite plainly."

"That might show that one was asleep. Not—both!"

"If they had chanced to overhear a few words, they would know it meant nothing—just fun! They would understand."

"If only, only you had not done it!" Bee despairingly murmured. "I feel as if I could never bear to see either of them again."

"Why, Bee, really you are making too much of a small matter. What does it signify? Just a jest between two girls! Any sensible man would know what it was worth. If I had had a notion that anybody was there, of course I wouldn't have teased you; but I had not. And till this moment I didn't know their names. But now we do know, we can be perfectly sure that if either of them was awake, he would never have listened. He would have done something to let us know he was there."

"Not if he were taken by surprise—if he woke just then and heard his own name! How could he speak? I dare say it isn't likely; but it might have happened! I do think that sort of joking is very very wrong and unkind."

"Well, I won't do it again; I promise I won't. And I wouldn't think any more about it if I were you. Things can't be helped now; and the only way is to take sensibly what's done and can't be undone. You may depend upon it Mr. Ivor heard nothing."

Bee felt that it was easy for one person to be philosophical about another's trouble. She bent over the book with a troubled face, and read aloud a short note scrawled after the two names—"Going to try the Blümlisalphorn, descending from the col to the alp above the Oeschinensee."

She carried the book inside the Hut, and drew their guide's attention to this memorandum. Steimathen uttered a gruff word of disapproval. It was in his opinion a difficult and dangerous deviation from the ordinary route. The Herren would have been better advised, he said, had they kept to that route—with the snow in none too sound a state. Naturally, Peter was not particularly pleased with the enterprise of guideless parties, on mountains which he looked upon as his preserve.

All the way down, as far as the Oeschinen Hotel, Beatrice walked in thoughtful silence. She was pondering, partly, the dread that Ivor might have been awake, and so might have heard Amy's imprudent utterance; but also her mind was a good deal occupied with Steimathen's observations. More and more the possibility took hold of her that those two were in danger. The guide's suggestion might, it was true, have been to some extent dictated by jealousy; yet such a suggestion from a first-rate guide, who was also a good and dependable man, could not be lightly dismissed.

What if things were as Peter seemed to fear—if they had chosen a perilous route—if the snow was in an unsafe state—if something should happen to them on their way down? Nay, what if something were happening at this moment? The fear came between her mind and Amy's talk. For once she wished that her friend were capable of silence.

She made an opportunity to tackle Peter anew on the subject, asking fuller details about the nature of the proposed descent, and the reasons for his uneasiness. Peter's explanations were the reverse of comforting.

Very much more quickly than they had gone up, they regained the little hotel on the shore of the Oeschinensee. No sooner were they there, than Bee made straight for the telescope. She called Peter, got him to show her by which way the English gentlemen had planned to descend, and found that, from her present position, the entire route from the col—including a risky descent towards a very undesirable bergshrund, the nature of which he had already enlarged upon—could be swept by the glass.

Whether they had yet passed in safety that yawning chasm, Bee could not know, Peter could not tell her. If they had not, there was no reason why she should not actually watch their progress, could she but once "locate" them—or, as she expressed it, "get hold of them."

A good hour went by, during which she searched in vain. The guide wished to continue their descent to Kandersteg; and Amy was growing impatient; but neither of them could induce Bee to stir.

"I can't just yet," she pleaded. "There is no hurry. I have such a feeling that something is wrong. Do let me try a little longer. Yes—it may be all fancy—but I want to make sure."

Remonstrances fell on deaf ears. The usually compliant girl was resolute. She said little, but she clung to her post.

"What an imagination you have!" pettishly complained Amy, who by this time was both tired and cross. Yet still Bee gazed, searching the white slopes, regardless of her own or the other's fatigue.

"Just a little longer, Amy! I shall find them soon. I am sure I shall. If you cannot wait, please go on with Abraham; and I'll follow with Peter."

"Thanks. If I go, I'd rather have Peter. Of course I don't mean to leave you. But it is such nonsense!"

"Peter must wait, in case anything is wrong. He would have to go and help them."

"Why on earth should anything be wrong? It's more than likely that they have kept to the usual route, and are at the Hut by now. It's ridiculous your bothering about them like this."

"I can't help it, Amy. If anything happened to Magda's brother—"

"Oh, you needn't pretend, my dear! It's not—'Magda's brother'—" mimicking her tone—"that exercises your mind."

Beatrice lifted her face for one moment to look steadily at the other girl.

"I don't think that is quite like you," she said gravely, and she went back to the telescope.

Amy broke a lengthy silence, as if it had not existed. "No; it isn't like me. At least, I hope not. It isn't like my better self. I'm in the grip of the Green-eyed Monster to-day. Can't you see? It's hateful."

Bee's hand came softly on hers.

"Yes; I know. I've got to conquer. But all the same—oh, bother—I wish they'd turn up and have done with it. I'm tired."

"I'm so sorry," was all Bee said; and another ten minutes of patient scanning went by. Then her attitude changed, as—"There they are!" escaped her lips.

"Really!" with awakened interest.

"I see them! I see them plainly. Two little dots on the snow. I'm sure it is they." She called eagerly to Peter. "Oh, come!—come and look. I've found the Herren. What are they doing?"

She relinquished her post as he eagerly advanced. "My lady, she has good eyesight. She is right. The Herren are there. Nicht wahr?"

"Let me see again. One moment, please. Just to make sure!"

Unwillingly the guide complied, for Bee could not control her impatience.

"I see them now—quite plainly. Is that the part you said was where the snow might be bad? How fast they are coming down! Is it safe? But they are not so very high up. It's all right, isn't it? Oh! Oh, what is happening? What is it?" She seized Peter, and thrust him vehemently into her seat. "Tell me—what does it mean?"

Peter drew a long audible breath. He was just in time to catch one clear glimpse of the rolling figure of Ivor, before it vanished.

"Something is—not right," he answered gravely. "Yes; there is a mishap. One of the Herren has fallen. It may be—not far—but he is gone down. Nein, nein, Mees—one moment," as she grasped his arm. "Permit me, Mees—it is better that I look. Mees will not understand. The second Herr does not move. He stays there. He does nothing."

"You will send help! You will go yourself! You will not leave him to die!" urged the girl. "Peter—what can be done? Oh, please make haste."

She wrung her hands together, waiting for his next words, which did not come at once. Peter's gaze was riveted.

"The fallen Herr is out of sight still. The Herr above stirs not. He stays in one spot."

"You will go—will you not?" implored Bee.

"It is so. Mees may rest assured. All shall be done that man can do. They shall not be left to perish." Three minutes longer he studied the far-off scene.

"Peter—tell me—which Herr is it that has fallen?" She put the question faintly; and in her heart she chided herself for hoping that it might be Magda's brother—poor Magda!—and not the other.

"Ach! How can I tell?"

"Is he—is he—dead?"

Peter stood up. "We must not waste the time, Mees, in talk. It is that we must act. You, ladies, will wait here—is it not so?—till a rescue-party shall return from going to the Herren?"

"Yes, yes—only don't delay!" pleaded Bee.

Two other guides had happily arrived within the last hour from an expedition with three ladies, who at once agreed to manage the rest of their descent under the leadership of their porter, since they were unable to wait. A hurried consultation then took place; and it was decided that the three guides should start immediately, taking ropes and restoratives, and going by the shortest possible route. Peter, from his intimate knowledge of the district, had divined that one of the "Herren" must have fallen into the bergshrund, though he would not say as much to Bee. He knew too well what it might mean.

For Beatrice there followed a period of suspense, such as she had never before gone through. The hours seemed endless. It was not her way to talk of what she felt. All she wanted was to be left alone, that she might carry on her watch, silently praying. Afterwards, when she looked back, she knew that her whole being had been concentrated into one continuous wordless petition.

Amy really was sorry, now that she knew true cause for fear to exist. But her anxiety was moderate and impersonal; while to Bee it seemed that all joy in life hung upon the result of the guides' expedition.

While daylight lasted, she sat at the telescope, searching and searching, till her eyes grew dim and dazzled with the strain. That one tiny dark figure was always there; moving from time to time, yet never straying far. Beatrice built much upon the fact. If the fallen man were dead, why should his friend stay? On the other hand, if the fallen man were alive, would not his friend go in quest of help? Hope was put to a severe test.

Amy, as she found her efforts to bestow comfort of small use, went indoors and fell asleep; but Bee could not rest. When darkness made the telescope of no avail, she walked up and down outside the hotel, scarcely conscious of the cold, turning gently from well-meant attempts on the part of the hotel people to cheer her up, and picturing to herself without cessation Ivor dying or dead, or at best waiting on the lone island of rock, in cold and hunger and discomfort, resolute not to quit his friend.

If only he might escape with life, she would be content to ask no more. He might never think of her; he might never care for her; they might never meet again; but still he would be alive. She did not know how to endure the thought of a world which would no longer contain him.

Mastered at length by Amy's entreaties, she too went into the hotel, and lay down under blankets, refusing to undress. When Amy again dropped soundly off, she arose and seated herself at the window, to gaze in the direction of the spot where, perhaps, Ivor still was; or looking up at the calm stars overhead, to wonder whether already his spirit might have taken flight to those sublime heights; and how soon—if indeed it were so—she might be permitted to follow. Would it be wrong to wish to go—not to have to wait very long?

Then, refusing to admit any such possibilities, she imagined the guides drawing near to the scene of disaster, and tried to see, as in a vision, how they would rescue the fallen man. Though Peter had not told her exactly what it was that he conjectured, she had been quick to put two and two together, quick to read his thoughts. He had spoken of the bergshrund before the accident; and she knew at least something of what might be involved. Scene after scene passed before her mind's eyes till her brain whirled.

Dawn at last began; and with the earliest gleams of light she again planted herself at the post of observation; long before she could hope to make out anything. Time slowly, slowly dragged by; and patience at length met with its reward.

As day grew into being, she found herself actually witnessing the cautious descent of the couloir by the rescue-party. They hugged the rocks on one side, avoiding the course of the avalanche; and Bee watched, with a trembling hope which could find no utterance, till they reached the islet of rock where that patient watcher had spent his night; and the solitary dark figure was reinforced by other little dark figures. They seemed to pause and consult; then movements took place. What actually happened was that one of the guides attached himself to the full length of the rope, and was let down towards the shrund by the others, till he vanished over its edge. Then, when he reached Ivor, he fastened the rope round him, and they were drawn up together, the guide undermost.

Bee, from her distant post, could make out something of this. She followed the descent of the small dark body, saw it disappear, and with shortened breath waited through interminable minutes till something became visible, coming up slowly out of the depth. Something! But was it one man or two men?

She strained her eyes to see. Yes, certainly—two specks, close together, yet distinct, where only one had been; both apparently being dragged upwards toward where the rest of the party stood. The second might be Lancelot Ivor—or Robert Royston—or only a lifeless form, taken from its snow-prison. Who could tell?

"Anyhow, they've got him," Amy remarked, when Bee in short murmurs told what she saw.

"If we had not waited—if I had not found them—"

"Yes. You were right. I'm glad now that you persisted."

"Nobody might have known till—too late! Amy, you were very patient."

"I didn't feel patient, I assure you."

More hours crept by, and still Bee watched. Amy at last protested—

"You are worn out, Bee. If you would but lie down for an hour!"

"I can't just yet. Please don't ask it."

Nearer and nearer drew the party; more and more distinct in the field of the telescope.

Then Amy heard one short sigh of relief. "Yes," she said. "I can count them now. They are resting. The three guides, and both the others. Both—both!"

"Yes, dear."

"He's not killed. He's—alive!"

She slid off her seat into Amy's arms; and for a moment Amy thought she had fainted away; but she pulled herself together.

"How stupid! What made me do that?"

"You felt dizzy. Come indoors now and lie down. They are all right; and they can't get here for ever so long."

"Yes; I think I will. I'm a little—tired."

She walked quietly, stumbling once or twice, as if uncertain of her footing. Amy put her on the bed, and covered her up.

"You are to go to sleep. You shall hear everything by-and-by."

Amy stooped for a kiss; and Bee held her down. "Dear—you have been so kind. Thank you. Please don't let anybody know that I have—minded!"

"No, of course not!" Amy did not add, as she felt tempted to do, that anybody might have seen. She knew that it would be easy to explain Bee's over-anxiety, by the fact that one of the two men was the brother of her intimate friend.

"He's safe!" dropped slowly from Bee's lips. She drew one long sigh; her arms slackened and fell; and already she was dead asleep. A look of childlike peace overspread her face.

Amy stood looking down upon her. "Poor little dear! That's all you care for now! He—not even 'they.' And will he ever care for you? And if not—will you break your poor little heart? People don't break their hearts now-a-days—some say. But Bee is not like the ordinary run."

Bee smiled in her sleep.

"I shall hate him if he does; and I shall hate him if he doesn't! A nice state of things! O you Green-eyed Monster!—How I despise you! But you've had the better of me to-day; though I don't believe Bee has found it out. And you've got to be squashed, you know!" Amy shook her fist as at an enemy.

CHAPTER X
THE RESCUED MAN

ONCE asleep, after her long watch, Beatrice slept profoundly—slept till long after the rescue-party and the two Englishmen had come in.

There could be no question of getting back that night to Kandersteg. Ivor was suffering from frostbite and bruises; and though, with a good deal of help, he had managed to walk part of the way down to the Oeschinen Hotel, he could do no more. Both he and Rob had to be warmed and fed; and for both a good night's rest was the first essential.

Bee saw nothing of them until next morning, by which time she was quite restored to her usual gentle self. That evening talk outside the Hut seemed to her dreamy and unreal, and as if it had happened years before. She had almost lost sight of it, under the great strain of anxiety; and she could not think of it now, for the joy of knowing Ivor to be safe. For this her heart sang a ceaseless song of thanksgiving.

Or at least, she would not let herself think of it. Probably, as Amy insisted, he had heard nothing. If he had caught a few words—the only course for her was to be utterly simple, utterly natural, free from self-consciousness. Then he would forget; he would think himself mistaken. Bee was capable of carrying out this rôle; as perhaps many girls, less practised in self-control, might not have been.

Ivor appeared last of an early party. He came to breakfast limping, and still pale, but with a smile.

"All right, old fellow?" Rob asked.

"Thanks—yes." His glance went straight to Bee, and without hesitation he crossed over, holding out his hand. "We have met before," he said; for he, like Bee, had resolved on complete simplicity as the only mode of "grasping the nettle."

She met the hand and smiled bravely; and before a word could be spoken, Peter Steimathen, who had followed Ivor in, to see how the "Herr" might be after his severe experience, made matters easier for both by breaking in—

"It is to the Mees here that you owe your life, Mein Herr!" He glanced at Bee with admiration. "The Fräulein she would have her way! She would not return to Kandersteg, till she should see where the English Herren were. Myself I had told her there might be difficulties for the Herren, and the Fräulein understood. Ach, but had she not so done, we should not so soon have gone in search. Nein, truly we should not."

"And that must have meant for me—just all the difference!" Ivor observed in a low voice.

He was not allowed then to say more. Rob insisted on attention to breakfast. But Bee had already heard from the others what was thought of her share in the rescue; and her feelings may be easily imagined. From Ivor she wanted no thanks. It was enough, and more than enough, to know that she had been the means of saving his life—as they all declared was the case.

After breakfast, when Amy was putting up their things and Peter was consulting with Rob how to get Ivor to Kandersteg—since he was clearly unable to walk any distance—she found herself, quite by accident, alone with the latter.

Bee took it simply; and her complete naturalness made the position of affairs easy for him.

"I am afraid you are suffering a good deal with your foot," she said.

"Rather numb still, thanks; but I'm getting back the proper circulation. No fear now, they tell me, that I shall lose even a toe." He smiled; then, putting aside his own hurts, he expressed his gratitude, in a few strong words, for what she had done.

"Neither Royston nor I can ever forget it. We owe our lives to your thoughtfulness. I—even more than he. I suppose he might have got back in safety; but I was helpless."

"Would not the guides have started in search of you—if I had done nothing?"

"Yes. The question is—whether they would have been in time."

"I am very, very glad!" The words sounded absurdly inadequate. She had never in her life been half so glad, half so thankful; yet she spoke quietly. "It was curious—I could not help waiting. Such a strong feeling came that something was wrong—that I had to wait!—Even before it actually happened."

"One may say, I suppose, that it was—Providential!" He spoke with shy English reserve, yet with real feeling; and this time her response was eager.

"Oh, I am quite, quite sure!" After a pause she went on. "I don't understand why Mr. Royston stayed there. Ought he not to have gone at once for help? Suppose we had not seen you? Suppose the guides had not started when they did?"

"That was the question—what he should do. The shrund was in no state to be crossed, especially by one man alone. He would have had to go back up the mountain, and round by the usual route."

"Could he not do it?"

"The danger of course is greater for a man by himself. But he is a cool hand, not soon flurried. He would have gone in the morning, if help had not come. Nothing would induce him to budge earlier, though I did my best. I knew that putting off must make the return alone much worse for him."

"Then it was for your sake that he waited?"

"Entirely. I could not persuade him to leave me. It would have pretty well settled matters, I suppose, so far as I was concerned; and that was what he felt."

Bee's eyes grew large. "You mean that he—?"

"He had made up his mind that, if I had to spend the night there by myself, I should be frozen before morning."

"But was it—was it—so bad as that?" Her breath grew short.

"I'm not sure that I could have held out, if it hadn't been for him."

"The cold—?" murmured Bee.

"Well, the cold was awful. Sometimes I seemed to be on the verge of slipping out of it all—losing hold of life. And then Rob's voice would rouse me, and I could fight on. But if he hadn't been there—don't you see?"

"Yes, I see." Bee had grown white, but she spoke quietly. "You might have just forgotten yourself, and not—not—"

"Not come to again," ended Ivor. "Yes, that was it. But of course I'd have given anything to make him go. I knew what it must mean, waiting hour after hour on that steep slope, with no shelter of any sort. He's a fine fellow! I wish you knew him better."

"Perhaps I shall some day. His sister is a friend of mine. Yes, he must be—splendid!" So was somebody else, thought Bee, and she did not mind the little glow which had come to her face, for he would only think it was called up by admiration of Mr. Royston. "And then—" she said—"then, I suppose, you saw the guides coming. I mean, Mr. Royston saw them."

"Yes; and his shout soon let me know. He had just been saying he must start soon. After that it was all right. I only had to be hauled up. But you understand now how much we owe to you—both of us."

"Not Mr. Royston!"

"Yes, both of us. I very much doubt whether, after that night, he would have been equal to the return by himself. He found it quite enough, even with the help of a guide. So I think we may pretty well say that you have saved both our lives!"

"I've always longed to be able some day to save somebody's life," she replied gently.

Much more he could have told her, and did not.

He might have described at length that interminable night in his dreary bergshrund prison, where he dared not stir, for fear of falling yet lower. He had found a lodgment on a narrow snow-shelf at one side of the great cleft. Black depths of mystery lay below; and steep snow-walls rose high before and behind him; and the projecting upper "lip" of the shrund overhung his head; and nothing was clearly visible except a strip of sky far, far above. At any moment a fresh fall of snow might overwhelm him; and time crawled on with leaden footsteps, as he waited in his constrained position, suffering acutely from the piercing cold.

He could not see Rob. He was without food, without restoratives, and in hourly peril of death. Vainly, from time to time, he urged his friend to escape while escape was possible, and to leave him to his fate. Or rather— and he put this forward for Rob's sake—to get help. But he knew well that such help must almost certainly arrive too late; and Rob, knowing the same, always cheerily refused, bidding him keep up a brave heart.

Through it all Ivor could not banish Bee from his mind. He saw her face; he was haunted by her soft tones; he recalled little talks with her in the spring; he heard again Amy's utterance outside the Hut. The consciousness of what she possibly felt for him, and floating visions of what in some future day they might become one to the other, alternated with a picture of his life cut short, his career abruptly ended. And with this came self-searchings as to the manner of life he had lived; not indeed a blameworthy life, weighed in ordinary scales; yet not all that it should have been, weighed in loftier scales, seen in the near prospect of the Life to follow. It had not been an irreligious or a prayerless life; yet now, looking back, he felt how much had been wanting in it of whole-hearted devotion to the service of God; and keen regrets for the past mingled with strong resolutions for the future—if he should be permitted to get through safely.

As the fierce numbing cold of night enveloped him, creeping from limb to limb, stiffening every muscle, gripping his very bones, he could hear Royston far above, stamping, stirring, ever and anon shouting words of encouragement.

And once—never after would Ivor lose the impression made!—once, without warning or introduction, in strong distinct tones, Rob repeated the General Confession. Heart and soul Ivor joined in, echoing each familiar petition, and finding in them the full utterance of his own deepest need.

A slight pause at the end; and then the emphatic tones went on, in words equally familiar, declaring that, "HE pardoneth and absolveth!" Sentence by sentence came soon the Lord's Prayer; the evening Collects; the General Thanksgiving; and the Blessing.

This, Ivor thought, was the end of their strange Evensong—a service amid unwonted surroundings, and with an unwonted audience. Silence fell upon the icy scene; and he thankfully felt that it had done him good. Death indeed might lie ahead; near at hand! But there was ONE Who "pardoneth and absolveth all them that truly repent and unfeignedly believe!" The words gained a new power and depth for Ivor in that hour.

Rob had not done. His voice pealed forth anew; and now in song. Words and tune were alike well-known. But never before had they carried such meaning to Ivor, as when he heard them from the depths of his snow-cavern.

> "O God, our help in ages past,
>   Our hope for years to come;
> Our shelter from the stormy blast,
>   And our Eternal Home!"

No wonder, as verse after verse rang through the still night-air, and rolled over the snowy slopes, and echoed from the rocks, that they brought a sound of hope and promise for the unfortunate prisoner below. At the end, Ivor had difficulty in controlling his voice, to shout a hearty—"Thank you!"

No, he would never forget! An experience such as this leaves its stamp on a man for life!

CHAPTER XI
PATRICIA'S AFFAIRS

"A LETTER from Magda, I declare! Again—already!"

Patricia laughed. She was lounging gracefully on a low chair, near the window of a good-sized first-floor bedroom. Outside lay that same mountain amphitheatre, which had enchained the gaze of Beatrice Major from two storeys higher. It did not enchain the forget-me-not eyes of Patricia Vincent—those eyes having been engrossed during an hour past with the latest "Tauchnitz" novel.

Opposite sat a good-looking and well-dressed elderly lady. She had in hand some light fancy-work, and she cast an occasional glance—like Amy Smith—at the view. Her chief desire was to talk, but Patricia was not in the mood for talk, preferring her novel, and the aunt had to wait.

An English maid brought in letters; and Patricia turned hers over, with the above remark.

"Three whole sheets. Gracious! And I shall have to wade through them. Magda always finds out if I miss a single sentence."

"I thought you heard from her two days ago."

"Well, about that. The day her brother turned up. This is another!" Patricia exhibited the trio of sheets, holding them up, fan-wise. "She writes an atrocious hand. It will have to wait."

"Till you have finished your novel, I suppose." Mrs. Norman had been resenting her niece's determined pre-occupation with the book.

"Till I have finished my novel," assented Patricia, quite understanding, and not in the least disposed to give way. She always expected, as a matter of course, that everybody else should give way to her.

"You and this Miss—what is the name?—seem to be great friends. How long have you known her?"

"Magda Royston. Oh, about—since March. She is years younger than I am; but she adores me."

"And you like to be adored!" There was a suspicion of irony in the level tones of the elder lady. Patricia failed to detect it; but she could always talk of herself, and the subject was of sufficient interest to make her lay down the book.

"Why, yes. Most people like adoration—when they can get it, aunt Ju! Magda's state is simply worshipping! You know the sort of thing."

"Perhaps I do. And you are fond of her?"

"Yes, of course." The manner was not enthusiastic. "She is a nice enough girl—in her way. School-girlish!"

"And that was her brother who was going up the Blümlisalp—the one you spoke to!"

Patricia had taken Mrs. Norman somewhat aback, after table d'hôte, by accosting Rob as the brother of her new Burwood friend. Mrs. Norman held certain rather old-fashioned notions, and objected to casual acquaintances.

"Yes. I had only seen him once before, in a freezing March blizzard; but I liked his face then—and there was no mistaking it!"

"Would you not have been wiser to wait for an introduction?"

Patricia yawned gracefully behind her hand, at the first suspicion of fault-finding; and to yawn gracefully is a feat possible to few. A widely-extended jaw shows most faces at their worst.

"People don't wait for introductions in foreign hotels."

"It might be as well if they did sometimes. Mrs. Framley is particular!"

"And practically I had an introduction, in knowing his sister. I assure you I am every inch as particular as aunt Anne. I know what I'm about, aunt Ju. The Roystons are right enough. Otherwise I should never have thought of noticing him." Patricia objected to the slightest implication that she had done wrongly.

"And his friend? You may find yourself in for him also."

"I don't mind. I know all about Mr. Ivor. He is a barrister—one of the most promising on the bench, they say—any number of briefs already. I believe he has money of his own, or else expectations—but he works like a horse, and he is tremendously liked. And he is a friend of those delightful people, the Wryatts of Wratt-Wrothesley."

"Rye—Ratt—Rott—what, my dear?"

"You may well ask! It is a mouthful of a name. Two unmarried sisters in a dear old country house; perfectly charming women. I don't know them well; I wish I did, for it is an ideal house to stay in. Anybody who goes there is sure to be all right. I met them once in a house-party, and heard all about them. Grand-daughters of an Earl, and cousins of a Duke, and all that sort of thing."

"Mr. Royston seemed to know that very sweet-looking girl nearly opposite to us—with the pretty delicate face, and nice brown eyes."

"No, he didn't. They were strangers, only they happened to be together, and people don't sit mum on those occasions. I shouldn't have called her 'pretty,' exactly!" Patricia seldom called any woman pretty. "But I liked her look—if only she had not such a queer little piece of goods for her travelling-companion!"

"Your friend, Miss Royston, will be interested to hear that you have met her brother."

"Magda! I'm not sure. I don't think I shall say anything about him till I get back. No use to rouse jealousies."

"Surely there can be nothing in that for jealousy."

"I can't tell. She is frantically jealous of every single person that I speak to. It is getting to be a bore. She wants to keep me as a close preserve for herself; and that is out of the question. Things were well enough for the first few weeks, when I knew very few people in the place; but I'm getting full up now with engagements, and I can't have Magda perpetually hanging round. However—I don't want to hurt her feelings. I wish girls wouldn't be so frightfully sensitive. But I like that brother of hers. There's something about him out of the common."

"Clergyman?"

"Curate in some big parish. I'm not sure where. South London, I believe." Patricia began to laugh. "Magda raves about him. She has made up her mind to live with him in the future—to keep house, and work among the poor. About as fit for it as our Persian cat! I never saw a more recklessly untidy person—and he is the very essence of orderliness. Every inch of the man shows it. If ever that plan came to pass, she would drive him demented. But of course it never will."

"Men don't invariably marry."

"Anyhow, Magda won't suit him for a housekeeper."

"What is all the stir about?" Mrs. Norman stood up to look out.

"One of the climbing parties coming back I should imagine. They have been away much longer than was expected." Patricia showed signs of interest. "Both parties together—yes, there are the two girls, and the two men. Mr. Ivor seems hardly able to get along. He must have had an accident."

She ran downstairs, followed more deliberately by her aunt. Everybody was hurrying out to welcome the returned climbers, and to hear the story of their doings.

Most of the way from the Oeschinen Hotel, Ivor had perforce submitted to be carried, but he insisted on walking into Kandersteg. It was as much as he could do, for his foot remained very painful; and a few days' rest would plainly be necessary before he could go farther.

To Beatrice this made no difference. She and Amy were leaving next morning; and of course they kept to their plan.

Bee had seen little of Ivor during their descent. The two girls had been together in front; Ivor coming behind with the guides; Rob taking turns with either. Nor did she see more of him this last evening. He had talked freely to her of his adventure, by the Oeschinen Lake; but he made no efforts to be thrown more in her path.

He recognised by this time the fact that he was very much drawn to Bee; that he had begun to look upon her as altogether different and apart from other girls; and he could not forget how she had haunted his imagination during this terrible time in the bergshrund. If not yet in love, he was fast nearing that condition.

But two strong reasons withheld him from immediate action. For one thing—she had saved his life; and it would not do to risk letting her think that he sought her out of gratitude. For another—she must be aware that he might have overheard Miss Smith's remark outside the Hut; and there again he sensitively feared that she would perhaps imagine his conduct to have been inspired by those careless words. His suit would have to come freely, naturally, spontaneously—if ever he did seek her.

Ivor put it thus cautiously to himself. Then, with a glow, he altered the words. "When I seek her—!" he said.

The farewell between himself and Bee next morning was entirely simple and commonplace. Bee said sadly in her mind—"I may never see him again!"

And Ivor went off to his room with a book, which he found supremely uninteresting. To make matters worse, he saw little of his hitherto constant friend. For the change in their plans which could mean nothing for Bee meant much to Rob, and something to Patricia. The two thereafter were perpetually coming together. They had endless talks, and Rob was captivated.

Patricia as usual welcomed with warmth another worshipper at her shrine. She lived for admiration, and she did not know how to get on without it. With her numerous devotees, both masculine and feminine, the question might always be asked whether what she really cared for was the person, or the person's devotion for herself. But she certainly did like Rob, and had liked him from the first. His personality took more hold upon her than was generally the case.

Mrs. Norman allowed matters to drift for three or four days, then suddenly awoke to the fact that this might mean something serious. Rob's absorption in her niece was patent to the most casual observer; and Patricia too showed signs of being for once touched. Mrs. Norman did not wish for the responsibility of an "affair," while Patricia was with her. Mr. Royston might be all that one could wish as a man, but a curate without private means or prospects would hardly meet with Mrs. Framley's approval. So she promptly decided to move on elsewhere, and she gave out this intention.

Patricia was not given to sulks, for sulks are not becoming; but she actually did treat her aunt to something not far removed from one of Magda's "November fogs" during the week that followed. Not of course in public, where she always smiled, but in private.

For obvious reasons Rob said nothing about Patricia, when he wrote to Magda; and for reasons perhaps less obvious, despite what she had said to her aunt, Patricia was equally silent. Beatrice followed the same course, simply because she did not write. Her last three letters to Magda had had no reply; and though hers was not a resentful nature, and she was slow to take offence, she had resolved to wait till she should hear.

Virginia Villa, in which she and her mother would now live, was within a quarter of an hour of Magda's home. It was clearly for Magda to take the next step.

CHAPTER XII
AN OPPORTUNITY LOST

MAGDA was unhappy, and distinctly cross.

She did not wish to be cross, and probably she would not have called herself so. But her world seemed all awry, and her temper suffered under the strain. Self-control was not one of Magda's prime virtues, as by this time you will have found out. It is quite possible for a person to feel desperately cross, and yet so to hold down the feeling that no one can guess its existence. But if Magda were cross, all around knew it.

Merryl certainly did. She came in, dragging her steps in an unwonted fashion, looking pale and heavy-eyed. Magda was alone, seated at a side-table of the school-room, with an ostentatious array of grammars and dictionaries. Since Patricia's departure for the Continent she had, in self-defence, taken violently to French and German.

"Please, Magda—"

"Oh, don't bother. I'm busy."

"Mother wants a note taken to Mrs. Hodgson."

"Well, I suppose you can take it." Merryl was the acknowledged family messenger.

"Yes—only—"

"Only what?"

"I thought perhaps you would—just for once."

"I can't, Merryl. I want to get this translation done before lunch."

"Couldn't you do it—after lunch?"

"No, I can't!" sharply. "I must bicycle over then to see if Patricia is back."

Merryl did not give up yet. "It's such a long way—and so hot!" she murmured.

"I don't see that it's any farther or hotter for you than for me!"

"No," rather faintly. "Only—if you could—only just this once."

"I've told you—I can't! That's enough."

Merryl said no more. She stood still looking at Magda. Then she dragged herself slowly from the room.

That was not like her. Ordinarily she was all sunshine, all readiness to do whatever anybody wished. Though not observant, Magda felt a little uncomfortable. It occurred to her that the child might for once be tired, and that she certainly ought to offer to go in her stead.

Instead of responding instantly to this inward suggestion, she sat still and debated with herself. Should she? Was it needful? It would be such a bother! She had made up her mind to do a certain amount that morning, and she hated having to change her plans. Besides, she felt cross and dissatisfied—unhappy, she called it to herself—and disinclined for a long hot bicycle ride in the sun. Such a dull straight road. And all the other way in the afternoon! She liked the idea quite as little as Merryl. Why should she have to do it, and not Merryl? Nothing ever hurt Merryl. And she couldn't put off going to Claughton. That must come first—sun or no sun, Merryl or no Merryl.

The translation was at a standstill. Magda leant back in her chair, lost in thought.

There was more than one trouble weighing on her mind.

Rob had written only a single short letter all the time he had been in Switzerland. True, he had sent a shower of picture-postcards; but what are picture-postcards when one wants a long delightful outpour? And since his return only one plain postcard! She felt deeply injured.

Worse still, she had written five long letters to the adored Patricia during her absence on the Continent; and only one scribbled note had come in response, with a list of places visited. She had poured out her soul for Patricia's benefit; giving the best gold that she had; and it brought in exchange a few coppers.

Nor was this all. Three days earlier, hearing casually that Patricia was expected, she had bicycled over beforehand, to leave flowers and an enthusiastic note of welcome, imploring to know how soon she might see her idol. No reply, no word of thanks, had yet arrived. It might be that Patricia's return had been delayed. She could not pass another night not knowing.

In addition to these worries was another, yet heavier. The Majors had arrived, and had taken possession of Virginia Villa. She had seen vans with luggage before the door ten days earlier; and by reference to Bee's last unanswered letter, she knew that Bee herself must now be there.

Action could no longer be put off. She would have to tell her mother and Penrose. She would have to ask them to call. She would have to explain somehow why she had kept silence so long. How she now wished that she had been brave and sensible, and had spoken earlier! It seemed so silly, so absurd, not to have done it—and so unkind to Bee. "Mean!" whispered a small accusing voice in her heart.

It was mean, and she knew it. Bee had been so good and true, always kind and helpful and ready to take trouble—surely, the least she could do now was to welcome her friend, and not to give way to foolish shame, merely because that friend lived in a small and unimportant house.

But—Pen's little contemptuous laugh!

If she could not stand a laugh for the sake of a friend, what was her friendship worth? And what was she worth? "Mean!" whispered again that accusing voice.

"Oh dear! I wish they had never come!" she sighed.

But they had come. It was sheer waste of time to sit wishing that her world had been ordered differently. The question was—not, how things might have been, but how she was going to meet them as they were?

Glancing out of the window, she saw Merryl bicycling down the road. So now it was too late to go in her stead. The matter was settled, and she might bend her attention to her work—that work, for the sake of which, ostensibly, she had refused to do a little kindness.

But the wandering attention failed to be bent. She had been beaten in one respect, and now she was beaten in another. The German translation made no further advance; and when the gong sounded for luncheon, she was still moodily nursing her grievances, still debating with herself what to do about the Majors—whether to put off, whether to speak, and if she did speak, what to say.

At luncheon she was to be taken by surprise—as one is apt to be, if one drifts along, waiting for circumstances to decide one's action, instead of simply resolving to do what is right.

Merryl did not appear. She had been some distance to take a note for Mrs. Royston, the latter said regretfully, and had not said that she was not well; and the heat had upset her. She was lying down upstairs. Mr. Royston was very much disturbed. He glared round angrily, and asked why on earth somebody else hadn't gone? It was too bad! They all made a regular Cinderella of Merryl, and nobody ever gave a thought to his poor little girl. What was Magda about not to do it, he wanted to know? He attacked the cold joint savagely, casting indignant glances.

Magda felt guilty and looked injured.

Pen tried to make a diversion. "I see that Virginia Villa is taken," she unexpectedly remarked. "People are arriving there."

"Oh, ever so long ago," piped Frip's little soprano. "There were two whole waggons there, and another next day. And, oh, such a funny lady, mummie—dressed all anyhow. She'd got a sort of big apron-pinafore all over her frock, and she stood outside the door in it giving orders. And she spoke in a sort of slow way, and made the men hurry, and told them just exactly where every single thing was to go. She was funny."

Magda writhed internally.

"And the Vicarage gardener was going by, just when they were getting the furniture down, and they couldn't manage the piano right. And she said to him—'Will you give a helping hand, my man?' John did it directly, and he didn't seem to mind. But it was funny of her, wasn't it? And there was one of those wicker things, like what Pen hangs her skirt on when she's making one."

"Another dressmaker, I suppose," Pen remarked. "I only hope she will be as good as the last. Such a pity she married and went away. I always liked her style. I wonder if this one will have any style."

Mrs. Royston half smiled. "Judging from Frip's description of her dress, that is doubtful."

"Any plate with a name on the door, Frip?"

Frip shook a wise little head. "I didn't see one, but she mightn't have had time to put it up yet, might she?"

Magda said nothing. She felt that she could say nothing. Not at all events just then. She wished with all her heart that she had spoken out sooner. Now—how could she? To have her friend's mother taken for a dressmaker! It was hopeless!

Luncheon ended, she felt scared and unhappy. The thought of Merryl went out of her head. She was bewildered, and perplexed what line to follow.

Claughton had to come first. Upon that point she was resolute. Nothing and nobody might interfere with it. But when she had been, when she had as she hoped seen Patricia, then no doubt it would be wise to go and see Bee. If she did not call soon, who could say whether Bee might not decide to come and see her? So she imagined, though no step was more unlikely on the part of Bee. She grew cold at the thought. What would Pen say?

There seemed to be nothing for it but to take the bull by the horns—by the wrong horn, be it remarked!—to go without further delay to Virginia Villa, and to put things right somehow.

She would have to make Bee and her mother understand the position of affairs. She would have to explain-or to hint—that though she herself would go to see Bee as often as she could spare the time, yet they must not expect to find themselves quite upon the same level, or look to have a welcome from all the circle of the Royston acquaintances. It was too horrid, too disgusting, to have to do anything of the sort. But how could she help it? Nothing else remained? After what had passed at luncheon, how could she ask her mother to call?

Was it really impossible? Even now, would not complete frankness be the wiser, the nobler, the better course? This thought came vividly; but Magda put it aside.

"I can't! I really can't!" she muttered impatiently. "I must wait! I must find out first what I can do with them. After that—perhaps—I suppose I must tell mother!"

And she did not see the cowardice of her decision.

CHAPTER XIII
VIRGINIA VILLA

IT was a broiling afternoon, and no mistake. No wonder Merryl had felt the sun too hot! Magda thought of this, and wished, with a touch of self-reproach, that she had gone to see her sister before starting. By the time she reached Claughton Manor, her face was the colour of a peony.

She rang and asked for Patricia. "Was Miss Vincent back yet?"

Miss Vincent had returned three days earlier.

"Could I see her?"

The man—an old family butler—was not sure. He believed that Miss Vincent had an engagement that afternoon, but he would enquire.

"I won't keep Miss Vincent long. Only just a minute!" pleaded Magda.

She was shown into the breakfast-room, and the man disappeared. Returning, he said that Miss Vincent would come presently, if Miss Royston could wait.

She was left in the breakfast-room, not taken upstairs, as she had hoped, into Patricia's boudoir—a sure sign that the interview was to be brief. There she sat, and waited long. Patricia often kept people waiting—those whom she counted to be of small social importance; but she had never kept Magda quite so long before. Gloomy forebodings attacked the girl. Did Patricia not care to see her, after all these weeks of separation? Had she said or done something that Patricia did not like? Could it be that some inkling had reached Patricia of the coming of the Majors to Burwood, and that she counted a friend of theirs no longer a fit friend for herself?

Magda had time enough in which to conjure up no end of direful imaginings. Nearly three-quarters of an hour passed, before a light step came down the passage, and Patricia appeared, wearing one of her daintiest frocks and most bewitching hats, evidently ready for some social function. She was drawing on a pair of white gloves.

"Well, Magda—how are you? So sorry to keep you waiting, dear, but I'm awfully busy since getting back. And I have had to dress early, so as to be ready in time. I can give you two or three minutes now." She just touched her lips to Magda's flushed cheek, eluding a proffered embrace. "Don't crumple me, dear, please. Well—are you quite well, and desperately busy too?"

"I'm never too busy to come here. Never!"

"You told me you were working very hard."

"Yes—but still—Patricia, when may I really see you? When may I come for a good long talk? I want to hear all about your travels and everything."

"Of course—yes. I have no end of things to tell you." Patricia slowly buttoned her left glove. "Let me see I'm afraid every single day this week is full. I must write, and name some afternoon—next week."

Magda's face fell, while Patricia was wondering whether and how much Robert Royston might have said to his sister as to their meeting abroad. It was her intention to avoid being catechised about it by Magda; but, perhaps, on the whole, some slight allusion now was desirable, all the more since there was no time for the said catechising. So, with a little laugh, she remarked—

"You must have been amused to hear of my coming across your brother at Kandersteg."

"Rob! Not Rob!" cried Magda, in deep amazement. "Why, he never told me!"

This meant a good deal to Patricia, as a token of Rob's feelings. She only said, with a smile—

"He did not think it important enough."

"Oh, it couldn't be that! It wasn't that! And you met—really! Were you in the same hotel?"

Patricia held out a hand. "Can you manage these buttons for me? They are rather difficult. Yes, the same hotel. Just for three or four days or so. It was when he went up the Blümlisalphorn with his friend, Mr. Ivor."

"He sent me a picture-card, I remember. But he did not say a word about you!"

"Too busy, my dear. Climbing takes a lot of time. And Mr. Ivor had a bad accident as they were coming down the mountain—fell into a crevasse, and might have been killed. That gave your brother more to do."

"I suppose so. But I do think he might have told me—if it was only half-a-dozen words."

"You shouldn't expect too much. Men hate writing letters on a holiday. By-the-by, thanks so much for those nice flowers, and for your note. So good of you! And now, I'm afraid, I really must say good-bye. But you will come again soon. I shall write and fix a day."

And that was all. Magda made her way out, mounted her bicycle, and set off for home; going slowly much of the way, and walking up the hills with a heavy step. She was puzzled by Rob's silence on what he must have known would be a great interest to her. She was conscious of a slight subtle change in Patricia—she did not use the word "subtle," but she felt it—which perplexed and weighed upon her. The manner was not less affectionate than usual; yet some new element seemed to have crept into their friendship.

Was it the Majors? Toiling up a long slope, she asked this question.

Anyhow, she would go at once to Virginia Villa, and would see how the land lay. No use putting off.

Thither she went direct, not calling at home by the way. She left her bicycle in the tiny front garden, and rang. A neat little maid opened the door and showed her into a drawing-room which took her by surprise. It was much larger than she had expected—yes, plainly, the front and back rooms had been thrown into one, making a room of good size, handsomely furnished. On an easel in the back window stood a half-finished painting; and work lay about carelessly. Magda recognised the tasteful fingers of her friend in the very sweep of the window-curtains, and in the mass of flowers piled upon a side-table. Bee was a born artist, and she carried with her an atmosphere of harmony.

Magda herself felt anything rather than harmonious this hour. She had never been more uncomfortable in her life.

The two ladies came in together; Bee, as always, gentle, slender, reticent, quietly affectionate, but rather holding back, as if not quite sure of Magda. The latter's constrained kiss was hardly of a nature to reassure.

There was no manner of constraint about Bee's mother. Of medium height, plain in feature, rather stout, wearing a short alpaca black skirt and a loose black jacket—she did in a fashion resemble the photograph with which Magda was familiar. Only, no photograph could reproduce the absolute ease and supreme composure of the original. In two points alone was she like her daughter—in the slender pretty hands, and the soft low-toned voice; but her speech was slower than Bee's, and she had the air of being much more sure of herself.

"So this is your particular friend, Bee!" Mrs. Major's eyes examined Magda kindly, as she shook hands.

Bee looked rather sad.

"I thought I had better come directly—though of course—though I was afraid—I thought you might be too busy—"

"Not at all, Magda. Mother was so good—only think, instead of waiting for me to come home and help her, as I expected, she did everything with the maids, and had the whole house straight before I arrived. It was such a surprise."

"Then Mrs. Major has been here some time."

"More than a fortnight. And how she must have worked!"

"Work does nobody harm. Sit down, Miss Royston. Tea is coming directly."

As Mrs. Major spoke, the neat young girl brought in a tray, placing it upon a small basket-table.

Magda murmured indistinct thanks, adding, "And you like Burwood?"

"It is not new to me. I used to visit in the neighbourhood when I was a child."

Magda was too much pre-occupied with her own line of thought to notice this, or to follow it out, as she might have done. How to bring in what she had to say she did not know; and the mental struggle kept her absent and dull. Bee waited on her, supplied her wants, and asked questions about things in general. Mrs. Major filled gaps with easy talk, never for a moment at a loss for something to say. She was evidently a well-read woman, and a clever one; much more so than Magda had been accustomed to consider Bee. She tried Magda on a variety of subjects, and had small response in any direction. For some time no loophole occurred for anything personal.

Tea was nearly over when Bee remarked—"I hope you will come in very often, Magda."

Magda seized upon the opening. "Yes—I should like it very much. Only, of course, when one is at home, there is a lot to do—and so many people to see—and—"

"We quite understand. I don't think you will find us at all unreasonable, dear."

Magda had an odd sense, of which she had never at school been conscious, that she was a good deal younger than Bee. The latter seemed, all at once, to have gained years in age. Not only was she older, but prettier, more dignified, more controlled in manner.

"But of course I do mean—" Magda came to a stop.

"No doubt you have a great many friends here, and perhaps not very much leisure," politely suggested Mrs. Major. It really seemed as if they were trying to help her out of her difficulty.

"And then, Magda, having Miss Vincent must make a great difference. You are always seeing her, are you not? And at first we shall not know all your friends, or they us."

The opportunity was not to be lost. Magda summoned up her courage. "I suppose—I suppose not," she said, with averted gaze. "People here are rather—are rather slow, you know—I mean, in calling on new-comers."

She looked up nervously to see the effect of her words, and intercepted one swift glance between mother and daughter. Not an unkind glance; not offended; but amused.

"No doubt," assented Mrs. Major. "It is always wise to be careful."

Bee laughed. "But even if we don't know your friends, dear, and even if we are out of it all, I hope we shall see you sometimes, when you can spare half-an-hour. You must not make a burden of it."

Magda felt ashamed. "Of course I shall come," she said. "And if—if my mother—" she stopped, hardly knowing what she had meant to say.

"I want so much to know your mother," Bee observed.

"But—but I'm not quite sure—" faltered Magda. "You see—mother isn't very strong—and she has so many calls to pay—and I'm not sure—if she—"

It was impossible to finish the sentence, in face of Bee's soft wondering eyes, still more in face of Mrs. Major's steady gaze and air of composed waiting. Magda found her feet awkwardly, with crimsoning cheeks.

"I'm so sorry, I can't stay longer now," she added. "I'll come again soon, if I may."

"Pray come any day that you feel inclined," Mrs. Major responded easily, with no apparent consciousness of what Magda had meant. "Bee's friends will always be welcome at Virginia Villa." She said the name in precisely the same tone that she might have used to say "Claughton Manor," or "Windsor Castle."

Bee went out to see Magda through the little front door, coming back with a shadow on her face.

"I'm rather disappointed in your friend, my dear. But she may improve on a further acquaintance. Is she always like this?"

"She was different at school. I don't understand her to-day—or what made her so. Unless—it is something perhaps that her mother has said."

"Probably. Mrs. Royston may not intend to call, till she has hunted out our antecedents."

"It may be that, mother."

"But after being your friend for two years, she might have said enough to satisfy even Burwood squeamishness."

"Yes—only—I never did tell Magda much."

"Not enough, perhaps."

"Mother, you have always hated snobbishness. And I know how you laughed at Miss Norris, for dragging in her rich relations at every corner."

"And you are your mother's own daughter." Mrs. Major's small dark eyes, clever and deep-set, rested lovingly on the girl. "However, one must take people as they are. Never mind. It will all come right. I have no doubt that there is a finer side to Magda Royston—and that this is a mere episode; not her fault."

"No. Only, I don't really think—if I had been in her place this afternoon—that I could have done just so!"

"I'm perfectly sure that you could not, Bee." Mrs. Major spoke with decision.

CHAPTER XIV
A REVERSION OF THOUGHT

LEAVING her machine in the bicycle-shed, Magda went indoors, to find herself face to face with her father. Up to that moment she had been entirely occupied with her own concerns—dissatisfied with herself, disappointed not to have seen more of Patricia, uncomfortable about Bee—and since leaving the house she had not once remembered Merryl.

The moment her eyes fell upon Mr. Royston she did remember. He was roving restlessly about, between hall and study and drawing-room, as if not knowing what to do with himself. At the sight of Magda, he faced round abruptly.

"So here you are at last! Time enough too! Where have you been all day?"

"I've only been away since lunch. Not all day."

"Pretty sharp you went off too, never stopping to see if you were wanted. Never a thought of your poor little sister, or how she might be!"

There was too much truth in this. She had hurried off, in fear that something might prevent that which she had set her mind on doing.

"Isn't Merryl well, father?"

"Well! Not likely!—treated in such a way! My poor little girl! Sent off in that hair-brained fashion, when she was only fit for bed! In this heat too! I'm not blaming your mother. She didn't know. Merryl took care she shouldn't! But you might have had more sense. Not a soul in the house sees to that child. She never complains—never thinks of herself—the most unselfish little darling that ever lived. And you—always so full of your own affairs, that you neither know nor care what becomes of anybody else!"

Magda swelled resentfully, for this of course was an exaggeration; but he went on wrathfully—"I'll take good care nothing of that sort ever happens again! I'll look after her myself in future—if—" and there was an ominous choke in his voice—"if—if she gets over—this!"

Magda's heart gave a great frightened throb.

"Is Merryl lying down still?"

"Lying down still!" growled Mr. Royston. "That's all you know! That's all you care!" He turned off, as if not trusting himself to say more, and disappeared in the study, shutting the door.

Magda stood feeling dazed. It was as if a small thunderbolt had fallen at her feet. If Merryl should get over this! She repeated the words to herself. Get over what? Something must have come to pass while she was away—something unlooked-for. All sorts of conjectures thronged up, none of which would fit the case. But Merryl was ill. Merryl must be ill. That "if she gets over this" could have no other meaning. She must have been ill in the morning—too ill for a long hot bicycle ride—and Magda had refused to go in her stead.

In one moment the world had changed; and she saw it from a new standpoint. No longer was Patricia the one and only person to be considered. Suddenly she found how much these home-ties really meant—how dear to her heart was this unselfish little sister, Merryl! Ill! Perhaps not to get over it! Oh, but that was impossible. It could not have come upon them with such frightful suddenness. And Mr. Royston was always an alarmist, especially in regard to Merryl.

Magda plucked up courage, and went to the school-room. She must hear more—must know what it all meant.

At first the room looked empty. Then she espied a small figure, curled up in one corner of the deep old window seat, with long hair falling like a veil and hiding the child's face.

"Frip!" The word came fearfully. Dread surged up anew.

Francie made no answer. Magda went close, putting an urgent arm round the little figure; and there was a slight shake of the shoulders, as if to repudiate her touch.

"Frip! what is it? Frip, tell me! I'm only just come in. What is the matter?"

Frip said one word—"Merryl!" and burst into tears.

"Go on! Go on!" commanded Magda.

"She is—oh, so bad!" sobbed Frip. "And the doctor has been. And he says—she never, never ought to have gone! Her head did ache so, and her throat was sore, and I begged her so to let you take the note. But she said you couldn't—you were busy—and she wouldn't let me worry mother—and I couldn't find Pen."

"She never told me her head ached," spoke Magda miserably.

"She didn't tell me; but I saw. Of course I saw. And I do wish now I'd told mother, though she said I mustn't. She said perhaps the ride would do her good. But it didn't. When she tried to get up, after lunch, she nearly fainted right off. And then she said she had tumbled off her bicycle twice, coming home; and the second time she banged her head against the gate-post, and it hurt her so dreadfully, she could hardly get indoors. And the doctor says nobody is to go into her room, except mother; and she's to be taken to the end spare room; and Pen has gone out to find a nurse. And I don't know what to do without Merryl!"

Magda felt guilty and unhappy. It was easy to see that even little Francie blamed her; and for once she had no words of self-defence to offer.

Penrose came in, grave and sad. "Is Frip here?" she said. Then—"So you have come back!" Magda heard reproach in the tone.

"Yes. What is the matter with Merryl?"

Pen did not at once reply. "Come, Frip, dear," she said. "You had better run into the garden."

"I don't want to go—without Merryl."

"Shall I come too? Run and get your garden-hat, and wait for me at the back-door. Don't go upstairs."

Frip obeyed, and Pen turned to Magda. "We don't want much said before Frip," she breathed. "Dr. Cartwright is afraid that it may be scarlet fever. There are one or two bad cases in the town."

"Then it wasn't going out in the sun that made her ill."

"That has made her worse. She never ought to have gone—if any one had had the least idea that she was so poorly. No one knew except Frip; and of course Frip did not understand. I can't think how it was that none of us saw; but mother and I were very busy; and she had such a colour. Frip says she turned quite white before she started—and when she asked you to go."

The words, though pointed, were not unkindly spoken; and Magda was too unhappy for vexation.

"I don't think I looked at her—particularly. And she never said she wasn't well. If I had known, of course I would have gone."

"It is such a pity you did not. She fell from her bicycle with her head against the gate-post, and it almost stunned her. That makes things so much worse. She was quite wandering before Dr. Cartwright came, and he found her in a high fever. He cannot know for some hours how much is due to the blow, and whether it really is scarlet fever; but he seems pretty sure. Poor dear little Merryl. If only we had known!"

Pen spoke tenderly and went away. Magda, left alone, with nothing to do, nobody wanting her, nobody turning to her, felt very wretched. When she thought of Merryl's plaintive petition, and of her own curt refusal, she hardly knew how to bear herself. It was too terrible to think that she might have refused Merryl's very last request—the very last time that she would ever see and speak with her sister. It was not her way to cry easily; but she sat long, looking straight before her, and feeling acutely that if that came to pass, she could never be happy again.

Yet nobody seemed to think that she was to be pitied. This dawned upon her with a sense of surprise. All the others were full of loving sympathy one for another; while towards herself there was only blame; and no one expected her to mind very much. It startled her to find things thus, and made her realise, more than she had ever done before, the manner of life she had been living.

For it was not that she meant to be unkind or selfish; not that she was wanting in real affection; but that she did not think, did not put others' happiness before her own, did not live for those around. There was any amount of real love and tenderness below the surface, but love of self had had the upper hand. And when she resented what they felt, she quite forgot how very little she had yet shown of what this trouble meant to her. The first impulse with Magda, as with many girls who pride themselves on their reserve, was to hide what she felt, and to put on an appearance of indifference.

This was only the beginning of a long stretch of anxiety. The doctor's fear proved correct. It was scarlet fever of a pronounced type; and the illness was greatly aggravated by the blow on the head, which had caused slight concussion. Day by day reports grew worse; and delirium was incessant.

The patient had been removed to a part of the house entirely separated from the rest, with a staircase of its own, and an outer door; so the segregation could be complete. There was at first some talk of the family going elsewhere for a time. But this was decided against. They had all been with Merryl; and any one among them might already have caught the complaint. So they remained where they were, all possible precautions being taken. Nothing could induce Mrs. Royston to remain away from the sick-room. A second nurse was a necessity, the case being so severe; so she and the nurse and child lived a separate existence from the household.

Complete isolation from friends and neighbours was involved for the whole party. It was a new experience for Magda. Everybody was most kind; notes and enquiries, supplies of beef-tea and jelly for the little invalid, arrived in profusion. But naturally and rightly, other people had to avoid infection for themselves and their children.

No going to church; no entering of shops; no seeing of friends; no engagements. The doctor of course came daily; before long twice and even three times in the day; but only Mr. Royston or Pen spoke with him; and though the Vicar called often, he and Magda did not happen to meet.

Patricia sent a little conventional note of sympathy, prettily expressed, and making it very clear that she intended to hold aloof as long as possible. Magda was requested not even to write to her, for fear of infection being conveyed through the post. Magda did think Patricia might have said less about the need for care on her own account, and more about her friend's trouble. It was the first real touch of disillusionment.

On the same day a letter arrived from Bee, so tender, so loving, so full of sympathy, that Magda could not but mark the contrast. Bee seemed to think of nothing, to remember nothing, except that Magda was in sorrow, and that she longed to comfort her. Magda could not but think of Miss Mordaunt's words—"Bee is a friend worth having, and worth keeping."

How little she had thought of late about kind Miss Mordaunt!—And still less of her own aims and aspirations, her desire to live a brave and useful life!

She quite longed to speak out, to tell her mother about the Majors, to confess her own folly in keeping silence. But Mrs. Royston was in the sick-room, out of reach. She had to wait; and meantime nothing could be thought of except that long life-and-death struggle going on upstairs in the distant end-room.

Then came a day when a few hours would decide the probable issue; when Merryl lay, powerless, feeble, unconscious, just breathing, and on the very borderland of the next world—when, hour by hour, they all knew that any moment might see the end. And of all in the house, none grieved more bitterly than Magda. For she knew, she could not help knowing, that her consenting to take the note might have made just all the difference. The great danger was that Merryl would sink from exhaustion. And but for the added complications, resulting from over-exertion and the fall from her bicycle, there could be no doubt that her rallying-power would have been greater.

If Magda had never prayed before—and probably she had at times, however fitfully—she did pray, fervently and passionately, in these days of suspense.

No one in the house thought now that she did not care. Little though she said, the burden was plainly written on her face. Even Mr. Royston had ceased to reproach her; and Pen was kind; and Frip often clung to her with childish pity. But there was no comfort. Magda felt that there never could be any comfort, if Merryl should die.

She saw life in truer colours than ever before. There are times when we get away from earth-mists, and gain clear views of the true proportions, the true values of things. This was one such time. Many a resolution she made in those sorrowful waiting hours—if only Merryl might recover!

Rob came down to see them. He thought nothing of infection for himself, being used to sick-rooms of all kinds; and he had hoped to see Merryl, but against this Mr. Royston laid an embargo. If Rob went to that room, he might not come back among the rest. Rob was about to agree, about to say that he would return home that evening, when his eyes fell upon Magda. He knew in a moment that she needed him more than Merryl.

No opportunity came before night for any word alone with her. Magda kept up and seemed resolutely to hold aloof.

And next morning the cloud lifted. Merryl was better. Definite improvement had set in; and the doctor, coming early, spoke in cheerful tones of recovery.

Until that moment Magda had not been seen to give way. But when Mr. Royston came in, radiant with the good news, and when she learnt that confident hopes might at last be indulged, she looked wildly round as if for escape. She rushed away, without a word, to the deserted school-room, and knelt down, hiding her face on folded arms, to sob out her vehement thanksgiving for this merciful escape from a life-long sorrow.

Pen found her thus; and she might as well have tried to stop a gale of wind with her hand, as to stay with words that tempest of weeping. As with many who seldom are mastered, when Magda was mastered, it was very completely. She did not even know that Pen had been, or was gone. But presently a strong quiet hand was on her shoulder, gently pressing it, and in time Rob's voice said—

"That will do!"

Magda sobbed on, and again came the words—

"That will do, Magda."

She was crumpled in a heap on the rug; and she allowed him to draw her to a sitting posture. With gasping efforts after self-control, she at length managed to stop.

"What is it all about?" he asked then. "Try to tell me—quietly."

"Rob—if—if she had died—"

"Yes. Go on."

"It would have been my doing."

"In what way? Hush—" as the storm threatened to return. "It would have been your doing—how?"

Gradually he induced her to pour out the whole—how she had failed all round, how she had lived for self only, how she had refused to help Merryl when asked, how that one ordinary slip in everyday kindness might have brought about tragic consequences. And when she had related her tale, she found that he knew it already at least in part, that he had divined what she must be going through, that he was here for the very purpose of bringing help.

Not help of his own. He was here to point her to ONE stronger than himself,—"mighty to save." Magda needed to be saved from her weakness of will, from her readiness to give in to temptation. For the past she needed forgiveness; for the future, power to fight and to conquer.

"But this must be no empty repentance," he urged. "You must let what has happened be a warning to you. It is in the small things of common life that we fail most grievously; it is in those small things that we often dishonour our Lord most, and do most harm to others. You have to make a fresh start now, to remember that you are bound to His service. It must not be any longer self-pleasing, self-indulgence—but—'Teach me to do the thing that pleaseth Thee!' When you get back into everyday life again, don't let yourself forget."

"I'll try," she whispered in a subdued tone.

CHAPTER XV
LIFE'S ONWARD MARCH

WEEKS and weeks had passed; all the long weeks of Merryl's acute danger, and of her slow recovery with its many drawbacks; and then of her absence at the sea-side with her mother. It seemed to Magda like years since the day that she had last called upon Patricia, for that short and disappointing interview from which she had hoped so much.

No one else had caught the fever; and it was now over a month that Mrs. Royston and Merryl had been away. The whole house had been thoroughly fumigated and disinfected; much painting and papering had taken place; and everything which could be suspected of conveying infection was destroyed. With the arrival of autumn, people were beginning to realise that the Roystons were once more "safe," though some of the more nervous still held aloof.

Mrs. Major and Bee had been for several weeks away from Burwood paying visits; otherwise, Magda could not doubt, she and Bee would have met. Not yet had she found opportunity to tell her mother about them; and she shrank from speaking first to her sister. Pen might set herself against the acquaintance, and might influence Mrs. Royston to refuse to call. A mistake again on the part of Magda!

The absentees were expected soon to return. Merryl was better, Mrs. Royston wrote, though not so much better as every one hoped; but they would not remain much longer away.

Patricia was among those who held longest aloof. If she chanced to meet any of the Roystons out-of-doors, she gave them a very wide berth; this, up to the last fortnight, during which she too had flitted elsewhere, Magda sometimes admitted to herself, though to no one else, that she in Patricia's place could not have shown quite such excessive caution to her greatest friend.

But was she Patricia's greatest friend? At one time she had felt sure. Doubts now troubled her often.

All these weeks of trouble, of anxiety, of self-searching, were good for Magda. It was one of those periods in life when one is taken apart from the ordinary round, and set upon a watch-tower on the mountainside, to gain new views of the landscape, new views of duty, new views of self. She had been compelled to pause, to think, to take stock of her own aims and objects, to examine her course. She had been humbled in her own eyes; had seen her failures; had made resolves for the future.

Now she was back again in ordinary life; and she found herself, as she might have expected, back also amid the old temptations, the old tendencies, the old difficulties. Nay, more—she was back amid the old views of life. A landscape, as seen from a lonely tower upon the hill-side, has a very different aspect from that same landscape looked upon from its own lowest level. She was assailed once more by the commonplace pleasures, the small distractions, the hourly inducements to self-indulgence, which surround us all; and she found resistance no easy matter.

Of course it was not easy—as Rob had frankly conceded. Life is not meant to be easy.

Though she would never forget what it had been to stand and wait in hourly expectation of news that dear little Merryl had passed away, conscious that she herself had had a hand in bringing about that peril—and though the shock of this experience had awakened and aroused her, and had made her look upon life with a new realisation—still, there was all the battle to be fought. Knowing that the foe is there, and must be conquered, is not at all the same thing as being victor. Magda knew; but the fight lay ahead.

One thing had become clear to her mind, in those weeks of graver thought—that there is a very definite danger in "drifting." She had to insist upon steady work for herself, of one kind or another. The resolution was for a time more easily carried out, because during their quarantine, few interruptions came, and social invitations were non-existent.

Her old favourite notion of a home some day with Rob was at this time strongly in the ascendant. While hardly willing to admit the fact even to herself, she was disappointed in Patricia; and being so naturally made her turn the more to Rob. She dwelt much upon this dream of the future, picturing the little house that she would share with him, and painting visions of herself as his housekeeper, his tried and valued sub-worker. Of possible trials and rubs and boredom in that life, she never thought. The whole view was rose-coloured.

Any day Rob might have the offer of a living. Though still so young, she knew that he had won golden opinions, that he had many friends, and that any of these friends might soon find just the right nook for him. When that happy day should arrive, he would want her. She never felt any doubt that this would be the case. For years there had been an understanding between them that when he needed her she would go—an understanding which no doubt was regarded much more seriously by Magda than by Rob. Still, though he had sometimes laughed, he had never discouraged the dream; and she looked upon it as a certainty. True, Mr. Royston might object; but if Rob wished it, Rob would get his way.

Magda decided that she would now, really and in sober earnest, begin to make herself ready for the life. A good deal would no doubt be needed. Not merely the study of music and history and languages—though Rob had intimated that all such learning might come in usefully—but, much more, habits of neatness, method, self-control, general usefulness. A mastery of cooking and needle-work suggested itself as desirable; and, during Mrs. Royston's absence, she went in for a course of cookery-lessons, much to Pen's astonishment. Also she set herself a daily task in plain needle-work, which hitherto she had disdainfully eschewed. Even darning and patching were included.

"Really, Magda is very much improved. Very much indeed!" Mr. Royston remarked one morning to Pen. His favourite notion of Woman presented her always as needle in hand, and he had never been able to reconcile himself to his second daughter's objection to sewing. "I found her yesterday in the school-room, making a child's frock."

"I wonder how long it will last," Pen could not resist saying.

"It will last; no doubt. She is growing older and more sensible. It will last," repeated Mr. Royston confidently. Breakfast was on the table, and the gong had sounded; but Magda unfortunately failed to appear in good time. No unusual event in the past, though lately she really had striven after punctuality as part of her preparation for the future. Mr. Royston expected everybody to be down before himself; and when she appeared, he showed displeasure. "Breakfast at such a reasonable hour as we have it—there can be no question of hardship," he declared.

Magda broke out in warm self-defence before she knew that the words were coming.

"I've not been late once for three weeks. But if I make one single slip, that always means a scolding; and there's never any praise for doing better."

The manner was not too respectful, and she knew it. Fresh blame was certainly deserved on that score. Happily, the entrance of letters made a diversion, and no more was said. There were two for Magda, one from Rob, one from Patricia; and she flushed with pleasure at sight of the latter, having given up all hope of hearing.

Neither letter could have immediate attention. During Merryl's absence, some of the little duties always before done by Merryl had fallen to her share. She undertook them at first, in the mood of self-reproach, and soon they were expected as a matter of course. Mr. Royston liked to be waited on and fussed over by his daughters. She had to boil him an egg in the silver egg-boiler; and because she was in a hurry, she turned the whole toast-rack over on the floor, scattering its contents far and wide. Mr. Royston growled out that Merryl never blundered, and he desired Magda to leave things alone, and to go back to her seat. She obeyed, feeling aggrieved; and Mr. Royston, no less aggrieved, took up one of his letters. Pen meanwhile was reading hers from Mrs. Royston.

"They hope to come next week," she observed, to divert attention from Magda's misdeeds. "Mother says Merryl is still weak, poor little dear, and gets tired out directly. But the doctor advises home for a time. Then there is something about Rob. He is paying a visit at some place—what is the name? Rat—Rot—W-r-a-t-t—"

"Not Wratt-Wrothesley!" cried Magda in amaze.

"Why, what do you know about it?" demanded Pen.

Magda was examining the postmark of her own letter from Rob. "He actually is there. I didn't know he had ever come across the Miss Wryatts."

"When did you come across them?"

"I've never seen them. They are Bee Major's aunts."

"Your school friend—Beatrice Major. You used to be always talking about her. By-the-by, I meant to ask you—are these Majors that have come to live here related to your friend? I'm told that they are delightful people."

Magda gasped. It was the last thing she had expected to hear from Pen. There was nothing for it now but to speak out.

"It's they—themselves!"

"Nonsense!"

"It is, Pen. Beatrice and her mother."

"Why in the world haven't you told us? Why, they have been here—months! We ought to have called at once."

"I did mean to tell mother. But I felt so sure you wouldn't like the idea of the house—Virginia Villa. You are always so particular."

"Particular! As if it signified about the house! Mrs. Major is a person who can live where she chooses. What does that matter? Why, all the county is calling on them. Really, Magda!—To let us wait and come in at the end, when we might have been the first to call! It is too bad!"

"I don't see how I could know! I was afraid you would keep mother from knowing them."

"The last thing I should do. But you never do understand! We only heard about them just before Merryl fell ill; and then of course we could do nothing."

Magda was at a loss what to say. She felt that she had been not a little foolish. Pen went on—

"I don't know how far it is all true; but everybody is talking about them. They say Miss Major is one of the sweetest girls ever seen. And as for Mrs. Major—of course you know that she is an Earl's granddaughter, or something of that sort. A Duke's cousin, some say."

"I don't know anything about it."

"And yet you call Miss Major your friend!"

"She never told me."

"If I had been you, I would have found out."

Which was undoubtedly true.

Magda began opening Patricia's letter. "Why—she is at Wratt-Wrothesley too. I can't imagine what has taken Rob there."

"I can tell you that. Mr. Ivor, who went up the mountain with Rob, and fell into the crevasse, is a great friend of the Miss Wryatts—and mother supposes that they wanted to thank Rob for saving his life."

"And Mrs. Major and Bee are there too," murmured Magda, feeling rather dazed; for this meant Patricia and Bee meeting under one roof in hourly intercourse.

"I dare say! Mrs. Major is their sister. Mother seems very much pleased that Rob should have had the invitation. You don't seem to have made much use of your openings at school."

Magda did not hear. She was suddenly engrossed by Patricia's letter, which indeed contained something altogether unexpected and astounding. No exclamation passed her lips. She read on in stupefied silence, at first hardly able to grasp the full meaning of the words, which ran as follows:—

"Wratt-Wrothesley."

"Tuesday."

"MY DEAR MAGDA,—"

"You will be rather surprised to find that I am here, in the same house with your brother, and with your friends the Majors. Why did you not tell me about their coming to Burwood, you dear little goose? Did you think I should be jealous? My aunt and I went lately to call at Virginia Villa—not dreaming that you knew them! And we were just charmed with them both. Mrs. Major is quite unique; and the daughter so pretty and charming. Of course everybody knows all about Mrs. Major, directly it oozes out that she is a sister of the Miss Wryatts'; and I believe it is solely through them that I have this invitation to Wyatt-Wrothesley, where I have always longed to come—though certainly I knew the Miss Wryatts slightly before. They are about the most delightful people I ever came across; and the house and its surroundings are simply perfect."

"I am enjoying myself here more than I can tell; and for more reasons than one—as you will understand! You are such a devoted sister, that you have certainly read Rob's letter before giving a look at mine; so you know the news, and there is no need to tell you again. We are very, very happy—he and I. How happy I cannot explain, or hope to make you understand, since you have never yet been through the same. He is such a dear fellow! I can hardly believe in my good luck! And it is nice to think that one day you will be my sister. Not that we talk of marriage yet. That must wait till Rob gets a living. But everything is so far settled—except that Rob is writing to his father and mother and I am writing to my aunt. Everybody here congratulates us both—each on having the other—which is all right!"

"Your affectionate friend,"

"PATRICIA."

With dazzled eyes and beating heart, Magda tore open Rob's letter, not trusting herself to speak. As from a distance she heard Mr. Royston's excited exclamations—

"Hallo! So Rob has stolen a march on us all! Engaged! And to Miss Vincent! Well, well, he knows a pretty face when he sees it. Pretty manners too, and a nice girl; and there is money in the background. Might have done worse for himself."

Magda was reading, or trying to read, Rob's short letter, brimming with suppressed joy and tender gladness, which found no echo in her heart. He spoke of his darling—of his supreme happiness—of his certainty that Magda would rejoice with and for him. Not one word about that discarded dream of the future, now never to be anything but a dream. Not a thought of her disappointment! For him and Patricia—all might be sunshine. But— where did she come in?

She stood up hastily, sliding her chair back. "Where are you off to?" Mr. Royston asked. He disliked any one leaving the table before himself. "Did you hear about Rob?"

"Yes—I know."

Before another word could be said, she was gone. It was impossible to stay, impossible to hear them lightly and with laughter discussing that which was the death-knell of her hopes. Again it was as if a small thunderbolt had crashed down at her feet; not this time from any fault of her own, which might have been a comfort, had she only seen it. To bear a trouble which comes straight from a Father's Hand is always easier than to endure one which we have brought upon ourselves.

Still, it did seem very, very hard to Magda; and not less so because it was Patricia who had stolen Rob from her. Till now she had never quite realised what that dream of the future had been in her imagination—how fixed and stable it had seemed, how it had coloured all her outlook, how it had comforted and helped her in little daily frets and worries, how it had filled the horizon of her mind. And lately she had worked so hard, so eagerly, to make herself ready! And now—now—she was nothing to Rob; now Rob would never want her, would never again turn to her for sympathy. He had Patricia; and in Patricia, he would find all he needed.

And she—Magda—had nobody! Not even Patricia remained to her. Patricia had Rob. She was left alone.

The ground seemed cut away from beneath her feet; and she found herself stranded.

She had escaped from the house, in dread of being questioned, and either pitied or laughed at; and she walked with hot impatient steps up and down the path at the far end of the kitchen garden. She was angry with Rob; angry with Patricia. And she did not see in this wreck of her dream one of Life's opportunities for real heroism—for putting self manfully aside, and dwelling only on the happiness of others.

CHAPTER XVI
THE THICK OF THE FIGHT

SOME days later, in the afternoon, Magda lounged in the old school-room basket-chair, with a novel on her knee. She failed to find the tale interesting, and she did not care to do anything else. Of what use now to practise or work or study? The future for which she had been toiling was at an end. No delightful little home with Rob lay before her—a home into which no troubles or worries were ever to find admission. The dream was dead; and life was a blank.

Her mood, of course, was wrong, and she knew it; but she would not admit that it might be conquered. She only indulged in self-pity.

Everything had gone astray to-day; and she had nothing to which she could turn in contrast.

The room looked untidy. This week it was in Magda's charge; and she had left arrangements to care for themselves; a mode not conducive to order. The green window-curtains hung awry; chairs stood crookedly; books lay about in confusion; and the table-cloth had collapsed in a heap on the floor.

Presently she stood up and went across to a side-table. In her present mood of self-compassion, she wanted further food for unhappiness; and it had come to her mind that Rob, no long time since, had spoken in one of his letters about that future which now had ceased to be. She unlocked her desk, and fished out a bundle of his letters, which she began glancing through.

The one she wanted did not appear; but she found a doleful enjoyment in reading one after another, and in contrasting their tone with what she knew she had to expect in days to come. He would write to Patricia instead of to her; he would tell Patricia everything, instead of telling her. That was the keynote of her mental ditty.

Losing herself in the thought, she ceased to read, and her fingers played aimlessly with the desk. Unconsciously she pressed a small spring with force, and a piece of wood stirred. Yes; there was a secret drawer there, of course; but she had not opened it for years and years. A touch of idle curiosity made her open it now; and she found within a sealed envelope. At the moment, memory brought no associations with the packet; but out of it dropped a small photograph. Then recollection flashed back.

"Why—Ned Fairfax!" she uttered.

It was the face of a boy of sixteen or seventeen; good-natured and sensible. She was a trifle amused, in spite of herself; recalling the long-past day when, in a fit of childish wrath, because her last letter to him had remained unanswered, she had tragically closed and sealed and put away his likeness, resolving to forget his existence.

"Seems to be my fate!" she muttered. "Everybody gives me up in turn."

A familiar voice outside the door broke upon these musings. "All right, Frip. I'll come presently. I must have a chat with Magda first."

And Rob came in; sunburnt, healthy, glowing with happiness.

Magda stood up reluctantly. She resented his manifest and supreme gladness, in which she had no share.

"Well, Magda," as she returned his kiss in limp fashion. "I have come for your congratulations. Why did you not write?"

"I—meant to. Are you going to stay?" So different from former comings did this seem, that she had to swallow a lump in her throat.

"I'm sleeping at Claughton. Came back with Patricia yesterday. I want to hear how Merryl is after her change. Not strong yet, I'm told. Well?" And his quiet happy eyes looked into hers.

She was silent, gazing on the ground. "Not one word!" in a tone of surprise. "Why—Magda!"

"I don't see how you can expect—" She spoke resentfully.

"Not expect congratulations!"

"Of course—I do congratulate you. One always has to say that, I suppose," and there was a hard little laugh. "All the same—Rob, you did tell me—"

"What did I tell you?"

"That you didn't mean to marry."

"I told you that I had not seen the right girl—and I had not. While that was the case, I was a non-marrying man. But now, I have seen her! Which makes all the difference!"

"Yes, it means that you'll never want me!"

Rob laughed outright at the injured tone. It was too comic—from the point of view of a man, and especially of a man over head and ears in love!

"My dear Magda!" he said. "You are not a child any longer. Don't you see that this alters everything—must alter everything? If I had not met Patricia, I might have gone on single for years, perhaps even for life. But—I have met her."

"Oh, I know! Of course, I understand. It's all quite right and sensible, I dare say—only it does just make all the difference to me. You'll never want anybody now except Patricia."

It was Amy Smith over again, but without consciousness of the "green-eyed monster." Magda was seeing things solely from her own point of view.

"Magda, are you an infant still?"

"No," shortly. "Only—I have looked forward—"

"I would not look forward any more in that spirit! I am sorry if my happiness means disappointment to you. Why, I thought you would be delighted—Patricia being your particular friend."

"I'm not."

"Don't make other people uncomfortable, pray, by treating them to a November fog."

Magda was silent.

"Come—be brave and sensible," he urged. "Some friends are expected there to tea this afternoon, and Patricia sent a particular message, hoping that you would come."

She murmured something like assent, and he went away evidently disappointed in her. No sooner was he gone, than she felt ashamed of her own moodiness, realising that if she should show any slight to Patricia, it could only end in a breach between herself and Rob.

The others were invited also; and not long after four o'clock they arrived at Claughton. A goodly company was already assembled on the large lawn, under shadow of some ancient cedars. It was a scene, and Magda felt secretly grateful to Pen and her mother for not allowing her to go in less than her "best," though she had flung out indignantly at the interference after luncheon. In her then state of mind she had been disposed to think that "anything" would do. Why bother to be smart?

Patricia, a dainty nymph in white and green, stood upon the grass, dispensing smiles upon an admiring world. She was particularly gracious to Mr. Royston—Mrs. Royston had not been able to come—and she welcomed her future sisters-in-law with exactly the right degree of warmth, kissing each lightly on the cheek, and paying chief attention to Pen as the elder.

Pen and Mr. Royston stayed in the circle which surrounded Patricia; but Magda fell back to a retired position, half sheltered by bushes. She had no wish to remain prominently forward, under Rob's observation.

To her surprise, she saw Bee, apparently the centre of another little circle, farther off; and Mrs. Major, looking distinguished in a rich black silk, seated in the post of honour, and receiving pointed attentions from Mr. and Mrs. Framley.

It was all oddly the reverse of what she had pictured so often in earlier months, before the arrival of the Majors at Virginia Villa.

Her own inclination would have been to escape from the crowd altogether; but that at present was out of the question. A fear of annoying Rob restrained her.

But what to do with herself was the question. Plainly she was not needed by Patricia; and having done her duty, she would not go forward again. All the ladies were chatting together, and being waited on with cups of tea by the limited number of masculine guests. There was no one for whom Magda cared; and nobody who cared for her. So she told herself rather dismally, as she stood apart, watching the people, listening to the buzz of voices. Bee once had cared; and, but for her own folly, Bee would undoubtedly care still, since hers was no changeable nature. But things were altered. How could Magda expect that either Bee or her mother would forget the manner in which she had treated them?

She was saying this to herself, when a hand touched hers, and she awoke with a start, to find Bee's soft brown eyes looking into her own.

"Why did you not come to me, Magda? I could not get away sooner, but I've been trying. Don't stay here all alone. Would you not like some tea?"

"Oh, thanks—but it doesn't matter. I can get some for myself presently. It's all right—don't bother about me, please." Magda was annoyed to hear a tell-tale huskiness in her own voice. That would never do. She pulled herself together, with an air of indifference. "The people over there want you. Don't stay."

Bee kept her position, and Magda examined her with more attention. She was very pretty, in her white embroidered frock and shady hat—so pale and delicate featured, with marked dark brows and a gentle smile. Yet there was something of sadness in those sweet eyes; and a wonder assailed Magda—had she given serious pain to her friend by her recent conduct?

"Bee, I want to talk with you some day," she broke out impulsively. "Not here. Another time. I want to explain—"

"Any day. You are always welcome at our house. I think I pretty well understand already. Don't you feel very glad about your brother?"

"Bee! How can I? When you know what I always expected!"

The words ended abruptly. Bee slipped her arm through Magda's, and led her into a little side-path winding among trees.

"Come, shall we have a turn through the grounds? Tea will do presently. Yes, I know you used to talk of keeping house for him some day. But that was only a dream. One knew it might never come true. And surely you must be glad about this—if it means his greater happiness. You—who are so fond of your brother! How can you help being glad?"

She would not seem to see the struggle going on at her side. Magda was in danger of a breakdown.

"Don't you see—" Bee went on—"that it is the right thing for him? If she is the one woman who can fill his life and make him happy—then, surely, he should marry. And you must wish the very best for him. Not merely that you should have something that you would like, but that he should live the fullest and most useful life possible. I don't know Miss Vincent well yet; but one can't help admiring her. And he is devoted to her—quite, quite devoted."

Magda muttered something indistinct, and they walked on in silence. On one side of them the bushes grew thinner, and they saw a seat beyond, with two ladies on it. As they passed, a voice remarked, low but distinctly—

"All very well, my dear! This is the third! Patricia is never happy long without a man at her apron-strings. But how long will it last?"

Bee hurried her companion on, making a slight stir; and the sound ceased. Another ten seconds, and they were out of hearing.

"Patricia! The third!" repeated Magda.

"We were not meant to hear. People should be more careful."

"Who was it? Do you know the voice?"

Bee kept silence, for she did know. It was that of Patricia's aunt, Mrs. Norman—the sister of Patricia's mother, whereas Mrs. Framley was the sister of Patricia's father.

"Do you suppose it is true?"

"There is always gossip of the sort. We must forget it."

"You don't think I ought to tell Rob?"

"Certainly not. It is no business of ours. Magda, be wise—don't repeat it to any human being. I shall not tell even my mother."

"But if it is true?"

"Miss Vincent may have been engaged before—and she may have found it to be a mistake. Anyhow, one may always allow for exaggeration. Your brother must find out for himself. Try to forget it, dear. No one can see the two together without seeing how happy they are."

"Would Rob be happy if he thought this was true—if he were really the third?"

"We have nothing whatever to do with that!" Then Bee began talking about Wratt-Wrothesley and the house-party there. "Everybody admired Miss Vincent," she said. "And everybody liked your brother. My aunts were so grateful to him for what he did in the summer, when Mr. Ivor had that terrible accident. He is one of their greatest friends; and but for your brother, he never could have come through it."

"But it was partly you too, Bee."

"Oh, mine was the most commonplace help. I just looked through a telescope and used ordinary sense. But Mr. Royston—think what it meant for him to spend the whole night on those rocks, in such awful cold—waiting for the morning. We all felt that he was a real hero."

"I suppose Mr. Ivor wasn't at Wratt-Wrothesley, too, when you were all there."

"No." Bee spoke quietly, without the shadow of a sign that it meant anything to her. "My aunts did invite him, but he said he could not spare the time just then. He was going a little later."

CHAPTER XVII
ABOUT TRUE SERVICE

"I SHOULD like to get hold of that child. There is something out of time in her life."

The Rev. Osborne Miles, Vicar of Burwood, stood on a side-path in his garden, surveying with deep interest a group of seedlings, pushing their way upward. After weeks of severe cold, a mild spell had set in—quite time it should, people said, near the end of April—and the Vegetable World was responding with vigour.

He had been presented to the living scarcely a year before this date, and was therefore still "a new man" in Burwood. Thirty years of strenuous toil in a murky manufacturing town, with a parish of twenty thousand, had broken his health by the time he arrived at sixty; and after much hesitation, and many regrets, he accepted a country cure. Burwood, though called a "town," was to him absolute country. Sleepy country too!

He did not look ill, as he stood with squared shoulders and vigorous mien—being a man of natural energy, and one who would never, at his physical worst, carry himself with limp dejection. Strong in build, deliberate and capable in movement, with abundant grey hair and searching eyes beneath overhanging brows, he was not one to be easily overcome; but two years earlier he had been brought by long strain to the lowest possible ebb of vitality. Yet he rallied; and though sternly prohibited by doctors from returning to his old and beloved sphere, he never dreamt of leading an idle existence. So the Burwood offer was accepted.

One thing he found here which, through all his strenuous existence, he had thirsted for—a garden. The old Vicarage, built of the same dull-hued local stone as the ancient Church, stood in an acre of ground well laid out. He could at last freely indulge his passion for flowers.

Of course, even in quiet Burwood, his time was much taken up; but after the life he had lived, this by comparison was ease. He found time for everything, and for his garden besides—especially on Monday, always counted as far as possible an "off-day;" and this was Monday.

After working among thousands of men, it was a change to find himself chiefly concerned with elderly ladies, spinsters or otherwise. Not all elderly. There were many girls in the place; and he studied them with interest. They belonged to such a different type from the young business-women and rough mill-girls, among whom he had worked hitherto. The mild futility of existence among many of them aroused his wonder. It seemed so inadequate a use of life!

"What do they do with themselves?" he one day asked his wife.

"A good many things, dear. They go to tennis-parties—and play hockey—and bicycle and skate. A few of them hunt."

"You are talking of amusements. What work do they do?"

"Some don't do any work. Some are busy at home. Some have classes in the Sunday-school—or help in other ways with parish doings. Some make their own blouses."

The Vicar heard this in silence and went on studying the problem. He was gradually individualising Burwood folks; and lately he had individualised Magda Royston. The church was free-seated; but the Roystons had their own position, just in front of the pulpit, and he had early noted a fresh girlish face, with its rather unusual mass of reddish hair, and with a bright brisk bearing. Then he observed a change. The bright face grew dull; the spirited pose spiritless. Something was wrong with her, he decided; and he went to call, but failed to find the object of his solicitude.

Two Sundays back his attention had been awakened anew. Talking to his people of life, its claims, its duties, its abuses, he saw that listless face lifted, and a look of interest dawn.

"The child wants a helping hand," he thought. "I must get hold of her." But he had not yet succeeded.

"Osborne," called a cheery voice; and his wife came across the wet lawn—a charming little woman, fresh as a daisy, despite years in a manufacturing town; supremely neat in dress, and supremely happy in look, with smiling eyes and ready laugh. They had been married ten years, and were lovers still, though she was a good twenty-five years his junior.

"You are wanted, dear."

"Generally the case on Monday."

"I know. You ought to be left in peace. But I did not like to suggest another time. Girls are cranky beings."

"You speak of them from personal experience."

"Yes, I do. I was cranky at her age—always ready to be rubbed up the wrong way."

Mr. Miles did not count this conclusive as to girls in general, though he forbore to say so. He seldom argued with a woman.

"And if ever I had screwed up my courage to the point of wanting an interview with a clergyman, and had been turned away, I should never have gone again."

"I see. Who is it?"

"One of the Royston girls. The red-haired one."

"She has asked for me?"

"She brings a packet from her father; and she said—might she give it herself?"

"All right. Send her here."

A very clear sense came over the Vicar that he had had this girl not only in his thoughts but in his prayers.

"My dear—the grass is wet."

"Nothing but dew. It's delicious."

She tripped lightly off; and the Vicar waited till Magda approached—shy at coming, and half disposed to bolt at the last moment. He saw so much. Also, from long experience, he at once recognised that she had something in her mind, which she wanted to bring out.

"How do you do? All well at home?" Though the words were commonplace, his strong hand closed round hers with a fatherly grip which won her confidence on the spot. "I'm glad you have found your way to us. It is time that I should know you better."

She said only "Yes," but there was evident pleasure.

"Fond of flowers?" He drew her attention to a fine bloom. "Is not that a marvel of colouring? Something in the arrangement of those petals speaks of a Mind behind—controlling. A garden has much to say to us, if we will but listen. We don't always."

"I suppose we don't always understand the garden-language," she suggested.

He stooped to gather a daisy from the lawn. "Did you ever come across those lines? — "

> "'Small service is true service while it lasts;
> The daisy by the shadow that it casts
> Protects the lingering dewdrop from the sun.'"

"And here is the dewdrop—see! Able to last till now, because of the daisy-shelter. I have taken the daisy away for another and a higher purpose. But it did its little work first."

"Why higher?"

"It has sheltered a drop of water. Now it serves to illustrate a great truth. That is the more important."

"I see-yes. Was the other worth doing?"

"Certainly—if that was its appointed task."

"Things like that seem so small—as if it were all the same, whether they are done or not done."

"Ah, that is the mistake often made. Nothing in life is so small, that its doing or not doing does not matter. Everything is part of one grand whole. That gives dignity to the smallest duty."

"I suppose—" and she broke off. "Oh, it doesn't matter."

"Perhaps it does matter. What is your trouble, my child?" And the kind penetrating eyes studied her.

"I can't see what work there is for me. I couldn't take a district. Father says I'm too young—and, besides, I shouldn't know how to manage it. I did think of a class in the Sunday-school. But I hate teaching. And mother is so afraid of infection for Merryl and Frip."

"What about home duties?"

"Pen sees to all that."

"Leaving nothing for you?"

Magda did not at once reply. A recollection came up of sharp complaints from her father.

"I can't see that there is anything for me to do—worth doing!" she said at length. "Nor anything worth living for."

"Child!"—and he spoke in a moved tone. "Life is always worth living—in God! Everything is worth doing—in Christ our Lord."

"But if there really is nothing?" she insisted.

"If you have absolutely no direct work now, you must wait in patience, and train yourself for the future. You must educate your powers—make yourself ready for what may come by-and-by. Preparation for work is, in its way, as important as the work itself. The preparation in some cases lasts for years; the work itself lasts but a short time. That does not matter. All that matters is that we should be doing whatever God gives us to do, in simple obedience and love."

"And suppose one worked hard for years and years—trying to make ready—and nothing ever came of it?"

"Something will certainly come of it—in this life or in the next. No true work for God is ever thrown away."

"I don't see what I'm to do. It all seems so difficult." She sighed despondently.

"Don't be in too much of a hurry to see your way. Only make the best possible use of your days meanwhile. There is always something to be done for somebody. The smallest service may be 'true service while it lasts.'" Mr. Miles pulled out his watch. He knew that he had said enough. "Ah—I must be on the move. But come again soon. You will find my wife indoors."

He went with her; and as they met Mrs. Miles, she said—

"A letter from Lance. He wants to pay us a visit."

"He is always welcome. How soon?"

"In a week or ten days. I'm afraid he'll find it dull."

"Ivor's not given to dulness." The Vicar vanished, and Magda asked in an interested tone—

"Is that the Mr. Ivor who fell into the crevasse? Do you know him? His name is Lancelot, I'm sure."

"We are first cousins; and he has always been like a younger brother to me. He is a dear fellow."

"I've never seen him, but he is Rob's friend."

"Yes, he has spoken of your brother. Come and see his likeness."

She went into the dining-room, and produced a framed photograph, which the girl studied.

"What a fine face!" she said. Then putting it down, she took up a second, asking—"And who is this?"

"Another cousin of mine; on my mother's side. Lance is on my father's."

"He isn't so handsome. I seem to know the face."

"Ned never had much to boast of in the way of looks. He is a dear, kind-hearted fellow; always ready to do anything he can for any human being. So Is Lance, for the matter of that!"

"I wonder if I ever saw him," murmured Magda. "Perhaps he is like somebody I know." She turned away, remarking—"I once had a friend called Ned; but I haven't seen him for years. Not since I was eleven and he was seventeen. He never wrote."

"I'm afraid your friend was rather fickle."

Magda took up the photograph anew, and after a fresh scrutiny she glanced at the back.

"Why!" she cried. "It is! It's the same. It is Ned Fairfax!"

"Certainly; that is Ned Fairfax."

"But he used to be my friend. The only friend I ever made before I went to school. He and I were immense chums. How funny! Oh, how funny! I didn't even know where he was. We were always getting together, and I was a sort of pet of his for more than three years. I told him everything."

"How amusing! Now I think of it, his mother lived here for three or four years, when she first became a widow. He used to go to a school two miles off. I was sorry she did not send him to a public school. Still, he has turned out a good fellow; not so brilliant as Lance."

"We used to write just at first; and then he left off. People said he would, of course, because he was a boy. But it made me miserable. I dare say he has forgotten all about me now. I should like to see him again."

"You are pretty sure to do that. He visits us at least once a year."

"Oh, how droll to come across him like this!" Magda said again.

CHAPTER XVIII
TAKEN BY SURPRISE

IT had dawned upon Magda that the home-life of Beatrice Major was not quite so smooth and easy, as an outsider might imagine. Bee said nothing to lead to this impression; but it came into being.

Mrs. Major was socially delightful; "so distinguished and patrician!" Somebody said this; and the phrase "caught on." The Burwood ladies went about, remarking one to another—"what a very distinguished person dear Mrs. Major was; so very patrician, you know!"

But to be never so distinguished and patrician does not mean of necessity that the possessor of those adjectives must be always easy to get on with.

She certainly had plenty of originality, with a goodly allowance of brains, and really fine principles. But she was a woman very much accustomed to have her own way; and she expected to have it. She was sensible, even wise; and the "way" that she wanted might, more frequently than not, be both wise and sensible. Yet at times one would rather be free to go one's own foolish way than be forced, against one's will, into paths of wisdom.

If this was the state of things with people in general, much more was it so with her only daughter. She indeed had shaped and ordered Bee's life in true "absolute monarchy" style. Of the mother's devotion to the daughter, there could be no question; and the love was warmly returned. Yet even Bee, with all her innate and cultured gentleness, did crave for a trifle more liberty.

Despite her twenty-one years, she was treated precisely as a child in the school-room. She had an allowance; but she was expected to consult her mother about every shilling that she spent. She might not go out for a walk without asking leave. Her ways of thinking were naturally much the same as Mrs. Major's; but if on any point she differed—and, of course, she did sometimes differ—she was at once suppressed. She might not act for herself, might not think for herself. In Mrs. Major's eyes she was a child still, and likely to remain so.

"Bee, I couldn't stand it in your place! I really couldn't!" Magda broke out one day. Of late Magda had taken to going often in and out of Virginia Villa, where she could always be sure of a welcome. Her friendship with Patricia had dwindled into small dimensions. Patricia had a fancy for Pen, and the two were much together, while Magda was treated with kindness as a younger sister, for whom Patricia found scant leisure. In disgust, she threw up the attempt to see more of her former idol, and fled for comfort to the earlier companionship.

Bee never showed the slightest umbrage at thus acting as a pis-aller. Magda one day tried lamely to explain and excuse her own past conduct; and Bee listened, with patient attention, till the explanation broke down. After all, there was little to be said, except that Magda had not been faithful to her friend. But Bee did not seem to mind. She was gently affectionate as ever, though with a difference. She no longer "worshipped the ground" on which Magda walked. Rather she took her stand as the elder of the two, and was kind, solicitous, sympathetic—but independent. Her happiness rested no longer on Magda's smiles or frowns. While she still loved, it was with love of a different quality. She had been disappointed in Magda; and nothing could reinstate Magda in the old position, for no explanations could do away with facts.

On this particular day, Bee had just had a decided set-down from her mother on some little point of variance; and Mrs. Major, having administered the snub, without any conception that it was a snub, took herself smilingly off. So soon as the two girls were alone Magda broke out as above.

"Yes, you would. What does it matter? Mother is so good to me always. It is only just—not arguing."

"I don't see why you are never to have an opinion of your own."

"Nobody can help my having an opinion of my own."

"Only you've got to smother it down! I've always thought I was pretty closely kept in—but it's nothing to what you are. And you know how girls do have their way now—in some houses."

"I wonder if they are the happier for it—really!"

"Anyhow, they like it. Wouldn't you?"

Bee worked steadily in silence. She had clever hands and often made her own dresses. A half-completed blouse lay on her knees.

"Perhaps I might," she said at length. "But one can't always have everything one likes."

"If you stood up for yourself a little more, things would be different."

Bee shook her head. "It isn't my way," she said.

After a break, she began again—"And, besides, don't you sometimes think, Magda, of how things will look by-and-by—as the years go on?"

"How things will look!"

"Yes. Don't you see what I mean? I'll tell you. I knew a girl near my home, three years ago, who had home troubles. They were real troubles—not easy to bear, I dare say. But she fought for her own way; and she said hard things to her mother, and was so cold to her—I've seen her refuse to give a kiss! And then, quite suddenly, the mother died. There was no warning at all—it was all in a moment. No time for any last words or explanations. And I never can forget that girl's misery—how she reproached herself, and how she would have given all she had for just one word—just to be able to have one kiss, and to beg for forgiveness. For she knew then what the mother's love had really been all through—even though there had been little difficulties, and perhaps some things rather hard to bear. And I made up my mind that I would never be in her position—that I wouldn't let myself mind too much about little worries—and most of all that I would never, never treat my mother coldly. For I know how she loves me."

"I suppose one ought to feel like that—more than one does," observed Magda. Conscience gave a sharp little prick. "Well, I must be going. Oh, by-the-by, what do you think Mrs. Miles told me yesterday?"

"I don't know. You like Mrs. Miles?"

"I like her immensely. And him too. They are dears!" Magda spoke with enthusiasm. Bee had noted the beginning of this new friendship; and not being of a jealous temperament, she was honestly pleased at what seemed likely to make Magda more happy. The last two or three weeks a change had been visible in the latter, a return of vitality, a dawning of fresh interests, and a lessening of the dull indifference which had followed upon Rob's engagement.

"Mother thinks them delightful," she said.

"Oh, they are. I've been twice to tea lately, and I'm going again to-morrow—to help Mrs. Miles with some work. And only think, Bee—she is a cousin of that Mr. Ivor who fell into the chasm last summer. And he is coming to pay them a visit."

Bee, taken by surprise, sent up a startled glance, and flushed brightly. She so seldom changed colour, that Magda came to a stop, with arrested attention.

"Is he? How curious!"

"Why—curious? Quite natural that he should come, if they are cousins."

"Yes. I meant, it is curious that they should be related."

"Mrs. Miles is very fond of him. She says he is such a good fellow— always so kind and thoughtful about other people, and he never minds what trouble he takes to help anybody. She has always been his favourite cousin—a sort of elder sister, because he never had any sisters of his own. She must be a good many years older than he is."

"She will be very pleased to have him." Bee spoke the words quietly, but she did not feel quiet. Her pulse and her thoughts were running riot together.

Was he coming—could he be coming—because he knew that she was here? Did he care—ever so little—for seeing her again? No—no—she answered resolutely—no chance of such a thing! He had given her no reason whatever to think so, when they were together. He had made no effort to see more of her. He had shown no particular feeling beyond simple gratitude for what she had done. She might not allow herself to indulge in dreams. Yet, even as she so replied, the eager questioning leapt up anew, asking with insistent loudness—was it, was it, quite impossible that he might find a pleasure in meeting her once more? She had tried so hard not to dwell upon recollections of him, and had counted herself successful on the whole. Yet now, at the first mention of his name, at the mere thought of seeing his face, she was stirred to the depths.

"Bee, what are you thinking about? You have such a colour! I never saw you look so pretty."

Bee woke up to the fact that she was not alone. Actually, she had forgotten Magda's presence. The latter was examining her with puzzled eyes.

"What are you thinking about? Are you so glad that Mr. Ivor is coming?"

Bee pulled herself together instantly. She did wish that every pulse in her frame would not clang at such a furious rate; yet she spoke in a voice of entire composure.

"I've met him twice. He was very pleasant both times. Of course, it will be nice to see him again—and nice for you too, as he is your brother's friend. Did I tell you that Amy Smith is coming to us?"

"No, I don't remember?"

"We expect her early next week."

"Why Mr. Ivor comes next week too. I'm not sure which day. The place will be quite lively. Well, I suppose I ought to be off. Mother told me to be back early."

Magda vanished; and Bee sat deep in thought, thankful to be alone.

Would the two visits clash—that of Ivor and that of Amy? Bee shivered under the possibility. It was one thing to turn aside Magda's attention. It would be quite another thing to encounter Amy's preternaturally sharp observation.

She might meet Mr. Ivor happily alone, when Amy was not there! But suppose he should come to call, and Amy should be present!—noting her every look, her every change of expression!

The Hut scene was again before her mind's eyes, vividly as if at that moment it was being enacted. She heard again her own talk with Amy; saw herself stand up in displeasure; caught afresh the words called out as she retreated—

"Much better confess that your poor little heart has been taken captive! I have it now! Of course—it's that Mr. Ivor! Wretched man, to rob me of my Bee!"

Words which—if Ivor chanced to be awake—could not fail to reach his ears! In which case he could say nothing!

At the time she had met this knowledge calmly. The after terror for his life had dwarfed its importance; and when he was safe, the after joy and relief carried her through their first meeting.

But now, at the thought of again seeing him, she was far more keenly affected by this realisation of what he might have overheard. Fear had her in its grip lest, when in his presence, she should fail to hold herself well in leash. How if he were indifferent, and if she should betray the fact that she was not indifferent? How if some look or word of hers should reveal that Amy's utterance had been true, while yet he could not respond? It would be too dreadful.

Extreme care would be necessary, not to go one inch farther than she intended—or than he would go. She Would have to be simple, natural, easy, kind—no more. And with Amy present, the difficulty would be magnified tenfold.

Till this hour she had not known the strength of the hold that he had upon her; the overwhelming intensity of her love for him. Would she have power to go through such an ordeal, and to emerge triumphant?

Bee almost felt that she could not endure the strain—that she must somehow make her escape.

But if he did care—if he were coming with the expectation of seeing her—how could she be absent?

CHAPTER XIX
IF HE SHOULD COME!

"BEE, I'm wondering—is it one-tenth, one-hundredth part as much to you as it is to me—my being here?"

The words broke into a long silence, rousing Beatrice out of her dream; by no means the first of the kind since Amy Smith's arrival two days before.

They were together in the little morning-room of Virginia Villa, sometimes called "The Green Room," because of its prevailing tint. It was a foggy afternoon, not tempting out-of-doors. Mrs. Major had an engagement, so the two were alone; and in the midst of a lengthy talk about "old days," Bee had dropped out of it, forgetting to answer Amy's last remark, leaning a little forward, her eyes fixed on the fire, lost in a vision, which seemed to be half-sad, half-glad, but certainly profound.

Amy knew that she herself had no share in this dream. Somebody else reigned there, and she was forgotten. She saw far more than Magda in her place would have seen. In her passionate devotion to Bee, she had accustomed herself to read each turn of expression, each inflection of voice. It was pathetic, this intensity of her love for the younger girl; for she paid away her whole self, and Bee could not give back an equivalent. Amy Smith, however estimable and good and unselfish—and in the main she was all these,—just did not possess that undefinable gift, the power to win great love. All that Bee was able to give in return was a kind and sincere affection.

Perhaps for the first time, as she sat gazing this afternoon upon Bee's absorbed face, Amy realised it. As the outcome of her troubled realisation, she broke into the above words. Bee, wrenched back to the present, lifted startled eyes.

"Why—of course—"

"There's no 'of course' in the matter. Are you glad to have me? Do you really care? Would it have been better, if I had not come? Tell me—truly. Shall I go back to-morrow?"

"Amy, what nonsense! How can you say such things?"

"Because I think them! Because I never have any secrets from you. Because I don't choose to live in a Fool's Paradise! There are fifty 'becauses,' any one of which will do. But most of all, because it is so much to me to be with you again; and I should like—foolishly, perhaps—selfishly no doubt—to be sure that you are the least little bit glad to be with me. Are you glad—honestly glad? I want the truth, please."

An embarrassing question! Bee had so wished that Amy's visit could have been delayed, just until Ivor's was over. Only that; no more. It was not that she did not wish to have her old friend, but that she dreaded the conjunction of the two. All day she saw Ivor with her mental vision, pictured their first encounter, and longed-for, yet feared the moment. And Amy was here—to look on! That alone was what she craved to alter. She was not and could not be glad to have Amy this particular week. Any other week—only not this. For sole answer, she put her hand on Amy's arm.

"Yes; I know. I'm unreasonable. All the same, remember—I had you for years and years; and nothing ever came between us. If ever the Green-eyed Monster had a valid excuse, I do think he has with me. It isn't as if I had dozens of friends, like some people,—or as if new ones with me could be more than the old ones. But circumstances are different. Once in love, I suppose everything else goes down before it. Do you think I don't know what is in your mind, when you look as you did just now? Know! I should think I did. It's—Mr. Ivor!"

"I would rather talk of something else, please."

"No earthly use. You can't think of anything else."

"You make me sorry I ever let you know that I had any sort of feeling—of that kind!"

"You didn't, my dear child! I found it out for myself—in spite of all you could do."

Bee's pale cheeks were slightly flushed. "And if I had not found it out before, I should find it out now. You are different—different altogether from the Bee of old. Do you think I don't see? Do you think I don't feel? You are away from us all—living in a separate world of your own. Oh, I don't complain. It's natural, I suppose,—and you are just as sweet and kind and thoughtful as ever. There's nothing to complain of—only—you are not here! Nothing is anything to you, except—Of course I see! Bee—look at me." She took possession of the slight hand, lying near, and was instantly aware of the hurried throb of Bee's pulse. "Look at me! I want to see into your eyes."

Bee obeyed gravely, but withdrew her hand. "Amy, if you want to make me really sorry to have you—you will go on saying this sort of thing."

There was a short silence. Amy was a good deal surprised, and her little snub nose reddened.

"You are developing," she said at length, with a touch of constraint. "I never knew you to take quite such a tone before."

"Was I unkind? I am sorry." Bee spoke with difficulty. "I did not mean to give you pain."

"I suppose all is fair in love and war—but you are older."

"Of course I am older. What else can you expect?"

"I didn't expect that, somehow. I thought my Bee would be my Bee still. And she isn't. She is—some one else's Bee now. There's nothing of you left for me."

"Indeed there is, Amy. I never could alter to old friends. How can you suspect me of such a thing?"

"I don't suspect. I know. It's not that you are changed to me, but that you are changed in yourself. You can't help it. You are another being. Quite as dear and sweet as the old Bee, but not the same."

"I'm sorry. I'll try to be my old self. We'll go back to what we were talking about. It was—" She stopped, in perplexity.

"Yes. Go on. It was—"

"I don't quite remember."

"No, of course you don't. Well—if we are to drop the subject of that individual—how I detest the man! Suppose you tell me about your friend, Magda. Are you as absorbed in her as ever?"

"Was I absorbed in her?"

"Every letter that you wrote from school rang with 'Magda' all through. I don't notice her name so often now. But then—you are no longer a school-girl. Do you like her as much as ever?"

"I'm very fond of Magda—really. There's so much that is fine in her. I think she's going through a sort of phase that girls do go through—she's unsettled, and never certain what to do with herself or her time. But she will come through. She does really wish to be useful."

"You might be King Solomon, my dear! It wasn't your way in the past to analyse her, as if you were her granny. You tried to give me the impression that she was a perfectly angelic being. I have always wanted to make her acquaintance."

"So you can. There she is!"

"Not coming here! What a plague! I did think I should have you to myself for this one afternoon."

Bee did not echo the regret.

Magda entered briskly, looking her best. She had for once arranged well her mass of reddish-gold hair; and the quick walk had given her a bright colour; and her golden-brown eyes had their happy light, often lacking in less cheerful moods.

"Bee—" she cried, and stopped at sight of a stranger. "Oh, I forgot!" As it recurred to her mind that Bee had expected a friend.

Bee performed the introduction, and the two shook hands, each critically scanning the other.

"What a plain uninteresting person!" was Magda's inward comment.

"Shouldn't have thought her the sort of girl to suit Bee!" Amy voicelessly said.

"I'm afraid I'm interrupting."

"Not at all. Do stay to tea with us. Mother is out for the afternoon." The words had no sooner passed Bee's lips than she wished them unsaid. She had carefully refrained from saying aught to Amy about Ivor's presence at the Vicarage; and Magda might bring it up. But the thing was done. Already Magda was accepting the invitation.

Bent on keeping clear of the one topic, Bee threw herself into conversation, taking the lead in an unwonted fashion, bringing up everything she could think of to interest her companions. For a time she was successful, though Amy looked curiously at her, and Magda more than once sought to introduce something of which her mind was full. Three times she tried in vain. But a slight pause at length occurred, when tea was brought in, and Magda used her chance.

"I've just been to the Vicarage, Bee. I had to leave some cards that I had been copying out for Mrs. Miles. And—"

"You are always going there now, dear, are you not?"

"Well, sometimes. Not always. I like going, and I like them. And I saw your friend. He arrived late last night."

"Did you? What will you have? Cake or bread-and-butter? Did I show you this photo of our house, Magda? It was taken the other day by a passing photographer—as a specimen of Burwood architecture." She tried to laugh.

Magda glanced casually at the proffered view. "Yes—very good. Bee, I like your friend. He is a handsome man. I never saw a handsomer, I do think. And awfully nice too!"

It was useless to resist. The situation had to be accepted. But Bee found it difficult. She was seated facing the light; and she knew that Amy's eyes were full upon her.

"Yes, he is nice," she said quietly. "You don't take sugar, do you, Amy? I haven't quite forgotten your tastes, you see. I can recommend these cakes."

"So—that is the meaning of the dreaminess," thought Amy, in a flash of comprehension. She instantly recognised that the 'friend' must be Ivor. But she would not spare Bee, feeling vexed that she had not been told of his coming, and she asked pointedly: "A friend! What friend? Who did you say it was?"

Magda answered this. "Why—Mr. Ivor. The one who fell into the bergshrund last summer—don't you remember? Rob always declares that Bee saved his life; and Mr. Ivor says the same. He says that but for her he wouldn't be alive now. I should be awfully proud in your place, Bee."

"I don't see what I have to be proud of. It was little enough that I did."

"Other folks didn't think so at the time," remarked Amy. "If you had seen her, Miss Royston—simply glued to the telescope for hours! Nothing would induce her to budge, till she had spotted the climbers. I should never have thought of staying. But then—they were not friends of mine! Don't you see? That makes all the difference."

"How horrid of me! How small of me!" Amy said to herself, as these words slipped out. She knew that she had said them in revenge, because Bee had not informed her of Ivor's coming.

"But, Bee—that was before you had seen Rob. You didn't know him then!"

A slight clash of the milk-jug against a cup showed that Bee's hand was trembling. It seemed hard that Amy, her own old friend, should make things more difficult for her!

"No," she said. "But I knew that he was your brother!"

"And you knew Mr. Ivor?"

"I had met him—once."

At this moment, of all moments, came a ring at the front door. Bee instantly guessed—nay, knew, as a matter of certainty—who the caller was; and her inward trembling increased. She was not surprised when the door opened, and the little maid announced—

"Mr. Ivor."

CHAPTER XX
THROUGH AN ORDEAL

IT was a severe trial for Bee. Amy there—Magda there—both looking on critically; one certainly knowing, and the other possibly half-suspecting, what she felt for him; while she had no knowledge whether his feelings for her went beyond ordinary friendliness, and gratitude for the part she had played in his rescue. That in some measure, he owed his life to her, none seemed to question. Under the circumstances, a call from him, when he happened to be in the place, was only to be expected, and might mean absolutely nothing.

Had she been alone, or with her mother only, she could have met him again as before—perhaps not quite so easily as then, yet with much the same simplicity. But Amy had been putting her to a severe strain. Already her heart beat fast, and her cheeks were flushed. If she allowed herself to show pleasure, there was danger that she might show overmuch pleasure; and those watching eyes would see! If she smiled in his face, she would be taxed afterwards with undue warmth. Besides—if he indeed had overheard Amy's words outside the Hut, he would understand only too well.

These thoughts rushed pell-mell through her mind, as she stood up to greet him. She knew that there was nothing for the emergency but self-restraint and composure. And in her present condition of overstrain, such composure could hardly fail to be over-done.

He came in quickly; looking well and handsome; and very glad, it would seem, to see her again. If so, he met with an immediate check. Bee received him coldly, distantly, as she might have received the veriest stranger. As he passed the door, the pretty flush in her cheeks died out, leaving her pale and apparently unmoved; and her chill quiet might easily be mistaken for utter indifference. Could he have seen the surge of joy which swelled below at the first glimpse of his face, he would not have been so taken in. Yet her eyes scarcely met his; and his warm grasp found limp fingers.

She overdid it completely, as many a woman in like circumstances is apt to do. And he had not the clue.

His own mind by this time was made up. He had thought incessantly of Bee, had grown more and more impatient to see her again, had craved to know her better. For the purpose of so doing, he had proposed this visit to the Vicarage. Her gentleness, her thought for others, had left a powerful impression; and he had begun to know that she was necessary to his happiness. More perhaps than aught else, the semi-consciousness that he might already be enshrined in that girlish heart recurred again and again, with an ever-growing sense of restful delight.

And now he was flung back on himself, and was made to feel that he had been all along cherishing a delusion.

She introduced him to her friends, then returned to the tea-tray, and busied herself with downcast eyes, leaving Magda to do the entertaining—a task which Magda was not slow to take up. Ivor submitted to what Bee apparently desired, though he sent more than one questioning glance towards that still face, wondering what it meant. Once she met his gaze; and a throbbing tide of joy swelled up, so fiercely that she dared not let herself meet it a second time.

She found him suddenly by her side, holding a cup and saucer. "For Miss Royston," he said. And then—"Are you thinking of Switzerland again next summer?"

"No—I am afraid not." She spoke in a low suppressed voice. "Not— likely. I hope you have quite got over—that night—no ill effects!"

"None at all, thanks."

"No sugar, I suppose," Bee remarked, with a glance towards Magda. Then she felt that she was restraining herself too much, was going farther than necessity imposed, and she lifted one eager wistful look—but too late. He had turned away, and was carrying the tea to Magda, beside whom he again seated himself.

The two were soon in a full swing of talk; for Magda liked Ivor, and found him entertaining. Besides, he was Rob's particular friend, which made a link and supplied a topic; and she could talk well enough, when she chose to take the trouble. She did choose to-day.

They got upon the subject of mountain-climbing; and since most of his ascents had been done in company with Rob, she was delighted to draw from him tales of difficult passages and hair-breadth escapes. He was not a man to say much ordinarily about his own doings; but this meant telling about Rob to Rob's sister, which made a difference.

Amy listened with dissatisfied annoyance. She might be vexed and jealous with Bee; she might even stoop to a momentary revenge; but she did not wish her darling to be unhappy, or to be ousted by "this red-haired upstart of a school-girl," as she contemptuously stigmatised Magda in her mind. Yet, looking on, she knew that the "red-haired school-girl" was not without charm, and also that Ivor was not unconscious of that charm. There was a touch of unwonted brightness about Magda, both in colouring and in manner; and the contrast of Bee's impassive pallor was marked.

Now and again the latter made some slight remark, just enough for politeness, and no more. Amy grew annoyed. Why did not Bee exert herself to be agreeable? Why leave the field clear for "that conceited child"? Amy had abundance of adjectives at command, and she often found them a relief to her feelings.

"I should just love to go up a Swiss mountain," Magda was saying. "No, I've never been to Switzerland. I've done some scrambling on English cliffs and places, with Rob—and once he took me to Scotland, and we had some real climbs there. That was three years ago. Only rocky places—not ice and snow."

"Rock-climbing may be quite as difficult, and may need as much care. There is many an English rock-face, where a slip might be as fatal as on a Swiss mountain."

"Only it doesn't sound so grand. That climb of Bee and Miss Smith last year sounds much more than what I did with Rob in Scotland—but I don't believe it was really. When they went to the Hut, I mean."

They both looked towards Bee, and she said mechanically—

"No, I dare say not."

"It was fortunate for me that Miss Major should have undertaken the expedition," observed Ivor.

"If I had not, somebody else would have been there," Bee murmured; and Amy put in an impulsive word, kindly meant—

"My dear, nobody else would have been likely to glue herself to the telescope for hours, as you did: You should have seen her—" this was addressed direct to Ivor—"hour after hour, watching and watching. Nothing would make her stir, when once she settled in her mind that you were in danger. She held on 'like grim death,' no matter what the guides or I might say." It suddenly dawned upon Amy that the "you" which she perhaps meant in the plural might be taken as in the singular; and she made matters worse by hastily adding, as an after-thought, and with a little laugh—"Of course I mean—you both—you and Mr. Royston."

Then she knew that she had doubly blundered; that it would have been far better if she had said nothing. Ivor for a moment was perfectly still, looking down; and it was Bee who broke silence, in her quietest tones—

"I don't see that any one else in my place could have done differently."

"No—perhaps not! Oh, well—I suppose it was just a sort of instinct," explained Amy, feeling guilty.

"And a most kind benevolence towards two fellow-climbers in difficulties," Ivor added.

He stood up then to say good-bye; and Bee did not relax. She longed to do so, longed at this last moment to infuse some warmth into her manner. But Amy's latest interference had made it impossible. She felt frozen and rigid. Good-byes were quickly over; and he spoke no word of seeing her again. His manner too was cold by this time.

As he walked back to the Vicarage, he was conscious of deep disappointment. Bee had been perpetually in his thoughts of late. He had dwelt upon her constantly in imagination; and—much more than he was aware of till this hour—he had counted on the truth of Amy Smith's assertion. He had believed that Bee would be easily won, that she was at least disposed to care for him.

All that was at an end. She did not care; she felt no pleasure in meeting him. Recalling again the Hut scene, he realised how easily he might have misunderstood or exaggerated the meaning of the speech he had overheard—also how, even if Bee had been a trifle touched, she might by this time have lost the slight impression once made.

It was quite evident that she did not care any longer. No girl could put on so icy a manner towards a man whom she loved. So he told himself— little knowing! He could imagine no cause for such a manner, save one— indifference! Probably, she felt that she had been too kind to him at the time of his accident, and she wished to make him see that clearly.

If so, she had succeeded. He did see. He had no further expectations. The dream was dead. He wished that he had not come to Burwood.

CHAPTER XXI
AND AFTERWARDS

BEE went quietly through the rest of the day, saying little, doing all that was needful. She looked white, Amy thought. But any attempt at confidential talk, any reference to the past scene, on the part of the elder, was decisively checked by the younger girl. For once, Amy found herself powerless.

Mrs. Major did not seem to remark anything unusual; and the hours wore away tardily. How tardily, how drearily, with Bee, Amy might have seen. She was no longer a young girl herself; but she had known something of life. She had had her own love-affair, many years back, caring too much for one who did not care for her; and this ought to have given her power, to read and sympathise. But she had found consolation in that past trouble, by pouring her rejected devotion upon Bee; and somehow, though she did see something, she failed to estimate fully.

Bedtime came; and Bee was alone. At last!

She had longed for this moment, through those leaden hours of the interminable evening. Till now she had not dared to let herself think. A heavy weight pressed upon her; but she might not analyse it. She could only struggle on, minute by minute, holding herself in with a firm hand.

The others had gone to bed; and her door was locked; and she no longer feared interruption. She stood in the middle of her pretty room, dazed and motionless; her hands clasped, her eyes fixed on a far distance.

She was seeing again, hearing again, all that had gone on that afternoon; feeling again her own coldness to him; enduring again that terrible strain, and the sense that she might not, could not, let herself go—that she might not, could not, let him see what his coming was to her.

And she had driven him away; had rebuffed and repelled him; had made him think that she did not care, that he was nothing to her. She had read in his face, that he understood it so. He would never get over it. He would never again come forward. She had ruined her happiness, once and for all!

It had been unavoidable. Not knowing what he felt, and recalling what he might have overheard, how could she take any forward step? Things might have been so different—but for Amy! Magda mattered less. Magda saw little below the surface. She could have managed Magda. But Amy— her life-long friend and devotee, Amy who professed to love her more than any other—Amy had done this. Amy had worked the mischief. Amy had laughed at her; had twice said the wrong thing at the critical moment; had upset her self-control; had interfered unkindly, when she might have helped; had driven her into doing that which had destroyed her hope, that which had spoilt her life. If Amy had not been there, or if Amy had acted otherwise, when he came in, she might have met him so differently!

Bee was startled at the force of her own passionate resentment, under this consciousness. Hers was not a resentful nature. That, is to say, it was not one of those natures which are for ever taking offence at nothings, being annoyed at little things. But if resentment were once aroused in her, it was no light matter—just because such arousing was so rare, and would never be without some real cause. To-day it had been aroused, intensely, deeply. Her whole being as she stood in the centre of her room, seemed to swell and surge in vehement bitter wrath. How could she ever forgive this—this which meant the wrecking of her life's happiness?

Somebody turned the handle of her door—in vain. Bee held her breath. She guessed it to be Amy; and she did not want Amy. She wanted nobody,— Amy least of all. Now that she had let herself go, she could not regain the dropped reins.

"If Amy comes, I shall show her—I can't help it!" she muttered despairingly.

Again the handle rattled, and a tap was followed by—

"Please, Bee—please!"

Bee moved nearer to the door, and said in a distinct tone—

"Good-night."

"I want to speak to you."

"No use. I'd rather not. It is too late."

"You are not in bed yet."

"I shall be—soon."

"But I want a word with you first . . . Let me in, please. I must, Bee!"

The wave of resentment again rose high, and Bee pressed both hands on her chest, as if to hold it down. But she had always given way to the elder girl; and habit is strong. After some further hesitation, she very slowly withdrew the bolt. Amy opened, and hurriedly entered.

"What is it that you want?" Bee asked icily.

"I want you. What made you keep me out? That is not like my darling."

She came close, and folded both arms round Bee; but there was no response. Bee seemed an image of snow; as white, as chill; not resisting, but simply enduring the embrace. Never, in all the years that they had known one another, had Amy seen her like this.

Releasing the passive figure, she stood looking, with troubled eyes— herself a small being, in a crude red dressing-gown, her limp light hair hanging loose in rats' tails.

"Bee dear—what is it?"

"Will you please leave me alone!"

"Why were you so stiff to him this afternoon?"

The question was unexpected, and heavy throbbing in Bee's throat answered quickly to it. She said only—

"You made me."

"I! But of course I didn't mean—"

"How could I be anything else—after all you said! With Magda there! It was—impossible! You did it!"

Amy caught one of Bee's hands, and it hung in her grasp like a thing without life.

"I was wrong—I knew I was wrong at the time," she said penitently. "It was horrid of me. That was why I couldn't sleep without seeing you again. I suppose—I suppose it was jealousy. Just a touch of it, you know. Bee—" and she caressed the cold fingers—"of course jealousy is always horrid. But don't you think there is just some little excuse for me? You have always been mine, and nothing before has ever come between us. And now—Oh, I see, it has to be. I see you can't help it. Nothing and nobody is anything to you, in comparison with—him! I must make up my mind to it, and learn to play second fiddle. Or rather—to play no fiddle at all. That's what it really means—" and she tried to laugh. "I shall be out of the orchestra altogether. But it isn't quite easy for me—is it, darling? You'll forgive—won't you?

Though I was rather horrid this afternoon. I'll never do it again. And things will soon come right."

"Please leave me alone!" was all that she had in reply.

"Won't you just say first that you forgive me?"

The silence following seemed long. Bee's head dropped.

"I—can't!" came at length. "I—can't—yet! If only you would go!"

"It makes me wretched to think of leaving you like this."

"Why should it? You can do nothing for me—now. You could have helped this afternoon—and you did not! You spoilt everything—made me drive him away—for ever! It was so cruel—so cruel! And now—to pretend—"

"Oh, Bee! Pretend!"

"I can't help it. You must give me time. I can't forgive you yet."

Bee turned away, with a low moan, and went towards the window.

Amy came close behind.

"Listen to me, dear. I promise you that I'll put it right. I'll explain—"

Bee turned fiercely, gripping her wrist. No limpness about her now!

"Never! Never! Not one word. Amy—if you dare—" and her breath grew short. "Have you no sense? Don't you see what it would mean for me, if—if he doesn't care? Promise—promise faithfully—that you never, never will say a single word to anybody about it. Promise!"

"Can't you trust me?"

"No, I can't—after to-day!—after what you did say! You must promise. Amy, I tell you plainly—if ever—ever!—you interfere again—it will be the end of our friendship."

The usually gentle girl was strangely wrought up; and Amy, quite subdued, gave the required promise. She had to repeat it three times, before Bee was satisfied.

"And now will you go to bed? Will you try to rest, darling? And do believe that things are not so bad as you fancy. You will see it to-morrow morning."

"Oh yes,"—came languidly, not in assent.

Life's little stage | 135

"And I do think you will soon believe that I did not mean to be cruel!" That word had gone deep. "Bee darling, if you only knew one-half of how I love you, I think you could not suspect me of ever meaning to be unkind."

Bee was listlessly silent.

"One kiss," pleaded Amy. She folded the other in a warm grasp, and Bee again submitted; no more. Amy released her, sighing.

"Well, good-night, poor darling. I'm much more to be pitied than you are. I've done the harm, and that is worse than only having to bear it."

Met again by uncompromising silence, Amy stole away, closing the door with circumspection, lest Mrs. Major should hear. She lay awake in bed, tears dropping at intervals. Had she indeed forfeited Bee's love by her folly?

Sleep under the circumstances lay outside the range of possibilities. An hour passed; and another hour.

The house was very still. A tiny creak startled her; and then a soft footfall.

"Bee!"—she said instantly.

A slight figure bent over her in the darkness, and a smothered voice murmured—

"I'm come—to say—good-night."

Amy held her in a long close clasp. Neither could speak at first; and one tiny sob might be heard from Bee.

"And you forgive me, my darling!"

"I—had to! I—couldn't say my prayers. I couldn't say—Forgive me—as—"

Bee broke down.

CHAPTER XXII
"COULDN'T BE TIED!"

"I REALLY did think that dear boy had more sense," quoth Mrs. Miles, as her busy fingers arranged rows of tucks in a small frock. Two little maidens of seven and eight brightened the Vicarage home, and she made all their clothes herself.

"Ivor! What has he done?"

"He has done nothing. It's what he is going to do."

"Where is he to-night?"

"Gone to dine at Claughton. I thought you knew. That is not the point! Imagine his taking to Magda, more than to Bee Major!"

"You think he has?"

"Quite sure. When he came back from his call yesterday, he had nothing to say, except what a nice bright girl Magda was. And so she is; and I like her. But you can no more compare her with Beatrice Major than—" Mrs. Miles paused for a simile, as she measured the width of her tucks, and failed to find one. "Not that Magda isn't attractive in her own way. But I wish one could bring her to a point. She is all loose ends, and vague dreams, and general discontent. Nothing that one suggests in the way of work seems to be the right thing. I suppose girls are often like that when they first get away from school; but it is time she should settle to something."

"I thought she had given you some help of late."

"In a casual fashion—when nothing that she likes better happens to turn up."

"That seems to be the way with a good many of the Burwood ladies—older as well as younger."

"I've tried my best to rouse them; and some respond all right. But with most of the girls, it is—'Oh, I can't be tied!' Those Hodgson girls, for instance—five of them, strong clever young people, and well-educated. And they're just running to seed. They do absolutely nothing for any human being except themselves. A house-full of servants—no help wanted there; abundance of money; and life one endless round of pleasure! Riding, hunting, motoring, golfing, dancing, paying visits, travelling—nothing but amusement! I tackled them one day in good earnest, and asked if one wouldn't help in the Sunday-school, and another in the night-school, and another in the shoe-club, and so on. And one and all made the same reply. Oh dear, no, they couldn't be tied! They liked to be free. Which means—free to amuse themselves without stint."

"One wonders that any human being, with brains and character, can be content with such an existence!"

"You see, dear, the point of the matter is that, if they undertake any regular weekly task, something may turn up at that particular hour, which they don't like to miss. An invitation, perhaps."

In the Vicar's strenuous life, work had habitually barred the way upon pleasure. But then he had found his pleasure in his work.

"And if it does?" he said.

"Why, generally they accept the invitation, and toss up the work. I tried to get the Hodgsons to see that they might perhaps owe a duty to other folks besides themselves; and they took it very well. They really are nice girls, you know, only so fearfully useless. One of them actually consented to help me in the library once a week for an hour. And she came twice. Then something turned up that she didn't wish to lose; so she sent an excuse. Next time she sent no excuse, but simply stayed away. And then she wrote a pleasant little note, saying she was so busy-busy! That she was afraid she must give up the library."

The Vicar had put down his pen, and was gravely attentive. He knew it all, of course—probably better than his wife; but she liked to pour forth and he liked to listen.

"There are delightful exceptions, I'll allow. Bee Major, for one. But she has been trained to do her duty; and the others have been brought up from babyhood to think of nothing but themselves. No real sense of duty! The Royston girls are different—except Magda. Whatever you propose to her she doesn't want to do. She can't manage this, and she doesn't 'like' that. Anyhow, I never came across a nicer girl than Bee Major. She would make an ideal wife for Lance!"

"You can't choose his wife for him, my dear."

"More's the pity!" she retorted. "One could often choose for a man so much more sensibly than he chooses for himself! However—since he likes Magda, he shall see her again. I'm asking her and Pen and one or two others—Bee included—to spend the evening here the day after to-morrow. You love having young folks about."

Ivor was already seeing Magda again. She and Pen had been invited to dine at Claughton Manor; other guests being there also.

Bee was asked, and she accepted; and just at the last she had to send an excuse. Nothing short of absolute necessity would have kept her away, since she realised what it might mean. But that very afternoon Mrs. Major was taken with an acute attack of illness, to which she was occasionally subject, connected with the heart, and serious enough to mean actual danger. Bee could not leave her. Neither could she fully explain; for Mrs. Major had an extreme dislike to being counted delicate; and Bee was under strict orders never to say a superfluous word about her mother's health. The doctor had similar instructions; and he alone, beside Bee and the faithful old "Nurse," knew how grave these attacks were, or might at any time become.

Nothing could have been more unfortunate than one happening just now. Ivor, on hearing of the excuse sent—that Mrs. Major was "very poorly," and that Bee could not be spared—naturally drew his own conclusions. Coupled with her cold manner, it meant of course that she wished to keep out of his way.

Partly, perhaps, in self-defence, and in consequence of the wet blanket to which he had been treated, he turned a good deal of his attention to Magda that evening. She was again at her best, in a prettily-made frock of thin black material, which suited the red-gold of her hair, and the bright curiously-tinted eyes. A spray of variegated leaves, chosen and fastened in by Merryl, gave exactly the right tone; and there was no other colouring to compete with it. She talked well too. She and Ivor exchanged ideas, played upon words, discussed opposite views, laughingly. He found her unformed, but clever, and on the whole refreshingly simple. It went for little, so far; yet the fact that she was the sister of his most intimate friend meant that they had many subjects in common.

For once Pen was in the background. Patricia showed herself, as always, daintily charming, moving amid a circle of admirers. The personality of the admirers mattered little, so long as they were there.

Magda was entirely occupied with Ivor—or rather, with Ivor's attentions. He managed to draw her out, as she had not been drawn out before. He made her sparkle, and showed her to herself in new and agreeable lights. A feeling of delighted gratification, which she did not attempt to analyse, filled her mind in consequence.

Two days later they again met at the Vicarage; and once more Bee, though invited, was absent, since her mother was still too ill to be left, though she might only hint at this. Ivor had no further doubts.

"A convenient excuse!" he said bitterly to himself.

Amy, full of remorse, would gladly have taken Bee's place in the sick-room; but it was not allowed; and, she knew Mrs. Major too well to venture on any full explanation to others. She too had been invited, and she had to go, since Bee was bent upon her having the pleasure. It was an evening which, for Amy, spelt the reverse of enjoyment.

Magda this time really shone. She seemed at one leap to have grown older, to have become less school-girlish, more handsome, more taking. A slight consciousness made her voice softer, her manner more restrained, than usual; yet with this came also a touch of increased confidence. She found in herself a power to please, which she had not known before; and the experience was delicious. Others watched her with a mingling of surprise and amusement. Magda was developing, they said. She was "quite coming out."

Amy Smith's sensations included no amusement. She grew inwardly furious, more and more furious, as the evening wore on. Bee's friend—to step in, like this, in Bee's absence!—To try deliberately to win Ivor's love away from her! It was scandalous! Disgraceful! Amy found it hard work to hold her wrath within bounds.

Nor did she—altogether. Early hours were the rule at the Vicarage; and by half-past ten a general exodus took place. Wraps were donned, amid talk and laughter, in the breakfast-room; and Amy, standing grimly apart from the rest, found Magda offering a good-bye hand, all smiles.

"Hasn't it been a delightful evening?" Magda was saying.

Amy had always been impulsive; and she was so still, though fast leaving girlhood behind. Without an instant's pause for thought, and not so much as remembering her promise to Bee, she spoke words which leaped up in her mind—

"To you, I dare say! But—I couldn't—in your place! I call it—poaching!"

Then, with sudden contrition, as a flame of colour rushed into Magda's face, she knew what she had done. "What do you mean?" came involuntarily.

"Oh, nothing!" Amy tried to laugh. "I'm talking nonsense. Good-bye."

Magda hesitated an instant; then walked off, holding her head high.

"I can't endure that Miss Smith," she said disdainfully to Pen, as they drove home. "Such a stupid ordinary little person! I can't imagine what Bee sees to like in her."

Pen made some chilling reply. She was not pleased with Magda's prominence during the two past evenings.

But Amy had blundered again. She had opened Magda's eyes.

CHAPTER XXIII
HERSELF OR HER FRIEND?

ONE may be walking on a most ordinary path, plucking flowers by the way, and doing—or not doing—one's everyday duties. And suddenly temptation comes!

But in the meeting of that temptation it makes just all the difference, whether the everyday duties have been faithfully carried out, or have been shirked. In the one case, previous weeks have strengthened one's power to stand firm; in the other case, previous weeks have lessened it.

Going to bed this night seemed to Magda almost impossible. There was so much to think about. Life had assumed a new colouring.

A vague sense had dawned upon her—vague at first, but rendered more definite by Amy Smith's unwise speech—that she had some sort of power over Lancelot Ivor. Power, it might be, to make him like her. He seemed to enjoy her companionship. She had found that she could interest him, could amuse him, could make him for the moment grave at will. And Amy's remark set the seal to her discovery. If others saw the same, then it must be real—then she could not only have fancied it.

The thought was immensely exciting.

Not that she cared markedly for Ivor himself. Magda did not know what real love meant. But he was handsome and much liked; and her vanity was flattered. Hitherto she had counted for little, either in her own home or among Burwood friends. His attention lifted her upon a pedestal of importance.

He had deferred going away for another night or two; and next evening he was to dine with them. She would see him again. She would have another chance to deepen the impression which—perhaps—she had already made.

And—it meant—temptation!

She woke up to the fact slowly; and it was partly from what Amy had said that she recognised the temptation as such.

Magda was not keenly observant. Thus far she had not known what Amy knew—that Bee's heart belonged to Ivor. It was the last thing Bee would have wished her to know. Here again Amy had betrayed Bee.

Not indeed directly. Her hasty speech at first only aroused Magda's ire, on her own account. She disliked Amy, and she hated to be lectured and interfered with. But as she restlessly walked her room, going over the evening in her mind, and as she thought again of Amy's words, a new sense came into them.

"Poaching! What nonsense!" What could Miss Smith have meant? Poaching in another person's preserve—that was the idea. What—in Bee's preserve? How ridiculous! As if Bee had any particular rights over Mr. Ivor! And as if Bee cared!

But did Bee not care? She recalled her own announcement of Ivor's expected arrival, and Bee's unwonted flush—then her absence, her dreaminess, her look of happiness. It all seemed rather suspicious, even though Ivor had received no especially warm welcome afterwards. Bee was always so funny about things—so slow to show what she felt. Perhaps Miss Smith knew that Bee really did care—and perhaps that was why she had meddled.

If indeed it were so—what then?

Was Magda to cut in between, to steal Ivor, to destroy her friend's hopes of happiness? It might mean all this! If left to himself, Ivor and Bee were not unlikely to draw together. But if Magda should exert herself to win him—should use the power which she believed to be hers—she might draw him on to like her more. And then—Bee might lose for ever the man who perhaps had already won her heart.

"Well, I suppose, if she does care, it would be rather mean of me, on the whole," meditated Magda.

That ought to have settled the matter, but it did not. Magda went on reviewing pros and cons.

If she now decisively drew back, and took no further pains to make herself attractive to him, she might thus secure Bee's life-long joy. Ivor, no longer drawn ever so slightly in another direction, would probably turn to Bee. Why not? They were well suited, each to the other. And Bee had saved his life!

It was all conjecture; yet grave possibilities were involved. And whether the conjectures were right or wrong, Magda's duty stood forth clearly.

One more of life's opportunities lay before her. An opportunity for self-denial, for self-forgetfulness, on behalf of her friend. She had so wanted in the past to do something great, something grand, something worth doing. Here was her chance. Self-sacrifice is the grandest thing possible in the life of man or woman.

Nor was it of so severe a type as to be overwhelmingly difficult. She liked to be the prominent person, winning attention and admiration. She also liked Mr. Ivor, and her vanity was pleased. But that was all. Her heart was not affected. To draw back would mean no question of heavy loss, still less of heartbreak.

Miss Mordaunt had spoken of "rehearsals" given beforehand of greater opportunities to follow. What if this were one such "rehearsal"? What if the faithful carrying out of this might mean something greater to come after? So it often is in life.

The thing looked worth doing, apart from any question of rehearsals. Magda thought she would do it. For the sake of right, for the sake of honour, for the sake of her friend—she would hold herself in the background. She would no longer exert herself to be delightful. Mr. Ivor should find her dull and uninteresting. That would put things straight for Bee. She got into bed at last, seeing her own conduct in rosy hues, self put aside, love for Bee victorious, principle getting the upper hand over inclination.

But she forgot to look for Divine help in the carrying out of her good resolution. Some perfunctory prayers had been said earlier—only said with wandering attention. That was all. She had not asked to be made able to tread this path.

And when she awoke in the morning, things wore a different aspect. The road she had marked out for herself had lost its sunshine.

A quiet background is no inviting place for a lively girl, who has just discovered her power to please. And what if Mr. Ivor really were inclined to like her—more than others—more even than Bee? What if he really did wish to see more of her? This thought flashed up vividly. Was she to fling aside such a dazzling possibility, merely because she fancied that Bee was perhaps in love? Why, it would be quite absurd!

Besides—how could she be so rude as to neglect Mr. Ivor, when he came to their house? It would be her duty to make herself agreeable.

Not that Magda was usually bound by any obligations in this direction, when the guest happened to be not to her liking!

Swayed to and fro by such opposite considerations, she went down to breakfast; and the first test came soon.

"Would it be of any use to ask Beatrice Major here this evening?" Mrs. Royston inquired of Penrose.

"I don't know, mother. Mrs. Major has been poorly, but I should think she is better now. Magda will know."

Mrs. Royston looked at Magda, and the thin rope of her last night's resolution snapped under the strain.

"I shouldn't think it would be much use. Bee has been nowhere yet."

"You might find out. She knows Mr. Ivor, and I dare say she would like to come, as he goes to-morrow."

Would Bee not like it? Was her mother not well enough by this time? Magda was aware at least that she might be able. But with the thought came a further temptation, as Pen said—

"What has been the matter with Mrs. Major? Not influenza, I suppose? We don't want to get that in the house."

"Something of the sort, I dare say!" Magda replied carelessly.

"Mean! Mean!" cried conscience. She knew she had done it now! Mother and elder daughter exchanged glances, and the subject was dropped. No more chance of an invitation for Bee! And Magda did not want her to come. She did not wish to have Bee as a rival. But how contemptible it was! All her visions of a noble self-forgetfulness had faded into smoke. Everything had given way before her desire to shine. And she knew that she had not spoken the truth. She knew that Mrs. Major was subject to such recurring attacks, though unaware of their exact nature.

When evening came, things did not go as she had hoped. In their own home Pen, as eldest, was automatically more to the fore; and Magda, as the younger, had to submit to being second. Mr. Royston too engrossed a large share of their chief guest. One brief ten minutes' chat with him Magda had towards the close; only enough to make her want more; and then Mr. Royston again took possession, and her enjoyment was cut short.

So she gained little by her disregard of Bee's interests. She had been worsted in her fight, and had flung away another of life's opportunities; and all for nothing. She went to bed feeling indignant and very flat.

And next day the young barrister returned to his busy life in town, without having again met Bee.

That morning Merryl and Frip, as they walked down High Street, saw her coming out of a shop; and she stopped at once to speak to them. Frip was still a small child; but Merryl, since her illness, had shot up rapidly. She had grown much slighter; and her face, though perhaps not strictly pretty, was very attractive, with its look of sunny repose.

"I hope Mrs. Major is better," she said. "We were so sorry to hear about her."

"Thanks, dear; she is getting all right again. She had quite a long drive yesterday."

Frip's shrill little pipe made itself heard before Merryl could reply.

"Why!"—came in astonished accents. "Why, mother wanted to have you to dinner last night. And Magda said it wouldn't be any use, because you couldn't come. And she thought it was influenza."

Bee flushed.

"No, no—Magda only fancied it might be that. She wasn't sure," explained Merryl, always anxious to smooth things down. "She had not been to ask for a day or two, I think."

"No, she had not been. It was not influenza." Bee spoke in a mechanical voice, and her smile was rather forced.

"I suppose—some one must have told her," ventured Merryl.

"People always say that sort of thing, don't they?" Bee remarked. Then, a little hurriedly, she said good-bye, and went on.

"Frip, you shouldn't have told!"

"But I do wonder what made Magda say it. I should have thought she'd have wanted Bee to come. And I'm almost sure Bee is sorry. I'm almost sure she'd have liked to come."

Merryl was quite sure, but would not say so; and the matter dropped. It did not, however, end there. At luncheon some remark was made about Mrs. Major; and Frip, pricking up her ears, put in a word which Merryl, at the other end, had no power to check.

"Mummie, we saw Bee to-day."

"You shouldn't call her 'Bee,' Frip. You should say 'Miss Major,'" admonished Pen.

"But she told me I might call her 'Bee;' so I may, mayn't I? And Mrs. Major is almost quite well again; and it wasn't influenza, not one bit; and

Bee could have come yesterday, if you'd asked her, mummie. And I told her you wanted to, only Magda said it was no good. And she looked—I don't exactly know how—only as if she was sorry."

"You do meddle, Frip!" burst out Magda.

"Frip was not very wise to repeat things. But why should you have said what was not correct?"

"I thought it was—of course! How could I know?"

"It would have been kinder to Bee to find out."

That was all that passed; but Magda was much disturbed. It had never crossed her mind that what she did might come to Bee's knowledge.

CHAPTER XXIV
SOMEBODY'S LOOSE ENDS

FOR a fortnight past—ever since Ivor's departure—those "loose ends" had been very apparent. Magda had dropped into a state of hopeless inertia. There was energy enough in her constitution, when it was aroused by a sufficient stimulus; but, like many strong and energetic people, she could be unspeakably lazy. And that was her present condition.

Everything seemed dull and stupid, "stale, flat and unprofitable." Work went to the wall. All that she cared to do was to sit before the fire, reading or pretending to read novels, and going over in imagination those two delightful evenings, which had somehow demoralised her, making nothing else in life worth consideration.

She had fallen back into her usual standing of a "nobody;" and she could not see why it must be so. Other girls were made much of, admired, put forward. Why should it not be the same with herself? She had found that—given certain conditions—it was in her power to be taking. She wanted those conditions to recur. If only Mr. Ivor would pay another visit to the Vicarage, she might again enjoy that delightful sense of power. There was nobody now in the place for whom she cared or who cared for her.

So she made herself far from agreeable to her home-folks, for whom in reality she cared very much; only, a cyclone was needed to reveal the fact. She forgot what she had to do, and refused what she was asked, and replied snappishly, and resented being found fault with, and behaved altogether like a querulous child.

"What are you doing, Magda?"

Mrs. Royston, coming into the morning-room an hour after breakfast, found her second daughter lounging before the fire, with an open novel on her knee, and eyes fixed dreamily on nothing.

Magda slowly stood up. "I'm—reading."

"I think, at this time of the day, you might find something better worth reading than that," as she glanced at the title. "I want you to leave one or two notes for me."

"Isn't Merryl going out?"

"No; not at present. What is the matter? Are you poorly?"

"No, mother."

Mrs. Royston stood looking at her. "Have you practised the last few mornings?"

"I do—sometimes."

"And you look 'sometimes' at your French and German, I suppose. It is a great pity that you let yourself get into such idle habits."

"It's so stupid—practising for one's self alone."

"Why for yourself alone? Why not give other people pleasure. See how pleased your father was yesterday with Merryl's playing."

"He wouldn't have cared for mine. Father hates classical music, and I hate jigs. Merryl only strums. She hasn't a spark of music in her."

"At all events, she does her best; and you do not. You have a real gift for the piano, and you are neglecting it."

"Whatever Merryl does is right, and whatever I do is wrong."

Mrs. Royston sighed. "You always have an answer ready, Magda. I did think at one time—when we so nearly lost our darling Merryl—that you meant to be different. But you go on now just the same. I should like these notes taken, please, at once—and you can ask for the answers."

"Verbal?" Magda spoke in a hard tone, all the more because her mother's words had struck home.

"I don't mind; only, if you bring verbal replies, do bring them correctly."

Magda took up one of the notes. "All the way to Claughton!"

"You used to think nothing of bicycling there two or three times a week. Why should you mind it now?"

"Patricia was fond of me then."

"Patricia has a good deal to think about. I do not believe she has changed to you. Is anything really the matter? If you are not well, tell me frankly."

"I'm quite well, mother."

"Then please take the notes."

Mrs. Royston left the room, and Magda stood staring out of the window—stirred uncomfortably.

No doubt it was true that she had "gone on" lately, and especially in the last fortnight, "just the same" as before Merryl's illness. She had lost sight of her remorse and her resolutions, and had again been wrapped up in her own concerns, living an idle and purposeless existence.

"This must be no empty repentance," Rob had said. "When you get back into everyday life again, don't let yourself forget."

But she had allowed herself to forget. She had been beaten again and again, in the strife between right and wrong.

She echoed her mother's sigh, and took up the second note.

It was to Mrs. Major; and strong distaste seized her. She had seen very little of Bee lately. The two had met once or twice in public; but not in private. Magda had been careful to avoid the latter. She knew that she had not been true to her friend; and she knew that Bee must know it. Frip's words could not fail to be enlightening.

And now she was as likely as not to find Bee alone. And she had to go in—had to wait for an answer.

She threw her book impatiently on one side, and left the chair with its crumpled cushions before the fire. Which house to take first was the question. She decided on the nearer, because then she could plead a need for haste.

As she went up the garden, she caught sight of Bee's head within the front room, bending over some work. And when she rang the bell, Mrs. Major came out.

"How do you do? Have you come to see Bee?" Mrs. Major scanned the girl critically, having remarked the rarity of her calls.

"I've come to bring a note from mother. She said a verbal answer would do."

Mrs. Major glanced down the page. "Yes—your mother wants an address. Will you ask Bee to look it out in my address-book, please. I have an engagement and cannot wait."

So Magda had no choice. She made her way in, for once so noiselessly that she had time for observation, before Bee awoke to her presence. Something in Bee's bent head and quiet look impressed her—something of resolute patience in the sweet face, with its downcast eyes and dark brows. It made Magda feel uncomfortable—almost guilty. She stirred, and the other glanced up.

"Why, Magda! It is quite an age since you came last!"

Magda explained her object.

"Yes—I know where the address is. Sit down. I'll look it up."

"I mustn't wait. I've to go on to Claughton."

"Are you in such a hurry? You once said you could bicycle to the Manor in twenty minutes."

"Did I? Oh, I couldn't quite have meant that. It takes half-an-hour at least—and more! And I ought to get back in time to practice."

Bee went to the davenport, where she hunted out the address and wrote it down.

"Will that do—without a note?"

"Oh yes, thanks!"

Magda stood up, and Bee came close, studying her gravely.

"You used not to seem so impatient to be off!"

"I've got to take mother's note."

"Yes, I know—but it is quite early still." Bee sat down, and a light touch on Magda's wrist somehow made her do the same. "I don't think there can be such terrific haste, that you cannot spare a few minutes. I want to ask you what has been the matter lately?"

Somehow, Magda had not expected this; and she flushed up.

"The matter! Oh, why—nothing! Of course not! What do you mean? Why should anything be the matter?"

"You have not been quite the same lately. And I never like to let misunderstandings run on. There is some misunderstanding—isn't there?"

"No! Nothing of the sort!" Magda spoke vehemently. "I don't know what you mean."

Then she felt that this was not true.

"Don't you, really?"

"No, of course, I—What do you mean?"

"I have noticed a difference, and I want to know the reason. We are old friends now—and it seems such a pity to let anything come between us, when perhaps one word of explanation—"

Magda broke in. "But there's nothing to explain. There isn't, really. I—it's only—I've been—busy!"

"Busy about what?"

"Oh, I don't know. Heaps of things. Perhaps—more lazy than busy." She tried to laugh, but could not face the wistful eyes bent upon her. "Oh, bother—why must you be so inquisitorial?"

"Am I? Well—if you would rather not tell me—"

"I can't. I've nothing to tell."

"Are you sure? Things haven't seemed right. If you would rather drop the subject, I must let you. Only, if I have hurt you in any way, or if you have thought me unkind, I am sorry."

"Bee! It isn't—"

Magda choked over the words. She hardly knew what to say; for the contrast between herself and Bee was not pleasing to vanity.

"It isn't what?"

"It's not you! If either of us is wrong, it is I—not you!"

She remembered afterwards that Bee did not contradict the assertion.

"Anyhow, it need not put us apart."

"I suppose not, if—if you don't mind. But—only—" Magda spoke disjointedly, fidgeting with a cushion-tassel. "Only—you know—one does feel horrid sometimes; and Frip told me she had told you—and of course—though I really didn't mean to be unkind—"

"When didn't you?"

"You know. You heard what Frip said. And I suppose you would have liked to come—and I ought to have known. And I dare say I did know, really—only one can't always decide rightly, just in a moment. Well—if I'm to make a clean breast of it—I didn't want you that evening, Bee. There! It's out!"

"But why?"

"I liked talking to Mr. Ivor. He was so jolly and amusing. And on the whole I rather thought he liked talking with me. He is Rob's friend, you see. And he somehow sort of made me able to talk—you know! As some people can, and only a few. And I wanted it over again. And I knew I should have no chance if you, were there. He would only have cared to talk with you."

Magda was not looking up, as she jerked out her little confession. Had she been, she could not have failed to see the swift flash of response in Bee's face. It was quickly subdued, and Bee asked mildly—

"Why?"

"My dear, you're dull to-day. You don't seem to understand anything. Why, of course—because you are you! He would be after you fast enough, if you would let him. You can be stiff—most people can, I suppose. But everybody says how pretty you are, and how taking. It's not like Patricia's prettiness. Quite a different sort of thing. But I couldn't help noticing that afternoon, when Mr. Ivor came to call here—though he and I were talking a lot, his eyes kept going back and back to you, as if he couldn't help it; and twice he didn't hear what I was saying."

"I didn't see!"

"Well, anyhow, I did. I declare, Bee, you are looking oceans better than when I came in. You were so white."

"Just a little tired, perhaps. It does one good to have a chat. Don't worry yourself any more about—that—or keep away. Come in as often as you can."

Magda stood up. "All right; I will. But I really must go now, or I shall be late for lunch."

"Yes; I won't keep you. But I am glad you came, dear."

Her good-bye kiss in its tender warmth surprised and touched Magda: for she did not feel that she deserved it.

"I wonder what made me say that—about Mr. Ivor?" she debated, as she bicycled out of the town. "But it was true. I'd forgotten, till the moment when I said it, how he did look at her."

And Beatrice, left alone, stood in the room, with both hands pressed hard over her face.

"Oh, if it is! Oh, if it is!" she whispered once or twice.

Then she drew a long breath, and went back to her work quietly, but with a glad light in her eyes.

"What a child Magda is still!" she uttered aloud, with a little laugh. "I seem to be years and years the elder!"

CHAPTER XXV
MAGDA'S OLD CHUM

"SO you know the Roystons," remarked Edward Fairfax to his cousin, Mrs. Miles.

He had arrived the evening before, and had been occupied for an hour past with the newspaper, near an open window. It was a fine day, late in July.

There was nothing restless or impulsive about him. Though only six years Magda's senior, he might have been well over thirty, judging from his outlines, his immobility, and his scanty hair. He was neither small and slim like Rob, nor tall and muscular like Ivor; but of another stamp altogether. Medium in site, and solid in make, he had rugged features, yet a very pleasant face. As he sat thus, silent and motionless, a looker-on could hardly have imagined the possibility of Fairfax out of temper. He seemed to be made up of kindliness and good sense. A queer little twinkle in his light-grey eyes gave promise of the "saving sense of humour," which alone goes a long way; and he also had a well-shaped head. As he spoke, he glanced over the edge of his newspaper.

"We know them well. Especially the second girl."

"Magda?"

"That is the one. She says she knew you in old days."

"Yes. Odd little scarecrow of a being, when I first came across her. She'd got into a way of talking all over the shop about her troubles. I cured her of that—made her tell me instead. I used to chaff her fearfully, and she took it well."

"Perhaps she wouldn't have taken it well from everybody. What sort of troubles?"

"Oh, a rum lot! She was always in hot water, somehow. I never could make out who was to blame. So I just told her to keep a stiff upper lip, and not to worry. She had ripping hair—all down her back."

"She has lovely hair now—rather wild sometimes. And she isn't bad-looking. The advice given sounds extremely like Ned Fairfax."

"What else would you have had me say? I wonder if she remembers what chums we were."

"Why—of course. It was she who told me first, when she happened to see your likeness."

"Yes—but still, it was she who dropped me, not I who dropped her. I wrote last, and had no answer. So I stopped."

"You might have tried a second time, if you wanted to keep it up."

"I might—but I didn't."

"Some day soon you are sure to see her. She is rather fond of dropping in here. And you will pay us a long visit."

"Anyhow, I think I'll look up Magda—presently."

"My dear Ned, you have not seen her since she was a child. Wouldn't you rather call her 'Miss Royston'?"

"She is not 'Miss Royston.' And 'Miss Magda Royston' is such a mouthful."

"I should imagine that she would expect it."

Fairfax returned to his paper for another half-hour. Then he put it aside, and went out, aiming for Magda Royston's home.

It was quite true that he and she had been great chums, in the days when he was a big schoolboy from fourteen to seventeen, and she an excitable little girl from eight to eleven. He had made a pet of her, and she had made a hero of him. She had confided to him her every thought and trouble; and he in return, from laughing and pitying, had grown to be fond of the impetuous warm-hearted difficult child, whom nobody seemed to understand. He was rather curious to see what manner of being she had grown into.

Reaching the house, he decided against a formal entrance by means of the front door. It was not an hour for a stiff call; and as a boy, he had been free of the garden. He saw no reason why he should not revert to old habits.

So, following a path amid bushes which led round behind, he found himself close to the kitchen garden; and a few yards in advance of him, their backs turned in his direction, he saw two girls; one small and long-haired; the other rather tall and slight.

"Yes, dear," the latter was saying in a soft voice. "But I don't think it does to mind that sort of thing too much. It isn't worth while. Shall we go and feed the chickens?"

"She needn't be so cross, though—need she?"

"I don't think she means to be cross, darling. Perhaps she is worried about something. That often makes people seem a little cross, you know."

"I beg your pardon—" Ned interposed, with lifted cap; and they turned promptly.

"No—not Magda!" Ned instantly decided. That serene brow, those smiling eyes and happy lips, could hardly appertain to his quondam chum. Unless, indeed, the years had remade her! But this girl was surely younger; hardly more than sixteen, with smooth dark hair. Another sort altogether. Not pretty perhaps in the ordinary sense of the word—but something in the sunshine of that childlike face enchained attention.

"I beg your pardon—" Ned was saying aloud, while such thoughts flashed through his mind. "I fancied you might be Miss Magda Royston."

"Oh, no, I'm only her sister. I'm Merryl," came in frank reply. "Do you want to see Magda?"

"She and I are old friends. I am afraid I have taken rather a liberty in coming this way; but it all looked so familiar that I—well, I came. You don't know me, of course. You must have been one of the little ones in those days. I am Ned Fairfax."

Merryl's hand came out cordially.

"But of course I remember. I'm only two years younger than Magda—though we did seem so far apart then. Of course I remember. You were always so good to us little ones. Will you come indoors, and shall I call her? She has gone to the other end of the kitchen garden."

"Then perhaps I might find her there. I should like to discover if she will recognise me—unannounced."

"If you like—please do. But I am sure mother will wish to see you too."

"Hadn't I better choose a more orthodox hour for calling? One afternoon, perhaps. I've come to the Vicarage for ten days."

"Yes, we heard you were coming; and Magda was so pleased."

"Then she has not quite forgotten me. And this of course is little Frip!" Ned's hand grasped Francie's pleasantly. Children always took to him, and Frip proved no exception.

"Frip is our baby still," observed Merryl. "I sometimes think she always will be. We are going now to feed the chickens. You are sure you would rather find Magda yourself?"

Ned was not quite sure. He felt tempted to ask if he might not first interview the chickens; but this suggestion was resisted.

Merryl smiled a good-bye; and as the two went off, he overheard a shrill little voice saying—"I like that man! Don't you?" Followed by a—"Hush, darling."

"That's a nice girl," Ned murmured. He recalled the plump plain-faced little Merryl of former times, and marvelled over time's developments. Would Magda be equally transformed? And if so, in what direction? She had been better-looking than Merryl, despite her "scarecrow" outlines. Whether she would be so still remained to be seen.

Ned knew well the walk at the end of the kitchen garden. It had been there that Magda was wont, in past days, to take refuge from a troublesome world, when in one of her injured moods. He wondered whether she kept the habit up still. Then Merryl's words recurred to his mind; and he questioned—was it Magda who had been "cross"?

There she was—pacing hurriedly along the grass-path, just as in old times. Something had plainly gone wrong with her. She was walking away from where he stood; and he examined the restless movements, contrasting them mentally with the repose of the younger girl's look. Like many men, perhaps most men, Ned loved repose.

Now she was coming back, moving still with a quick impatient swing, as if working off indignation. Her eyes were bent on the ground and he had time to analyse her further, before she looked up. Improved in some ways, he told himself. Height and figure were good; and she held herself well; and the sunshine, catching her hair, lighted the red-gold into brilliancy. But the face at that moment was not a happy one.

Suddenly—as a result, perhaps, of his gaze—she glanced full at him. There was a momentary hesitation; and then a glow of pleasure.

"Ned!" she cried, and drew back. "Oh, I beg your pardon. I mean—Mr. Fairfax."

"Since when have I ceased to be 'Ned'?" he asked, as their hands met.

"Since we grew into strangers," she replied readily. "Ages ago! But I heard you were coming, and I wondered if we should come across one another."

"Was it likely that we should not?"

"How could I tell? Those are such far-off times. But it is nice to see you again. Have you seen mother yet?"

"I did not suppose she would be grateful for so early a call."

"But how did you get round here?"

"Usual mode of progression—on my two feet."

"Oh, how like you are to what you used to be! We always talked nonsense together."

"Did we? My impression is that we discussed endlessly your heart-breaking trials and dismal views of life."

"But then you always made them out to be nothing."

"And then you used to howl and be the better for it."

"Girls always are the better for it, I suppose. I don't howl now. And really I did not often then."

"Not more than three times a week, on an average."

"Oh, I didn't! That is too bad."

"It was a safety-valve. You would have gone off in steam, otherwise."

"But what are you doing now, N—Mr. Fairfax? I mean—what are you—if you don't mind my putting the question? I know nothing of your history."

"Yet we seem to meet very much on the old level."

"I always fancied we should. We were such real friends!"

"Though the friendship has been in complete abeyance!"

"Fizzled out into nothing," she rejoined. "Well, it wasn't my fault. I wrote last."

"I beg your pardon; I wrote last, and had no answer."

"N—Mr. Fairfax! You didn't."

"Miss Magda Royston—pardon me! I did."

"But I do assure you—"

"I sent you a lengthy and most interesting composition, full of sympathy for your bereft condition. And that was the end. I had no reply. So I came to the conclusion that you had found another Ned, and wanted no more of me."

"But indeed, indeed, I wrote last. I wrote sheets; and you never answered them. So I was dreadfully miserable, and I knew you were tired of me, and delighted to get away. And so—"

"So it meant a long gap. But old friends can always begin again, just where they left off."

"It's very nice," murmured Magda. Then she wondered what her mother and Pen would say if she kept N—Mr. Fairfax all to herself out here. "I think I ought to take you indoors," she remarked. "Wouldn't you like to see the others?"

"I'm glad to see everybody. You asked a question just now."

"Yes. I thought you didn't mean to answer it."

"Why should I not? My mother has made a home for me in town, and I have a post in a bank."

"I see—" with a note of disappointment.

"Not romantic, is it? A good many useful things in life are unromantic."

"But you like it?"

"One must do something, and that turned up. It seemed as good as anything else was likely to be."

They began to move towards the house. Magda had suggested this, but it was Fairfax who took the first step. Magda talked eagerly, bringing up one reminiscence after another, and he responded sufficiently to keep her going.

Perhaps his interest was a little less keen than hers; for when they came across Mrs. Royston and Merryl in the flower-garden, and Magda muttered an impatient—"Oh, bother!" Fairfax showed no reluctance. He even quickened his pace to meet them. Magda wanted to keep him longer to herself, for she had no notion of sharing her friend with others.

CHAPTER XXVI
WHERETO THINGS TENDED

"WHAT is all this about, mother?" Rob asked three weeks later. "I mean, of course,—the girls."

He had run down for a few days, spending the greater part of them with Patricia. Mrs. Royston thought him looking pale and worried, even unhappy. But he said nothing which could give a clue to the cause; and she was reluctant to force confidence by direct questions. Rob, whatever his own cares might be, was not too much wrapped up in them to note other people's concerns; and he very soon put the above query.

The condition of things which led to it was as follows.

Pen had an affair on hand, which had suddenly reached a forward stage, occupying the whole of her attention. A recent acquaintance, the Honourable James Wagstaff, a sensible and agreeable bachelor, well over sixty, with plenty of money, had taken a fancy to "neat Pen," and was assiduously pursuing her. Pen showed no reluctance or hesitation. It became clear that she was simply waiting for the word to be spoken.

There was nothing romantic or misty about this affair. It was straightforward and business-like.

Ned Fairfax had been much in and out of the house. Having come to his cousin's for a fortnight, he was there still. From the first he had dropped, easily and naturally, into his old position of intimacy with the Royston family. Much as Mrs. Royston liked him, she would have preferred a more cautious advance; but she found herself powerless. Fairfax took it for granted that he might do as he liked; and he made himself so charming to her personally, that she had not the heart to administer a check.

He was Magda's especial friend. All her world admitted the fact. She had the first right; and she took care to claim it. When Ned came to the house, he of course came to see her; and she was always on the spot, never doubting that he felt as she did.

It was delightful to have him again; to revert at once to the old order; to pour out unreservedly in his hearing her aims, her wishes, her difficulties, her worries—to be laughed at and genially set to rights by him. She enjoyed it heartily. Each day her mind was more and more full of Ned—of nothing but Ned. As usual, her steed ran away with her; and she could think of nought else. When Robert arrived, she did not so much as notice his pale and altered look. Her whole world now consisted of—Ned.

So different, she told herself, from the time when she had that silly little fancy for Mr. Ivor! She had never given him another thought since he went away; and he had not again been to the place. But Ned was her friend—her property—and everybody knew it. Everybody appeared to recognise her right.

Just exactly like former days!

Well, no; perhaps not exactly. As time went on, it dawned upon her that a distinction did exist. Some measure of reconstruction in the manner of their friendship was needful. Things had to be different from the days when he was a big boy and she a small girl. She could not now rush after Ned, whenever she wanted him. She must wait till he chose to come. He was a man—and she a woman—which altered the whole outlook.

He did very often come. But was it only or mainly after Magda? This was a question which soon took shape in the mind of Mrs. Royston. He always saw Magda, it was true, for she managed to be invariably to the fore; and the one desire of unselfish Merryl seemed to be that Magda should thoroughly enjoy her old friend. So surely as Fairfax appeared on the scene, Merryl effaced herself and left him to Magda. Mrs. Royston, watching with a mother's solicitude, had doubts whether Fairfax was duly grateful.

No doubt he had at first thought mainly of Magda. He had even recognised a dim notion in his own mind that, not impossibly, his one time little chum and playmate might suit him for a life-mate.

But on his arrival, the first strong impression made upon him was imprinted, not by Magda but by Merryl. And unfortunately for herself, Magda did not go to work in the right way to counteract this impression, as she would have wished. She was making herself cheap. A man often values more highly the thing that he cannot too easily obtain. There was about Merryl a touch of the elusive which fascinated him. In Magda, he found no trace of the elusive. He had begun to grow—though he hardly yet acknowledged the fact—rather tired of her outpourings. And he could not but note that Magda always talked about herself—a subject direfully apt to become boredom to the listener! Whereas Merryl never did.

True, he was very pleasant with his former chum. It was his way to be pleasant with people in general, and he was not given to administering snubs. He treated her with frank kindliness, and was always ready to respond to her sallies. That did not mean much, Mrs. Royston thought; and she was troubled to see Magda so entirely absorbed in this revival of a childish friendship—far more absorbed, she feared, with Fairfax, than Fairfax was with her.

Sometimes she all but resolved to give a word of warning. But Magda was apt to receive such words tempestuously; and also she had a wholesome dread of suggesting ideas and feelings that had not yet taken shape. Ned Fairfax would soon return to London, and then things would go back to their normal state; except that Magda would pass through one of her uncomfortable states of discontent.

While she so debated, Rob came home, and before two days were over, finding himself alone with his mother, he asked—

"What is all this about?"

"I think it is genuine with Pen and Mr. Wagstaff," she said.

"He's old enough to be her grandfather."

"There is a difference in age, but not so much as that, Rob. And after all, Pen has always taken to people older than herself. And she is so staid and controlled—don't you think it may be better for her than a very young husband?"

"Such a thing does exist as the happy medium! But if it is for her happiness—and if you and my father are satisfied—"

"Your father likes Mr. Wagstaff. And I do think that Pen is—not exactly in love, perhaps, but really attached to him."

"And what about Magda?"

"I don't know what to think. I am rather sorry that Mr. Fairfax has turned up. He is such a good pleasant fellow; but Magda's head is completely turned. And I cannot see that it is his fault. She takes it for granted that he is just the same now as when she was a child. And really—such a friendship—after all these years—"

"That is all nonsense, mother."

"Magda doesn't see it so. She seems never to have a doubt. And his is not the manner of a lover. He lets her talk, and he chaffs her, but I don't believe he is touched."

"Whether Magda is touched seems more to the point!"

"It is my fear. But what can one do? Speaking too soon might do harm. I don't want to put the idea into Magda's head that he is after her."

"You don't suppose the idea isn't in her head already!"

"I really cannot say, Rob. She is still so oddly childish in some respects— actually in many ways younger than Merryl, since Merryl's illness. Magda seems to think of nothing beyond their old friendship. She is continually recurring to it. Mr. Fairfax must grow rather sick of the subject. And— perhaps I am only fancying—but I do sometimes think he is a little taken with Merryl."

"That infant!"

"Yes, of course she is very young, but she is old for her age now. And he is very discreet. It may be nothing. Anyhow, he goes home in three or four days; so I hope all this will be over. And Magda in time may forget."

"I wish Magda had more balance," he said with a sigh.

Mrs. Royston longed to ask him—"Is all right between you and Patricia?" Her cautious reserve, and fear of saying the wrong thing, held her back.

Fairfax did not leave so soon as was expected. He again deferred his departure, not leaving until the day after Rob.

Late that last afternoon he appeared; and for once Magda was not on the watch. She had been called away; and he followed his favourite route to the back of the house, coming upon Merryl. She met him with a little flush and smile of greeting, and he thought once more, as often before, what a happy winsome face hers was.

"How do you do? Have you come to say good-bye to Magda? I'll call her."

"Not yet," he replied cheerfully. "There's plenty of time. I'll get through my good-bye to you first."

"But Magda won't like—she will want to know at once!" Merryl showed uneasiness.

"Plenty of time," repeated Ned. He was not going to lose this opportunity. "Did you tell me a day or two ago that you had a little greenhouse of your own? I wish you would show it to me. It's all right," as she glanced round. "Magda will come after us directly." The old use of Christian names had been reverted to.

Merryl was rather distressed, but Ned's manner being positive, she could not see her way to a refusal. So she led him to the quiet corner of the garden, where she had a little piece of ground and her tiny "bit of glass," sheltering pet plants. Ned, with his cool and disengaged air, wiled her inside, and led her into a discussion about the names, the natures, and the particular needs, of her said "pets," and he succeeded in so enchaining her attention, that she forgot all else, and thought no more of Magda. She had not the least notion how long a time had passed thus; and both she and Fairfax were thoroughly enjoying themselves, when—the little door was pushed indignantly open, and Magda came upon them. There was barely space for the three to stand inside at once.

It was a shock to both girls. A shock to Merryl, to find that she had been depriving Magda of her expected enjoyment. A shock to Magda, to find those two in happy and confidential talk, and to see how much Ned liked it. More than this she did not see, but it was enough. She flushed up hotly.

"Ned! You here!" she cried. And then in a tone of sharp rebuke. "Why didn't you tell me, Merryl? It's too bad!"

The sound of that angry voice, the sight of Merryl's grieved face, made together an impression on Fairfax which time would not efface.

"I'm so sorry; I did mean to call you," faltered Merryl.

"You must not blame your sister," Ned said gravely. "She only did what I asked her to do. I particularly wished to come and see the little glass-house."

"Merryl had no business—your last day—and when she knew—"

"I'm so sorry!" Merryl repeated, tears in her eyes. "I quite forgot! But I'm going now, dear. Good-bye, Mr. Fairfax!" And with one glance at him, she literally fled.

That scene showed Ned more than he had yet discovered about his quondam "chum."

Magda cooled down when she had him to herself; and he noted that she did not seem troubled about her own outburst of annoyance. He said nothing, and allowed her to run on as usual; but his mind was very much astray—wandering after Merryl. He registered a silent determination that, next time he came to the Vicarage, things would have to be different.

CHAPTER XXVII
WHAT PATRICIA WANTED

"REALLY, my dear, I don't see that it can be helped. If Robert says he cannot come on that particular day, I suppose he cannot. Men generally know their own business. You will have either to alter the day, or to do without him."

Mrs. Framley stood near the door, in the Manor hall, and she spoke in her deepest voice—a voice which Mrs. Miles privately declared had its origin in her shoes. She wore her magnificent furs; and she looked more than ever like a big brown bear on end. But she smiled good-humouredly as she spoke; while Patricia, on the other side of the solid oak table, seemed the reverse of good-humoured. A frown puckered her pretty brow; and the charming smile was conspicuously absent. When Patricia was "put out," she could be very much "out" indeed.

"You see, he is a busy man, not always with time at his own disposal; and he has to consider his Vicar. If I were you, I wouldn't mind. It can't be helped."

"I do mind, and it can be helped. If I want Rob, he ought to come. And I intend that he shall."

"I thought you said it was impossible."

"He says so. Ridiculous! Rob can always get his own way, if he chooses. People have told me so, again and again."

"Why don't you alter the day?"

"Because it's not convenient, and I don't choose. Rob has to make his plans fit in with mine. Some stupid parish tea! Anybody could see to it."

"When you are Rob's wife, you will find that a parish tea can't be put aside for the sake of a charade."

"When I am Rob's wife, if that ever comes to pass, he will find that a parish tea has to give way to me."

Mrs. Framley doubted the fact, but forebore to say so.

"I am sure he would do what you wish, if he could. But if he cannot—"

"It only shows that slums are more to him than I am."

Patricia walked across to the fireplace and threw a letter into the flames. She watched the disappearance of Rob's signature, as it slowly blackened and curled.

"Does she mean to toss him overboard?" questioned the elder lady.

"I would not be too sure," she remarked with soothing intent. "He naturally feels bound to his work, even at some cost to himself."

"He ought to consider the cost to me. But he never does. I have seen that, plainly—and I have my doubts—"

Mrs. Framley repeated the last word.

"Whether he really wishes things to be as they are! Once or twice before he has refused to do what I wished. And it can't go on. I shall make this a test-case."

"Patricia, if I were you, I wouldn't do what I should be sorry for afterwards."

Patricia made a movement as of one flinging aside unasked advice.

"I shall make this a test-case," she loftily repeated. "I have told Rob that I particularly want him to be here that evening, and to take a part in the charade. If he cares so little for my wishes that anything and everything is considered first—then our engagement may come to an end. I shall tell him so."

"I wouldn't, my dear! I really would not. You know you are fond of him—and you can't expect always to get your own way in life. You had much better give in quietly and not mind. It would be such a pity to upset things for nothing."

"The question is whether Rob is fond enough of me—to do what I wish. If not, the sooner we part the better. If he does not choose to give in, he may find somebody else to act as his humble slave. That's not my style!"

Mrs. Framley shook a protesting head. "You are not wise, Patricia. You may do the sort of thing once too often. This is your third engagement!"

"If it were my thirteenth, I would end it, rather than go on with what we should both be sorry for in the end."

"Well, I believe you will be sorry soon for what you think of doing. But of course it is no business of mine! You must decide for yourself. Ah—there it comes."

"It" referred to her carriage, for which she had been waiting. Two minutes more saw her gone; and Patricia sat down, to write the threatened note to Rob. She tossed it off in haste; not weighing her words; put it up, and stamped it. Then Magda was announced.

"How do you do?" she said coldly, presenting a cheek. "A note? Thanks."

"From mother. I think it is only to say that we shall like very much to come to your evening—and to help as much as we can."

Magda spoke in a rather dejected tone, and sat down with the air of one who was tired of everything. Since the departure of Ned Fairfax a month earlier, in the end of September, no word of him, good or bad or indifferent, had come to hand. She began to feel again as the little Magda of old had felt, when her long letter brought no response. Only she was now debarred from writing, since Ned had not asked it. She wondered much and often that he had not! Here again was shown the altered nature of their relations.

Patricia read the note slowly, then seemed to ponder over it. Magda exerted herself to break the silence.

"We're all looking forward to your evening. But it is such a pity that Rob can't come."

"Rob will come of course—if I ask it."

"I've had a letter from him this morning, and he says it is impossible. He would if he could."

"I'm writing to say that I shall expect him."

Magda wondered at the confident tone. She thought she knew Patricia pretty well by this time—but she also knew that Rob was not in the habit of lightly changing his plans.

"It would be nice if he could," she said, with unwonted caution, aware that Patricia was not in a mood to be contradicted. "And you are going to get up a charade."

Patricia laughed. "I call it a charade!" she said. "My uncle has a mortal horror of theatricals, and wouldn't for any consideration allow them in his house. He doesn't mind a mild little charade—so that's what it is supposed to be. Of course I intend to do things properly. Pen says she can't act—so I want you and Merryl."

"I should love it—but Merryl can't act!"

"She'll do for dumb show—it will be hardly more than that. Mind you don't use the word theatricals before my uncle and aunt."

"But won't they know when the day comes? And—do you think you—ought?"

"That's my business; not yours! Of course they will know when the day comes. They can't help it then; so it will not matter. They can say what they like afterwards."

Magda succumbed. "What sort of play is it to be?" she asked.

"Written by a friend of mine—on purpose for me. Something quite uncommon. A Queen of Beauty, living on an island, and being wooed by two Princes from other islands. Not many characters, and I shall take the part of the Queen, of course. I want you and Beatrice Major for my attendants. Your colouring and hers will look well together; and Merryl shall be the waiting-maid. She will only have to say a word or two at a time. My part is much the longest of any. Yours will be easily learnt. But I must have two men for the princes; and Rob is to be the successful one."

"Rob never cares for acting."

"He will have to care—if I wish it."

Magda was again astonished.

"His part is not difficult. I thought of Mr. Ivor for the second prince; but he says he has no time for getting it up. It wants some one with a turn for the comic. I've been rather wondering—how about that other cousin of Mrs. Miles who was here—Mr. Fairfax?"

Magda flashed into animation. "Oh, he would do it splendidly."

"I'm not so sure. He is plain; and he can look dull."

"Oh!" and Magda barely held in words of indignant contradiction. "I should think he would be the very one for you. He once did Father Christmas for a lot of children, and kept them in roars of laughter."

"When?"

"Years ago."

"That is a very different sort of thing."

"But he can be comic, I know, and that is what you want." She watched Patricia's undecided face eagerly. "I've known him ever so long. He and I were great chums, when I was little. And we are now—too. He is such a nice fellow—everybody likes him. Mrs. Miles says so."

"Really!" in an uninterested tone. "Well—it might be worth thinking about, if I can't get any one else. I'd rather have had somebody a trifle better-looking."

Magda again bottled up her wrath. Ned not good-looking indeed! But she knew that if she annoyed Patricia, all hope of his coming would vanish.

Patricia then entered at length into the momentous question of what she herself would wear in the different scenes. It became clear that the part which she had selected was the dominant one of the play; and that all others, except those of the two lovers, would be subordinate and unimportant. She took out the MS., and read passages aloud, explaining by the way what would be required of Magda and Bee, but chiefly occupied with the impression which she herself expected to make. Her dress was to be arranged without regard to cost.

"White and blue are what suit me best; and I mean to make my first appearance in white and silver—a sort of silver sheen, which will sparkle— and my hair down over my shoulders. I've been making a sketch of the style of dress—a kind of medieval flowing robe. Yes—here it is. What do you think? But nothing suits me quite so well as blue; so I shall keep that for the last. I'm not sure about the second act. Something by way of contrast might come in there. I have a notion of pale mauve velvet, with gold trimmings and a long train."

"It will cost a lot," remarked Magda dreamily, her mind still on Ned. Would he come? Would Patricia ask him? "I'm afraid I can't spend much on mine. I shouldn't think Bee could either."

"I've spoken to her, and she is all right. She will run up her own things in no time. And I mean to help with you and Merryl. In fact, I shall give you both your dresses. Yours won't need to be expensive. The general effect has to be pretty; but so long as your colouring harmonises with mine, that is all that matters. For the first scene I thought of some soft material like delaine— either blue or mauve—for you and Miss Major. Then, in the second part, something dark—and in the third, just white. You see, if your frocks are simple, they will throw out mine the more."

Patricia spoke with serene unconsciousness; and this was the note which controlled her talk all through. For herself—the best, the most costly, the most becoming and effective that could be designed! For the rest—anything!

And she did not see it! She had not the faintest idea how this looked in the eyes of another.

Magda's mind wandered, as Patricia flowed on—still about self, all about self, how self was to be adorned, how self was to be admired. A sudden revelation had come to her of the great lack in the character of this girl, whom once she had adored and counted perfect. And with the glimpse into Patricia Vincent came also a glimpse into—Magda Royston. Being with Patricia to-day meant an unexpected vision of herself, seen as in a mirror, whereby she learnt something new as to "the manner of girl" that she was.

Weeks earlier, in a certain talk with Bee, a little previous insight had been given. Then, by way of contrast. Now, through an exaggeration.

Yet, was it exaggeration? Were Patricia's complacent self-absorption, self-admiration, self-preoccupation, really so much greater than her own? Patricia was the prettier, the more fascinating, and her temptations therefore were increased. But Magda too had lived for self.

And how essentially unlovely such a life was!

Another thought broke upon Magda with sudden force. Had Ned seen her as she now saw Patricia?

All the month that he had been in and out of the house, all through those long delightful talks she had had with him, through which he had patiently listened,—had not the keynote been the same with her outpourings—always Herself? For the first time she saw it with clearness.

What must Ned think?

"Oh, how could I?" she mentally cried, in extreme disgust. "How could I do it? But I must stop! I must change! I can't let myself go on so. I didn't know before how it looked to other people—how poor and mean and horrid!" She might have added—"Or, how it looked in the sight of God!" At this moment the thought of Ned's opinion blotted out all else.

"What on earth are you mooning about?" Patricia enquired. "I've asked you a question three times and had no answer."

"I'm sorry. What was it?"

Patricia declined to repeat her question a fourth time; and Magda found that she had to move, or she would be late for luncheon. When she was gone, Patricia took up the note that she had written to Rob, and stood weighing it in her hand with an air of consideration.

"Shall I send it? Yes, I think so. Why not? Rob needs to be brought to his bearings."

She dropped it into the letter-box in the hall, then mounted the stairs, singing as she went, picturing herself as the Queen of Beauty, and wondering which of the three costumes would be the most entrancing.

Half-an-hour later a qualm assailed her. What if her words should fail to "bring Rob to his bearings"? What if he did not yield? Then—she had said to him—they had better part. Did she really wish this?

She ran downstairs again, with a half intention to take her letter back, and at least to have a few hours for consideration.

But the letters were gone, and from the window she saw the postman trudging far down the drive. Should she race and overtake him? She could just do it.

Pride held her back, and she stood debating till it was too late. No chance now! "Oh well, it must go," she said recklessly.

It went, and later in the day she would have given much to recall it. She began to realise what Rob really was to her, how much more than either of her two former fiancés, whom she had discarded as easily as one discards old gloves. What if he should take her at her word? She grew cold at the thought. Then she tried to forget him in renewed attention to the charade costumes.

CHAPTER XXVIII
WOULD SHE GIVE IN?

TWO nights passed, and the early post brought no letter from Robert. Patricia might have heard, possibly, the evening before. She had felt secure of a reply, at latest, this morning, giving in to her demand. When Rob knew all that hung on his decision—and she had put it plainly—he could not hesitate.

Since no word arrived, she began to realise that it meant his coming down to speak. So much the better! She believed in personal power. To travel from London, and to return in the same day, meant a rush; but it could be done.

She knew at what hour to expect him, if he followed this plan; and as it drew near she was rather surprised at various heart-flutterings and nervous dreads. What if he should walk in, merely to announce that he had no intention of yielding.

But the idea was absurd. Rob had more sense!

She put on one of her prettiest frocks, arranged her hair with extra attention, and then busied herself with preparations for the charade—still keeping watch on the clock.

The time when she expected him went by, and he did not come. She was alone in her boudoir, waiting; and the minutes lagged. Even allowing for a tardy train, he ought to have appeared before now. With a sinking of heart she gave him up and determined to go back to her arrangements. A letter would doubtless arrive later.

As she moved towards the door it opened, and he stood before her— calm, stern, collected. Not the Rob whom she had known hitherto. She moved forward in welcome, but his manner checked her, and he offered no kiss.

"I have come to see you," he said. "That is better than writing. I must know what you mean."

"I meant of course what I said." Pride again had the upper hand as she stood facing him.

He had closed the door as he entered, and he too kept on his feet, looking pale but resolute.

"You said—or implied—that the continuance of our engagement must depend on my coming to that particular party."

"Yes. I meant that. I have told you how much I want you here—and it ought to be enough! If I ask it, you ought to come."

"For my own pleasure I should not hesitate, of course. There are other things to be considered. It is a question of duty, not pleasure; and I have told you already that I cannot be away from my post on that particular evening."

"Some stupid parish tea, I suppose."

"Yes, it is our parish tea; and I told the Vicar weeks ago that nothing should induce me to fail him."

"I think my wishes ought to rank first with you. If you love me—as you have said you do!"

She sat down, but Rob remained standing.

"Even for you, Patricia, I cannot put amusement before duty."

"But if your duty is to please me?" She lifted her eyes to his with their sweetest look.

"I cannot be away—even to please you—that evening."

"If you asked your Vicar, he would understand."

"It could make no difference. I have no doubt whatever as to what I ought to do."

She held up her head. "You can put slum-work before me! It shows how little you really care!"

"Is it not rather that you and I look upon life with different eyes? My first duty is to my Master—to the life-work to which I am vowed. Nothing may hinder that. Cannot you see things, or try to see them, from my standpoint?"

"Really, I don't see why I should try to do anything of the kind," she retorted, losing temper. "It ought to be your business to see things from my standpoint."

"Hardly—when yours is a question of pleasure, and mine is a question of duty. If I were a soldier in the king's army, could I let our enjoyment come before duty? It would be impossible. Neither can I here."

"Evidently you are much too good for me!" She spoke in a mocking tone.

"It is necessary that we should face the question." He said this with extreme quietness. "Better that you should see how things are now than later—too late! If you and I are to be one, we must be one in very truth. We cannot pull opposite ways."

"If you mean that I am always to be put second to every slum-child or dirty old woman who happens to want you—then—I agree! We had better part. That of course is what you mean."

"I mean only that you must see clearly what lies before you. At one time I had no fears. I believed that you thought as I thought—felt as I felt. I believed that my Master was your Master—that my aim in life was your aim in life. But lately I have doubted. You must remember that when I have a living, it will be the same. Year after year the same. Work before pleasure— work, for which you do not care—in which you have no interest. If that is indeed so—"

"If that is so, we had better have done with one another," she said impatiently. "Anyhow, I don't choose to be second. I suppose you made up your mind to this some time ago, and only waited for a good chance."

"I think you know that you are wronging me. Do you imagine that I find it easy now to make this stand? But there are some things that a man cannot do—and this is one. I cannot put aside a plain duty merely to come here on a particular evening, because you have set your mind upon it."

"I see! Oh yes, I see! My setting my mind on a thing isn't worth a moment's consideration. All that signifies is your work. We are happier apart!"

She stood up, flushed and excited. "Remember—it is your doing!" she added.

"Had it not better be yours?"

"Well—we both agree. Is that it? We feel that we don't suit, and can't get on together."

"If you make my coming that evening a sine quâ non!"

"I do make it!" she responded passionately. "I told my aunt it should be a test-case. And you fail to meet the test."

Rob's eyes met hers; quiet eyes, full of patience, full also of pain. She found it difficult to meet them, but anger helped her through.

"I don't believe you love me. If you did, you could not say 'no' to such a little, little request! It is absurd. You could come if you chose; and you do not choose. Once more I give you the chance! Once more, Rob!" She held out her pretty hands, and lifted her lovely eyes to his. "If you love me—if you care—give in this once. Just this once! I won't ask it again. I'll be good in the future. Only this once!"

The tone was almost entreating, but he said gently—"I am very sorry. It is impossible. I am pledged to the other."

"Very well! You've taken your choice. It's all over!"

She dropped her hands and stood facing him, a scornful smile on her lips—lovely still, in spite of the scorn. Rob remained motionless, drinking in her beauty. And well he might; for, though neither he nor she could guess what lay ahead, he would never again set eyes upon that rare and perfect colouring.

"Well—good-bye!" she said coldly.

She brushed past him, moving with unusual haste, and left him alone. Going upstairs she set to work, precisely as if nothing had happened, upon the dress arrangements for her acting.

Rob made his way out of the house. He knew that this had to be. He had feared for months that it might end thus. Patricia, if she were indeed what she had seemed of late, would act in his life as a deadweight, hindering the work to which he was vowed, dragging him constantly earthward. He had feared; yet he had waited and hoped. Now matters had come to a climax, and Patricia herself had settled the question.

Whether he was more grieved, or in a certain sense more relieved, he could not yet have told. Her beauty had an extraordinary power over him; so that, when with her, he found it desperately hard to offer opposition, not to let her have her own way. Yet the last few months had brought to him deep disappointment. Not even a lover's devotion could permanently blind him to the truth that, within that exquisite casket, little was to be found beyond mental emptiness. Or, if Mind were there—and at times he felt sure it was—it had never been exercised, had never been called forth. He found in her no companionship, no understanding, no sympathy, no true intercourse.

Rob had long fought against the knowledge, had viewed her with indulgence, had made all possible excuses. He loved her still, and the thought that she was no longer his made the whole world look blank, and robbed life of its joy. Still, far below the chill desolation which had him in its grip, there was also a dim sense of regained freedom. In years to come, he might well be thankful to have had things thus decided for him.

He did not go home, but caught the next train, and from London wrote a line to his mother, simply stating that "all was over" between himself and Patricia.

A cheerful note from Patricia to Pen endorsed this. "We don't feel that we are suited, so it is by mutual consent," she said. Then she expressed an urgent hope that it might make no difference as to her "little charade." She would still want the help of Magda and Merryl.

"How like Patricia!" somebody remarked, as Pen handed over the note indifferently.

Pen had that day become engaged, and she had small interest to spare for other people's concerns.

Somebody else suggested—"So now Magda will be able, after all, to keep house for Rob by-and-by!"

That set Magda thinking. She wondered that she had not at once remembered the possibility; and she wondered still more that the idea did not wear its old radiant colouring. It certainly did not.

Patricia, with undaunted courage, set to work to re-organise her plans. Ivor, after a good deal of persuading, at length consented to take that part in the charade which Rob had refused. Bee Major, thenceforward, looked as if her world lay under a June sky. And Ned Fairfax undertook the comic character; with a proviso that he could not come down till a day or two before the evening. He would learn his part in readiness; learning by heart was no trouble to him; and no doubt a single rehearsal would be sufficient. Patricia was piqued at what she called "his cool assurance;" but since she could find nobody else, she agreed.

One letter Magda sent to Ned on the subject, doing it avowedly to save Patricia trouble. She put much of herself into the sheet, writing and rewriting more times than she would have cared to avow. No direct answer was called for, though she felt sure that one would come. But Ned wrote instead to Patricia, and merely sent "thanks" to Magda. Her spirits went down to zero, and she became a burden in her home.

CHAPTER XXIX
SO AWFULLY SUDDEN!

FEW would have supposed, on the eve of Patricia's evening, that she suffered under her broken engagement. To all appearance, both then and during the weeks before, she was sublimely indifferent, fully occupied with plans and arrangements for her forthcoming "charade."

No, not quite "to all appearance." Those about her, Mr. and Mrs. Framley and the servants, knew that she was not her usual self. Excited, impatient, hasty, ready to take offence, difficult to please, hard to get on with—they had found her all this. But outsiders saw little of it.

Magda, annoyed for Rob, who she felt sure had suffered ill-treatment at Patricia's hands, would gladly in the first instance have drawn back from taking an active part; and Mrs. Royston shared the feeling. But since Patricia had made it a matter of personal request that all should go on, unaltered; and since she had been at some expense in getting dresses for Magda and Merryl, it was hardly possible for them to give the whole thing up against her will.

Both Ivor and Fairfax were induced to run down to the Manor for a night, some little time before the important day. Then of course Ivor met Bee, and Ned met Magda; but Patricia claimed everybody's time and attention. Bee was her usual gentle controlled self; and she and Ivor came together as mere acquaintances; yet each understood the other rather better after those few hours.

As for Ned, he was pleasant and friendly with Magda, her old chum still; but she somehow felt that she no longer had a monopoly of him. There was a slight indefinable difference; whether due to their altered relations as man and woman, or whether to the fact that he did not look upon her as he had once done—she was unable to determine. The perplexity weighed.

This little visit was soon over, and everything promised to go well. On the last evening a final rehearsal would take place; almost equal to the "real thing." Mr. Framley had a distant engagement, which ensured his absence, much to Patricia's relief. Mrs. Framley had begun to remonstrate, as she found how far from a simple charade the affair promised to be.

But Patricia by this time had the bit between her teeth. "It had to go on," she said composedly. "If uncle didn't like it—well, then it wouldn't happen again. Too late now to make any difference."

Ivor and Fairfax were again to sleep at the Manor. Dinner was over and all had arrived. Mrs. Royston had excused herself; and so had Pen, busy with her elderly fiancé. The men, in no haste to don their costumes, had gone to the drawing-room away from the large library, where, on a raised dais at the upper end, the acting would take place. Curtains, dividing the dais from the rest of the room, were now drawn back, and a door behind the dais led into a smaller room, which had no other outlet and was lined with book-shelves.

Magda, Merryl, and Bee were present; also three or four other girls with unimportant parts to play. Magda was alone, half-way down the library, in the broad gangway left between rows of chairs which had been placed for spectators. Two or three of the girls had grouped themselves on one side, some distance behind Magda, as she faced the dais. Bee and Merryl, still farther away, were talking together.

A spare woollen curtain had been flung down, just behind where Magda stood, ready for possible use.

She was gazing towards the figure of Patricia, visible within the smaller room; but her mind had wandered elsewhere. Would she see anything of Ned on the morrow, before he returned to town? Did he wish to see more of her?

Patricia, in white and silver, with long fair hair hanging loose, stood before a full length pier-glass in the inner room, looking flushed and excited and very lovely, while the maid vainly tried to arrange the silver-tissue veil to her liking.

"It won't do. It hangs all wrong. How stupid you are, Frost! It will not do at all."

"If I was to loop it up this side a little, Miss—"

"That is better. But you must have made the veil wrong. It hangs quite crookedly. Yes—so. You want safety-pins."

"I'll get some, Miss. I haven't got any more here."

"Why didn't you bring plenty? You knew they would be wanted."

The maid went away, not answering. As she disappeared through the door at the lower end of the long library, Magda stepped dreamily backwards, and stumbled over the curtain, just escaping a fall. Nobody else was near Patricia.

Then it was that Magda's "great opportunity" came; an opportunity for heroic self-forgetfulness, such as she might never have again.

Patricia, still before the glass, was studying herself, turning this way and that with hasty petulant movements. At the instant when Magda stumbled, a quick movement brought the hanging veil into contact with a lighted candle on the table, dragging the candlestick over. It fell—the candle still alight—upon Patricia's flowing train, which at once caught fire.

Though vaguely conscious of having made something fall, Patricia did not know what had happened. But the flame rushed up her robe and enveloped her. One instant she was twisting into a new attitude, muttering vexedly about people's "stupidity." The next instant, dress and veil and hair all blazed, and a burning tongue licked her delicate skin, bringing anguish and terror. With a frantic shriek, she sped into the library, aiming straight for Magda—across the dais, down the two steps.

Now was Magda's opportunity! She had longed for such a chance, and here it was. She stood nearer to Patricia than any other, and the heavy woollen curtain lay in readiness at her very feet.

But the thing came with such awful suddenness! There was no warning. The whole world seemed serene; everything going on quietly, just as usual. And then, all at once, that fearful piercing scream, and the living column of fire and smoke, with white arms flung high in wild appeal, bearing down upon her!

She was taken utterly by surprise—terrified—bewildered—startled out of her self-control. And her own dress was so flimsy as to mean added danger. Not that she thought of this, for she thought of nothing. There was no time to think! She only followed the first blind impulse, which urged personal safety.

Afterwards, she never could imagine how it was that she had not instantly snatched up the curtain, and thrown it round the fire-clad figure. There it lay, within touch; yet she did nothing. Terror overmastered her; and with an echoing cry of alarm, she turned and ran towards the farther end of the long library, as Patricia in agony came after her.

Such a simple obvious thing it would have been to do—though meaning no doubt danger to herself. Ah—but not so easy! The prevailing impulse at such a moment is determined by dominant habits of mind and thought. And Magda had not trained herself to act instinctively for others, to put self aside.

She had been beaten on countless small occasions before; therefore she was naturally beaten here again. She had not been faithful in those things which were least; and how could she now be faithful in this which was much?

So, without thought or pause, she fled, not turning till she had reached the door.

Then, with dazed senses, she became aware that Bee had rushed forward—had caught up the curtain—had flung it over and around the frenzied Patricia—had dragged her with desperate energy to the ground; that Bee now was kneeling over the prostrate form, pressing down the charred clothes, putting out the flames, and pleading for "Water! water!" While Patricia's screams had died into moans. Not Magda but Merryl—white as ashes and shaking like an aspen-leaf—flew to the inner room for a large jug, and poured its contents over the two, just in time to quench Bee's frock, which had become alight.

It all happened in a flash. Others were hurrying to the spot, and crowding around. Magda, already ashamed and conscience-smitten, was among them, asking—"Can't I help? What can I do?" But nobody listened, and the time had gone by. She could do nothing—now. It was too late!

Ivor, first to arrive, lifted Bee away in a half-fainting condition, and carried her from the room to an open window in the hall.

Fairfax somehow at once took the lead, and bent over that moaning form on the floor, warding off well-meant attempts to touch and raise her, and asking urgently for oil, which he knew might be safely applied, pending the doctor's arrival. In the general confusion he found it not easy to make his want understood; but Merryl caught the word, seized the elderly housekeeper, and dragged her off, to hunt out a bottle of salad-oil, with which she herself sped back to the scene of disaster.

Ned's eyes went to her face, as he received it from those little icy fingers; and a quarter of an hour later, when the doctor's coming set him free, his first move was in search of Merryl.

Magda, thinking that he would now surely speak to her, began—"Oh, can't I do something?" But he was gone before the words were uttered; and Magda wandered forlornly into the hall.

There she came upon two others who did not need her. Bee, rallying slowly from the faintness which had blotted out everything, found herself lying on the broad window seat, supported by somebody. At first she did not even wonder who it might be, but only whispered—

"Is Patricia badly burnt?"

"I hope not. You have done your very best to save her—you splendid girl!" A stirred and familiar voice replied; and then she woke to the fact that it was Ivor himself, and that her head was resting against his shoulder.

"My darling!" he breathed, unable to restrain himself.

For in that terrible moment, when he saw Bee on the ground, in a heap with the smoking figure which, but a few seconds earlier, had been a dazzling Queen of Beauty, and when he believed that she too might have been fatally injured—then in a flash he knew with no shadow of doubt all that he truly felt for Bee. And, strangely, in the same moment, questionings as to what Bee felt for him died out of existence.

"Oh!" she said, with a note of bewilderment and joy. "I didn't—think—"

And again he murmured—"My own brave, brave darling!"

Magda came near enough to hear this. It made no difference to them. They were entirely taken up, each with the other. Bee almost forgot the smart of her poor scorched hands, in the supreme gladness of learning that Ivor loved her.

CHAPTER XXX
IF ONLY SHE HAD—!

THROUGH the next two or three weeks Patricia's life hung on a thread. Bee's promptitude had indeed saved her from death; but shoulders and back, arms, and hands, were badly scorched, and all her pretty hair was gone. As she rushed from one room to the other the flames were driven back; yet her face had felt their touch, though to what extent the doctors did not say. For the greater part her burns were not deep, but the extent of surface affected made them serious; and she was suffering from shock to a degree which meant pressing danger.

As this peril lessened, another set in, with a threatening of septic pneumonia, barely warded off. Intense pain, restlessness, delirium, days of blindness from the swelled face, weeks of prostration in a darkened room—all these were her portion. Night and day nurses were in constant attendance.

Wide interest was felt in the poor girl's condition; and the news at length given forth, that she might be counted out of danger, was hailed with relief on all sides.

It oozed out slowly that the fair face, so much admired, had suffered more than was at first expected; and that she would in all probability never regain her old loveliness. This fear was still carefully guarded from Patricia herself, though she had begun to suspect, and to put many disquieting questions.

"She has cared so much for her beauty," murmured Bee. "If that goes, she will have nothing left. Mother, it is sad."

"I suppose it sounds rather hard to say—just now—that if she went through life caring for nothing but her own looks, that would be sadder still," Mrs. Major remarked.

Bee felt that it did sound rather hard—just then!—however true. She could only think tenderly of Patricia's feelings when she should learn her loss.

Everybody was talking about Bee's heroism, though Bee herself made nothing of it.

"Why, how could I do anything else?" she asked, when admiration was openly expressed. "Of course I had to try. And the curtain being close at hand made things so easy."

It had lain closer still to Magda! But about that nothing was said, at least in her hearing. Few quite realised what her position had been. Few perhaps knew that she had actually run away; and some who did seemed to think it quite natural. But Bee had suddenly developed into a heroine, going about with bandaged hands, unable to endure a touch or to do anything for herself, yet radiant in her new happiness.

Merryl too came in for praise, only second in degree to that which was showered upon Bee. For it was she who had kept her wits, and had rushed to the help of Bee. But for the jug of water, promptly procured and used, Bee might have suffered much more severely. Mr. Royston was exceedingly proud of his "little girl," as he still called her, and he could talk for days of nothing else.

And Magda, looking on at all this, felt bitterly regretful and very unhappy.

For, whatever other people might think, she saw—she knew—she realised. She had had her longed-for chance in life, and had failed to use it. She was humbled in her own eyes.

And it was useless to talk, to express regrets. The crucial moment had gone by. Such an opportunity might never recur. If it should—how different might be her conduct! But such chances seldom come a second time. Other tests, other opportunities, would no doubt arrive in due course; yet they would not be the same in kind.

In that moment of horror, she might have done just what Bee did do. She might now be the heroine of the hour; admired and talked about—a centre of notice.

Yet this is hardly fair to Magda. It was not only for the sake of lost praise that she so blamed herself, and so vehemently wished to have acted in other wise. Praise once had been her foremost aim; but of late she had made advance. She did now truly wish to live a noble life for the sake of living it; not merely that she might win good opinions. She began to see—a little—what it meant to do right for the sake of pleasing God!

And, looking back, she knew that she had not even tried to do this; she knew that her life had been the reverse of noble. Everything had gone wrong. Plans had failed. Resolutions had come to nought. Nothing that she took up had ended well. She was of no use to any one.

Was it that she had begun at the wrong end?—That she had not first yielded herself in heart and spirit to her Divine Master? That she had attempted things in her own strength alone?

As days went by, a longing took possession of her to pour out what she felt to somebody. But who would care? Fairfax was out of reach, having left within twenty-four hours after the accident, during which she had seen nothing of him. Rob was corresponding with his mother; not with her. Magda had refused sympathy in his happiness; and naturally now he did not turn to her in trouble. She could not go to Bee. Bee was so glad, so joyous! Bee had done just what Magda had failed to do. To seek help from her at that moment seemed out of the question. Not that Bee would be conceited or boastful!—But still, she could not!

There was the Vicar! Many times Magda thought of him, and almost went; but somehow she held back—perhaps mainly from pride. Perhaps unconsciously what she craved was not really advice, but soothing. So, unwisely, she put off that step.

It was no doubt well that she had no "soothing" friend at this juncture, to whom she could pour out freely. Much talk is apt to weaken conviction. She might have found satisfaction in enlarging on her own remorse, and comfort in making excuses for herself. Having no such vent, she viewed her own conduct more severely; and, from the lack of such comfort, she was driven to find help in prayer.

Thus weeks passed by, and Pen's wedding-day arrived. After which Pen was gone, and Magda found herself in the new position of eldest daughter in the house.

It entailed upon her a variety of new duties, new claims, new responsibilities. She had never guessed beforehand how very much she and everybody would miss careful quiet Pen in the little arrangements of common life. Everything at first seemed awry without her; everything out of joint. And Magda really did set herself, honestly, to learn and remember the hundred and one little things, which somehow had always seemed to do themselves, and which now she was expected as a matter of course to undertake.

It was not easy. The habits of years are not to be conquered in a day. But for Merryl, her faithful remembrancer, she would have failed much oftener than she did; and she forgot or let slip her new duties quite often enough. She could not but note that Mrs. Royston, perhaps half unconsciously, turned far more to Merryl than to herself, in the blank left by Pen; and this again spoke sharply to Magda, spurring her to renewed efforts.

Till late in February no one saw anything of Patricia. Even when the doctors gave leave, she steadily refused to admit any of her friends. Bee and Magda were often at the door, making inquiries, only to be denied admittance.

And each time that Magda went, she came away with a sense of relief; for she dreaded the first meeting. Words of sympathy never flowed from her with ease; and she could not feel at home in a sick-room.

So when a little pencil-note at length arrived, asking her to go that afternoon, her first exclamation was of dismay.

"What is it?" Merryl asked.

"Patricia wants to see me."

"Oh, I'm glad! It is so bad for her, being shut up as she is."

"I'm not glad. I don't know what in the world to say to her."

"Magda—how funny you are! I should have thought—so fond of her as you used to be—!"

"I'm fond of her now in a way. But don't you understand—if she is as much altered as people say—how is one to take it?"

"I can't see any difficulty."

"I dare say it would be easy enough for you. It isn't for me. And Patricia would hate to be pitied."

"But you needn't pity her—exactly. I wish she would let me go."

"I'm sure I wish you could—instead of me."

At the hour named, Magda reached the Manor, and was shown into the breakfast-room where, as she remembered, she had been taken on a certain day when wild to see her then idol. Patricia had put her off, lightly and indifferently, to her dire distress. That day seemed very long ago; and Patricia was her idol no longer. Enthusiasm, lacking food, had died a natural death.

A maid came to take her upstairs, and she went, feeling each moment more awkward and embarrassed, more uncertain how to comport herself. She had not yet acquired the gracious gift of self-forgetfulness.

Outside the door she was met by a pleasant-faced woman in nursing dress, who said in a low tone—

"Please do not let Miss Vincent excite herself. She wants cheering up."

They went in together; and at first, in the contrast of lowered blinds and semi-darkness, after brilliant sunshine, Magda could see nothing. Guided by the nurse, she stumbled towards a dim figure in an armchair, wondering whether to offer a kiss. A hand held out settled the question.

"Sit down, please," Patricia said. "Nurse, you can leave us for a talk."

"Not more than half-an-hour, I think."

"Magda will have had enough of me by that time."

Nurse went away; and Magda growing more used to the light, ventured on a glance—only to snatch her eyes away too hastily.

What she saw in one hurried glimpse was a thin pale face, with a patchy complexion, scarred on the brow, with weak eyes, and the skin on one side of the mouth slightly drawn. A light lace shawl over Patricia's head hid the absence of hair—though it had begun to grow again, like a baby's.

That—Patricia! That—the lovely Queen of Beauty!

CHAPTER XXXI
LOST LOOKS

"YOU don't seem to have much to say," Patricia languidly remarked, as Magda sat in a dazed silence.

"It was—so kind of you to send for me," murmured Magda.

"I didn't want to do it. I don't care to see any one—till I'm all right again. But they said I must have somebody—so I thought of you."

"Yes, of course—I—you were quite right."

"Bee Major has offered to come, again and again. But I can't have her yet. I'd rather not. Magda—I want you to tell me something—quite honestly. Tell me the truth. Am I much altered? Nurse won't let me have a glass. She says I am to wait—but I have waited so long. I did get a glimpse one day—some time ago. But my eyes were so weak, and the room was so dark, I could hardly see anything. Of course, I know there's a scar—and that must take some time to wear away. The doctors keep telling me to be patient. Patient! After nearly three months! It is like three years!"

"I dare say it does seem long."

"You don't understand, of course. You have never had anything of the kind to bear. It wasn't so bad at first when I was very ill. I could think of nothing then but the pain; and, in a sort of way, time didn't drag so awfully. But now I am better, I do long to be all right again—and just as I used to be."

Magda muttered something vaguely, playing with the handle of her sunshade. Would Patricia ever again be "just as she used to be"?

"You've not answered my question. How does my face look—seeing it for the first time? Tell me plainly—I want to know the truth. Is it much altered?"

"Of course you look different. Anybody would—after a long illness."

"That is not what I mean. I want to know if I shall be pretty again, as I was. Nobody will tell me. I am treated like a child. And I don't choose to be treated so." She spoke fretfully. "I want to know how I look—now."

Magda was very much at a loss. "It must take time, I suppose," she observed hesitatingly. "If I were you, I would try not to think about that. I would make up my mind to wait."

"I dare say! It's so easy to be patient for somebody else! If you had to bear it yourself, you wouldn't be so sensible. I'm sick of hearing that sort of thing. Everybody talks so—aunt and nurse and doctors, all round. Over and over again the same. My face feels horrid still—like a mask. Magda, do you know that it was Bee who saved my life? You just ran away and did nothing! It was awful!—to feel myself so horribly alone! I suppose it was only for one moment; but it seemed like ages."

"I wish I hadn't! I would give anything to have done what Bee did!" Magda spoke from the depth of her heart, and Patricia heard listlessly.

"Of course you were frightened. I dare say I should have done the same in your place. But if Bee had run too, they say I must have died. I should have been out in the hall in one second more, in the full draught—and then nothing could have saved me. I suppose I ought to have thrown myself down; but how can one remember anything at such a time? Bee was quick! Sometimes I wonder—whether—I wouldn't rather have died!" Patricia burst into tears.

"Don't cry, please," begged Magda, dismayed. "You don't really mean that, you know."

"Perhaps not, in one way. But in another way—if I'm never to be what I was—if nobody is ever to love me again—"

"People don't love one another because of their looks."

Patricia drew the little lace handkerchief petulantly from her eyes.

"Oh, don't they? I know better."

"Wouldn't it be wiser not to keep thinking about that sort of thing—just to wait till you are well again?"

"I dare say! I've nothing else to think about. If money would do it—would make me what I was—I would spend every penny I have!"

Magda thought she would try a change of topic. "Have you heard of Bee's engagement?"

"Everybody has heard it, I suppose. When are they to be married?"

"Not till next August. Mrs. Major says she can't spare Bee sooner. I'm to be one of the bridesmaids."

"And of course your brother will be best man."

Magda had not expected Patricia to speak of Rob.

"I dare say he will, if he isn't too busy."

"He always says he is too busy for anything." A pause, and then—"I sometimes wonder—if we had not broken off before all this—"

"You wonder what?" Magda's curiosity was aroused.

"How he would have managed. He would not have wanted me any longer."

"Patricia!" indignantly. "Rob would never never have changed—and for such a reason!"

"He did change. It was because I knew he had changed that I—oh, it doesn't matter! Nothing matters now. I dare say he would have put up with me still, as a duty. I should hate to be put up with, as a duty! And he only cared for me because of my face. I knew that all along, though he didn't."

"If that was all, I don't call it 'love.'" Magda spoke with decision, though an odd consciousness came over her that the devotion which she herself had poured upon Patricia might be described in those terms.

"You don't know anything about it. I'm glad we broke off in time. And he has his beloved slums. That is all he really cares for."

"He mayn't have them long. There's some idea of his going to Canada."

Patricia sat suddenly upright, and her pale face grew quite white. "Canada! Why! What for?"

"There's a great want for more men in the North-West—men of his stamp, it is said. The Bishop there has begged for Rob; and Rob is thinking what to do. He likes the idea. Mother is sorry; but she won't try to prevent his going."

"If he does, I suppose you will go too some day, and keep house for him. Your old notion!" There was a hard little laugh; but Magda, occupied with her own thoughts, did not notice it.

"Oh, I don't know," she said uncertainly. "I—perhaps I shall—some day."

"You used to rave about the prospect." Patricia leant back with a sigh.

"Are you tired? Would you like me to go?"

"It doesn't matter. Yes, I'm tired—I always am. And you can go as soon as you like. There's nothing to keep you here. I'm not going to be a bore to people."

Magda kept her seat uncomfortably; and the door opened slowly. "Who is there? Nurse?" Patricia asked.

"It's not nurse," a soft voice said.

"I can't see anybody. Go away, please. It is a mistake. Magda, you needn't wait. I'd rather be alone."

"It's Bee," the voice said. "I did not know Magda was here. The maid told me she was gone, and she said I could not come upstairs. And I have come—against orders. I wanted so much to see you, dear."

Patricia turned sullenly away, hiding her face with both hands. Bee came through the dim room to her side, knelt down, and took Patricia into her arms, holding her in a firm and tender grasp. Nothing more was said. Magda looked on in wonder. Bee remained perfectly still; and in a few seconds Patricia turned a little, so that her face rested against Bee's dress. She was sobbing now, hard convulsive sobs; and at first Bee allowed the passionate distress to have its way. Presently the nurse, coming in and finding them thus, murmured—

"She ought not. It is bad for her eyes."

"Some water, please," Bee said in a smothered voice; and a glass being brought, she held it to Patricia's lips.

"You poor darling!—take some," she said with a sob.

Patricia looked up in utter amazement, to see those brown eyes streaming.

"Bee! You don't really care!" she gasped. "I thought nobody—nobody—would ever care again!"

She flung her arms round Bee and clung to her as if in a despairing appeal for help; and the silence now was broken only by Bee's weeping.

"Don't cry!" Patricia whispered in her turn. "Don't! But—it's such a comfort! It has been—awful! And I mustn't even cry. They say—if I go on as I did—it will make me blind!"

Bee had hardly voice to whisper—"Poor darling!"—once more.

"Hold me tight! Bee—don't go. To think that you—care! I shan't feel so alone now! Hold me—tighter!"

Magda might have moved or spoken, not being tactful, but nurse's hand on her arm insisted on silence. Any sound or stir might break the spell. Presently Patricia's voice was heard again in a note of subdued passion and vehement appeal.

"Bee—Bee—help me! I want help! I don't know what to do. I don't know how to bear it! . . . Bee—I've been so wicked! I've been longing to die! And nobody helped me . . . I know—it was my own fault. I wouldn't see any one—who could. But I—I—couldn't make up my mind. You'll come now—sometimes—come and help me!"

That hand on Magda's arm bade her go. She obeyed without a word, and it did not seem that Patricia even remembered their presence or noticed their departure. Nurse closed the door softly when they were outside.

"If anybody can do that poor thing good—she will!" came with a slight break.

"Nurse, is Patricia getting on? Will she be well in time?"

"She gets on slowly. She would get on faster, if she cared."

"Cared to get well?"

"Yes."

"You mean—she doesn't care because her face is altered? Yes—I heard what she said. But will it get right in time? She has been so lovely. Will she be that again?"

"I'm afraid not, quite. She will improve; and the scar will get fainter. But that contraction of the mouth will be permanent."

"And her eyes—they seem so weak."

"Yes. They may improve a good deal. I hope they will."

Magda was conscious of a lump in her own throat. She went off, oppressed once more with a sense of failure. How was it that she could do nothing for Patricia, while Bee in two minutes had gained a hold, and was giving comfort? And a soft inner voice whispered—

"You were thinking of yourself! Bee thought only of Patricia."

CHAPTER XXXII
AFTER SEVEN MONTHS

ONE sunny August afternoon saw those two charming sisters, the Miss Wryatts of Wratt-Wrothesley, in their favourite "living-room," a square antique hall, with windows of mediæval coloured glass and ancient black-oak panelling, busily discussing with their other sister, Mrs. Major, the never-ending subject of Bee's wedding on the morrow.

Bee was to be married from the old family home—of course! So the Miss Wryatts had said from the first. That she should be married from Virginia Villa was, in their opinion, a thing unthinkable. Not only every spare room in the house—and there were fewer than might have been expected from its size, since a large amount of space went to reception rooms—but also every available bed in the neighbourhood, had been long engaged for the use of relatives and friends.

Miss Wryatt was tall and meekly dignified, with the sweetest and serenest elderly face ever seen; and Miss Emma Wryatt was short and plump and full of life. Both resembled Mrs. Major in a certain air of distinguished composure; and both also resembled her in devotion to and admiration for Bee, only daughter of the one, only niece of the other two.

Everything was by this time in train for the morrow; all arrangements were made; and nothing remained to be done. The staff of old and capable servants knew their duties to perfection in any kind of function; so that really they needed little telling, though Miss Wryatt kept the reins in her own hands, and trusted nothing to chance. She had just been going through with her sisters the list of guests expected that afternoon, naming the bedroom assigned to each, and discussing plans for making the hours slide by with smoothness and satisfaction.

Mr. and Mrs. Royston, Robert, Magda, Merryl, and Frances; Mr. and Mrs. Framley, and Patricia Vincent; Mr. and Mrs. Miles; Ned Fairfax, and two or three others, would arrive before tea; and carriages had already been despatched to meet them at the station. Ivor had come the day before, and was now with Bee in the grounds.

"Dear Bee!" Miss Wryatt said affectionately. "She looks the very picture of happiness! It does one good to see her face. Well, dear—one thing is certain—you will be gaining a son and not losing a daughter. And such a son! I really do not know a finer fellow than Lance—such high principles! All that we could wish for our dear Bee. And there are not many men whom one could count worthy of her."

"Lance is all right," remarked Mrs. Major, who had no trace of sentimentality in her composition.

"Dear fellow! And he will be a fortunate man—with such a sweet wife. My dear, I am glad that poor girl, Patricia Vincent, has made up her mind to be present. Bee was afraid she would not."

"Bee refused to let her off."

"And of course it is wiser—still, one can well understand that it must be a trial to come among all her old friends. Such a lovely creature as she was! And now, I suppose—"

"No, she is not lovely now. To my mind, she is more taking."

"Really, dear!" both sisters exclaimed.

Mrs. Major was turning down a narrow hem, in some useful work for Bee; and she paused to complete it.

"Much more," she said. "Patricia's prettiness was all outside—mere shape and colouring. Something else has come now. There is a great difference—but not all for the worse."

"Ah! Something of spirit-beauty, perhaps," murmured Miss Wryatt.

"You might call it that. A very pleasant look. Her expression in old days spoilt her—it was so self-centred."

"And now—it is otherwise?"

"Yes. The fact is, Bee was the saving of her. No one else could do anything. She seemed hopeless and broken, with no interest left in life; and she would see nobody—not even Mr. Miles."

"That delightful Mr. Miles! We are so pleased that he can come. And Bee did—what, dear?"

A slight moisture might be seen in Mrs. Major's small keen dark eyes.

"What the child always does! She crept somehow into the poor thing's heart, and got hold of her. It is a way that Bee has, you know. She was the first to carry a grain of comfort. And for weeks afterwards, no matter how busy she might be, she went there day after day—even if it were only for ten minutes, and generally it was for at least an hour—till Patricia was ordered abroad in May. Patricia would only go on condition that Bee should be with her for the first month. I have no doubt that Bee's influence has made all the difference to her future."

"Just like dear Bee!" murmured Miss Wryatt. "And—what about Robert Royston?"

"Well, he went to Florence after Bee came away. Mrs. Framley says it was a curious sight to see him falling in love again with Patricia—this time with herself, not with her face. For my part, I believe he has never left off caring for her. They say that after her accident, he looked ghastly. Then he had a breakdown, and the Canada plan had to be put off. In June he was ordered abroad—and he went straight to Florence. If he were not going to Canada, I don't see why that might not come on again."

"Why should not Patricia go too?" Miss Wryatt asked tranquilly.

The expected guests began to arrive and no more could be said.

Bee had indeed devoted much of her time to Patricia, through the late winter and early spring; spending hours in the dim room; putting aside other claims and many pleasures, that she might carry comfort and cheer to the stricken girl, bracing her to endure her trouble with courage, and gently leading her up to higher views of life and its duties, to a truer conception of what is meant by happiness, than Patricia had ever known before. These efforts had been crowned by a month with her on the Continent, and later by constant correspondence, while Patricia remained abroad till after the end of July.

The Roystons were among the first to arrive; and Rob was there when Patricia came. She walked in quietly—not as of old with the air of one who expected everybody to be looking at her, but rather as if shunning observation.

And she was, as Mrs. Major had said, much changed in more ways than one. She was thinner than in past years; and the exquisite colouring had vanished. The scar was already less prominent, yet it could not be overlooked, neither could the contraction at one side of her mouth, which altered her much when she smiled. The eyes were still weak, but very gentle; and her hair had grown into short curls, clustering closely over her head. But there was gain as well as loss; for if the delicate beauty of form and tint had disappeared, a new loveliness had dawned in the calm peace of her expression, the soft light in her eyes, never seen there before. It was, as Miss Wryatt suggested, a touch of spirit-beauty.

Rob had noted it already, in its earlier dawning; and he welcomed now its fuller development with a throb of joy. Few minutes passed before he made his way to her side; and neither he nor she had much attention to spare for others that evening.

Magda looking eagerly for Ned Fairfax, found him soon at her side, where indeed her face beckoned him; and they had a short chat. Her consequent high spirits, somewhat later, were rather dashed, when she saw him deep in talk with Merryl, showing at least as much interest as when he had been with her. An independent observer would have said that he showed much more interest, but Magda was not an independent observer.

She noticed enough, however, to feel a sharp pang of jealousy; and she recognised it as jealousy, which would hardly have been the case a year earlier. Jealousy was so mean, she told herself; it had to be kept down! And she really did try hard.

Soon she saw Merryl making signs to her to join them; and she at once responded, failing to note the disappointment in Fairfax' face. Bestowing herself gaily on a seat close by, she took the lead in a triangular talk, from which Merryl next slipped away, leaving her in possession.

That was delightful! Now she had Ned again all to herself; and there were a hundred things that she wanted to tell him. Merryl never seemed to forget for a moment that Ned was her friend, and that she had—as she would have expressed it—the "first right." That this view of the question made small account of Ned's possible wishes did not occur to her mind.

She began to pour out details of what she had been doing lately, of books she had read and people she had seen. As she rambled on, she awoke to the fact that Ned seemed less interested than he had been before she joined him and Merryl. His eyes and attention both wandered; and his answers went astray. Then, to her utter amazement, on some slight pretext, Ned himself was gone; and in less than a minute she saw him again by Merryl's side.

But she wouldn't be jealous!—She wouldn't!—She wouldn't! So she declared resolutely to herself. Jealousy was so horrid. And Ned had always been kind to the younger ones. Merryl was still only "one of the younger ones!" It was just like dear old Ned to go and amuse her, because she had unselfishly departed—when perhaps he might have liked better to stay and talk with his old chum. He always had been so nice and thoughtful!

CHAPTER XXXIII
THIS GLORIOUS WORLD!

"OH, it is a glorious world!" Magda exclaimed.

At six o'clock she had roused up, wide awake. Breakfast would not be until past nine. To waste two more long hours in bed, waiting for an "early" cup of tea was out of the question. The radiant sunshine, the dew-besprinkled lawn, the great cedar of Lebanon with its flat outspread branches, the distant blue hills, all enticed her. So she sprang up and dressed with speed; and after a short time given to her devotions, she ran softly down the wide staircase, meeting no one by the way, and slipped out at a side-door which she noiselessly unbolted.

Everybody else was resting or asleep, unless perhaps in kitchen regions. Only she out here, with sunshine and dew, birds and insects, enjoying herself. Why did not others do the same? If Ned should come, that would mean perfection!

Even without him it was very near perfection. Such a lovely place— such masses of flowers—such luxuriant trees with branches sweeping the ground—such velvet lawns! She set off at full speed, going from one part to another with ever-increasing delight, till she reached a little "view-spot" on the top of a hillock, where creepers had been trained as a background to a sheltered rustic seat, and a wide extent of country broke upon the sight. She stood drinking it eagerly in; and—

"Oh, it is a glorious world!" escaped her lips.

"Yes, it is," a voice said. To her surprise, there stood Mr. Miles.

"Isn't it lovely?" she exclaimed. "And you are up too! I thought I was the only one. It seems a shame to lie in bed and lose this!"

He pointed out to her some of the main features in the landscapes, naming two or three distant hills. Then they sat down, and somehow— Magda could not afterwards recall what had led to it—she found herself talking about the use she had made of life in this same wonderful world. Mr.

Miles certainly asked a question or two—but she forgot what the questions had been.

"I did mean once to study hard," she said. "When I first left school, I mean. There was plenty of time—then—and Rob said I ought, so as to prepare for future work. But somehow—I never kept it up. And now Pen is married, I am much less free. I'm supposed to do heaps of stupid little fidgets, and I never know when I shall be wanted. And—is it right? Ought I to be always doing such things, instead of finding time for more important work?"

"It seems that when you had the time you did not use it. What sort of 'things' are they? And what is the more important work that you propose to do?"

"I don't know. I've wanted for ever so long to find some work really worth doing. And the little things are—oh, just what Pen used to do. Things for the house; and going out with mother; and writing notes; and tidying up."

"Home duties, in short. Now that you are the eldest daughter, they must come first."

"Merryl could do them!"

"But if they fall to your lot, you must not shirk them. Think! Now is your chance to do all you can to brighten the lives of your father and mother. The opportunity will not last for ever!" Magda gave one startled glance, as if the suggestion had gone home. "And the duties which lie ready to our hands are generally the important ones in life—for us."

"They seem so poor—just frittering away the hours."

"If they are given you to do, it is no question of frittering away. It becomes a matter simply of obedience."

She repeated the word—"Obedience?"

Magda almost thought he had not heard, for he seemed lost in thought. Soon he aroused himself.

"Once upon a time," he said, "a carpet was being woven by hand in an eastern land. Many men were employed upon it; and to each his separate task was given. If he failed—either the whole would be spoilt, or his share would be given to another. To a visitor from far-off, who stood looking as they worked, it appeared a mere jumble of shapeless figures and ill-assorted colours, with no definite plan, not worth the trouble expended on it. But long after, when that same traveller saw the carpet in its completed state, he found it to be a thing of wonderful richness and beauty, of fine design and splendid colouring. For he saw it then on its right side—whereas he had seen it before on its wrong side. And those men, as they worked, could see little beyond the small portion under their own eyes. They could not judge of the effect of the whole, till the day when it should be finished."

Silence again; and Magda said, "You mean—?"

"A world-wide carpet is being woven through the ages. And only the Divine Master-Mind, having designed its pattern, can foresee what it will be like in the end. Many, many, are at work upon it. One little square inch of the weaving is given to me as my life-task, and another little square inch is given to you. Neither of us can see much beyond our own tiny share. What we have to do may seem to us out of harmony with the rest, or not worth the trouble of doing. Sometimes our whole work looks like failure. But we cannot judge. It is impossible for us in this life to see which task is the more important—still less, to decide which is the better done. We only know that it is in the faithful working out of our own appointed task, great or small— in doing it for our dear Master and by His help—that we may hope to win by-and-by His loving—'Well done!'"

"Only it's so awfully difficult to find out what one really has to do."

"Granted, in certain cases, such a difficulty! There is always the promise that he who wills to do God's Will, shall be shown that Will. He may have to wait; but in time it will be made clear."

"And till then—?"

"Till then—there are always the little homely duties ready to hand; small kindnesses, small self-denials. The one thing that we are never called to is—careless drifting. Never despise the tiniest deed which may add a feather's weight to anybody's happiness; or which may aid in the right shaping of our own characters."

"I suppose one ought to think about that."

"Certainly. We are put into this earthly school—this glorious world, Magda!—for the express purpose that our characters may be formed for the great Future. And while we are here, our God graciously uses us, if we are willing, to do some of His work. The more fully we submit to His training, and the more we strive with His help to make ourselves ready, the more likely it is that, at some crucial moment, He will find in us just what He needs."

Magda thought of her recent lost opportunity. Was Mr. Miles thinking of it too?

"And—if we fail—"

"Then we are losers. One thing is certain—that failure after failure in ordinary temptations must lead to failure when extraordinary temptations come. Each hour that we live helps to shape future hours."

"But I suppose—other chances do come, in time."

"Yes, my child. Don't be discouraged by past failures. Go on in hope and courage!" Magda glanced up into the kind face. "If Christ our dear Lord is your Master and Friend, there's no need to despond. Trust in Him more fully—lean upon Him more utterly—and that will lead to victory. That alone can. Without Him we are powerless."

"Is everybody called to—something particular?" Magda asked after a pause.

"Yes. God has need of us all—each for some particular task. We have each to live our lives, to do our work. And life is short; it comes only once. There are hundreds of people, kind-hearted well-meaning people, who let the years slide by, just pleasing themselves, and doing practically nothing for God. Don't be betrayed into that. Home duties come first, and ought to come first. But there are great needs, all over the world, for workers; and it is not necessary that three or four girls should give themselves to that which one could easily do alone. The chorus of outside calls must also be heard."

"And if—if one should want to go—and if—one's father should say No?"

"Then just put it all into the Hands of God and wait for His guidance. Wait!—But be ready to act, the moment the way becomes clear. And meanwhile, do your very best to make ready for an opening when it comes. Time given to preparation is never wasted."

Magda was musing gravely. It might be, in time, though Pen was married, that Merryl would suffice for the home needs, and that she herself would be free to go elsewhere.

Time was getting on; and Mr. Miles stood up. As they turned towards the house, he repeated aloud—

"'Birds by being glad their Maker bless,
    By simply shining, Sun and Star;

And we whose law is Love, serve less
By what we do than what we are.'"

"Not that the 'doing' is not needful; but that, to be, is what matters above all. Simple shining is often a great deal harder than active work. Still—there the work is, needing to be done; and it must not be neglected."

In the front flower-garden they came across two other early risers; Patricia and Robert. Both were smiling. Rob touched Magda's arm.

"I want your congratulations," he said.

She looked puzzled. "What for?"

"Patricia will go to Canada with me!"

"Oh, Rob! I am glad!" cried Magda. She was honestly glad, honestly delighted, both for him and for Patricia. But this involved no "opportunity," no contest with her own desires. Life with Rob had ceased to be the one thing wanted. She did not now even wish to keep house for him, since that would involve leaving England. A more absorbing attraction existed here.

Another and a very real test awaited her not far ahead. And, as often happens, it was to come from a quarter least expected.

Was she by this time better fitted to meet it? She had learnt to know herself more; she had found her own weakness; she had begun to look upward for help in the battle. Victory in small skirmishes of late might make all the difference in her next hard fight.

CHAPTER XXXIV
ONCE MORE TO THE TEST

WITHOUT a single hitch the wedding went off.

All agreed that Bee, in bridal white, with a veil of old and exquisite point-lace, presented by the Miss Wryatts, looked her sweetest; and that her handsome bridegroom was worthy of her. And though it might not be possible to find happier faces than those two, another pair could be seen, not far-off, which at least equalled them in sunshine—the faces of Patricia and Rob, that very morning re-engaged.

The little church was full to overflowing. Patricia had begged off being one of the bridesmaids, who were much admired in their graceful white and mauve. Of the six, Magda and Merryl were accounted the best looking; and indeed more than one observer was heard to remark that Merryl had grown quite pretty. Ned said nothing, but he gazed the more! And almost the only person present who did not notice his absorption in Merryl was unobservant Magda. Whether Merryl was conscious of it might be questioned. She looked serene as usual, but kept her eyes unwontedly cast down.

Perhaps her serenity was not quite as usual. For after the wedding service, still early in the afternoon, when house and garden were thronged with guests, and kisses and congratulations and cake-cutting had been gone through, and Bee was upstairs, changing her dress, Magda came across Merryl in a quiet corner—actually with tears in her eyes!

"Why, Merryl!" she said in amazement.

But Merryl put her off so lightly, that she fancied she must have been mistaken.

And then, in the excitement of watching for Bee's re-appearance in travelling-dress, ready for departure, she forgot all about it.

The send-off was enthusiastic; and Bee seemed all smiles, except at the moment when she said good-bye to her mother; while Ivor positively radiated gladness and pride in his new possession. Amid a shower of rice and a hurricane of cheers, the carriage drove away. After which came a pause, and a general sense of flatness.

Local guests disappeared gradually; but few departures from the house would take place before the morrow, since the Miss Wryatts were giving a large dinner-party that evening. The hours between had to be got through somehow—no difficult matter with at least two of the party.

Rob and Patricia promptly vanished, not to be seen again till nearly dinner-time. Mrs. Major was invisible. Mrs. Royston and other ladies went to their rooms to rest. Some of the more active individuals changed to everyday dresses, and started for a ramble.

Magda, watching these departures, knew that Ned was not among them. Where he might be she could not guess; but she was counting on his society that afternoon. It seemed only natural; she had seen so little of him thus far.

After waiting about for a while she went into the garden, hoping that he might turn up. Nor did she hope in vain. Suddenly, there he was—by her side.

"I want a chat with you, Magda. Free?"

"Of course I am. I should like nothing better," she said joyously. "Somehow I rather fancied you'd come, Ned. I've no end of things to say to you."

"All right. This way," and he turned towards a little shrubby avenue, leading from the flower-garden. "It will be quiet."

"We always did like tête-à-tête rambles, didn't we?" She felt perfectly happy. Ned to herself was all she wanted. Dear old Ned! He was just the same as ever.

"Did we?" absently. "I don't remember."

"Why—of course we did. It wasn't half so much fun if there was a third person."

"One doesn't always want a third person, certainly!" Ned spoke with feeling.

"That's just what I meant."

"Was it?" questioned Ned internally. "Well—" he said aloud. "You wanted to talk about something."

"But you had something to say first."

"Place aux dames! Mine must wait. Presently I'll ask you to do something for me. Yours shall be the first innings."

Nothing loth, Magda started off with one of her accustomed outpourings. She had, as she said, "no end" of things to enlarge upon— books she had read, people she had seen, things she had done, plans she meant to carry out. She was always sure of Ned's interest and sympathy; and it never occurred to her that he might grow tired of listening. But, as she flowed on, it dawned upon her that she had not his undivided attention. He twice said "No," when he ought to have said "Yes;" and when she put a leading question as to a certain subject, which she had fully explained, his silence spoke for itself.

"Didn't you hear?"

"I'm most awfully sorry!—No, I'm afraid—not quite all."

"You were thinking of something else!"

"Well, perhaps—just for a minute," admitted Ned, with an air of penitence.

Magda drew a long breath; for this was rather hard. So unlike Ned!

"I think you had better have your say first," she suggested, with great magnanimity. "I'll tell you the rest of mine presently—when you've got yours off your mind."

It flashed across her, suddenly and brilliantly—what if he wanted to ask her to marry him? True, his ordinary manner was not that of the typical lover. But this might only be because they were so entirely at ease in their intercourse. His present absence of mind and evident embarrassment had a suspicious look; and it might be so! He might wish it! The notion had never before presented itself to her imagination in so luminous a light; though at the same instant she realised that she had thought of it, had pictured it, had hoped for it, not on the upper surface of her mind, but in some shady half-acknowledged corner. And if he did—if it should mean this! She would have no doubt what answer to give. There was nobody like Ned—no, not in all the world.

Her heart beat fast, and her colour heightened. "Go on," she said carelessly. "Tell me what you want."

Ned was almost nervous. He said nothing, but walked slowly, poking his stick into the ground at regular intervals, as if marking out an embroidery pattern.

"Perhaps," and she paused, "you are in need of a pair of bedroom slippers. Shall I make them?"

"I'm in earnest. Don't talk bosh."

"No, I won't. I'll be sober. What is it, Ned? You needn't mind saying out what you would like. We're such old chums."

"Just so," assented Ned. "That's what I've been feeling—that I might ask your help, and that you wouldn't mind—you'd be sure to understand."

It did not sound precisely like the preliminary to an offer of marriage; but she replied cheerfully—

"Of course I shall. We always did understand one another—even in the days when I wore short frocks, and when you—"

Ned was in no mood for a plunge into schoolboy reminiscences.

"Yes, yes—that's all right," he said hastily.

"Well, you may as well tell me what it is that I've got to do for you."

Ned hesitated still. "You see," he at length said, "you see—I've wanted it so long! And the longer I wait, the more I'm set on it. That's the way one does, I suppose. And the time has come now when I needn't put off any longer."

Magda's hopes again went up. "Yes—I see!" She vaguely agreed.

"And there seems no possibility of getting hold—" one or two words were murmured inaudibly. "Always something in the way—preventing—"

"Why, Ned!" she all but exclaimed. "You haven't tried!" Happily she checked the words.

"It seems no use trying," he went on, with a touch of dejection. "I cannot get hold of her or make her understand. She slips away as soon as I appear on the scene—or at least, as soon as—" He left the sentence unfinished, and Magda could supply the missing words. "You must have noticed! And I thought I would have it out with you, and ask your help. You can put things right for me."

Once launched, he found it easy to proceed; and he did not observe her silence, nor the averted face.

"I believe I have had it in my mind from the first moment that I saw her again—you know! When I met her in the garden, on my way to find you. I believe I went in, over head and ears, there and then. She is the sort of sunny-tempered darling that does take hold of a man! But she was so young, I didn't venture to say anything. It was wiser to wait. However—I spoke to your father and mother a few weeks ago, when I was down in Burwood, and they gave their consent. The difficulty now is to get hold of Merryl. I seem to have no chance. You see—"

He paused again and had no response. Perhaps he hardly expected one yet, as he had not finished. Magda was in the thick of a fierce conflict which rendered her voiceless.

So Ned was not in love with her! He did not want her! He was in love with another—and that other was Merryl. Merryl—of all people! The younger sister—the quiet little useful nonentity—Merryl, who was not clever, nor charming, nor really good-looking—Merryl, who had no conversational gifts, no particular talents or powers—Merryl who was so far inferior intellectually to Magda herself! Yet here was Ned Fairfax, her friend!—professing himself to be deep in love with Merryl. Not only so; but calmly asking her to help forward his suit! A passion of wrath had possession of Magda—wrath towards Merryl, and wrath towards Ned.

"You see," he went on, "she seems to have got it into her head that she is an intruder if you and I are together. And that, of course, is absurd. I want her to understand."

"You want me to make love to Merryl for you!" Magda spoke with a curt laugh.

"Well, no—not exactly." Ned took this as a joke—a rather ill-timed joke in his opinion—but he echoed her laugh good-naturedly. "What I want you to do is to make her understand that she is not in the way—that she never can be in the way—that it is her dear little self that I want—always!"

"That, in fact, I'm the person in the way—not Merryl!"

Ned wondered for a moment—was Magda in one of her "moods"?

"If you must take it in that way, I shall be sorry that I said anything. I thought I might venture."

"Of course you might!" Magda was alarmed, lest he should discover too much. "Go on—you had more to say."

Ned obeyed, and did go on. He went through the whole again, with amplifications, explaining more fluently, and enlarging in lover-like style upon Merryl's unselfishness, and the spell which her face had laid upon him—that face of placid content, which would be a never-ending delight to the man who should be so fortunate as to win her for his own. For once, it was Ned who poured out, and Magda who listened.

Or at least, who seemed to listen. She heard only part, for she was fighting a very hard battle. The same hour which had brought knowledge of his love for another, had brought also knowledge of what he had grown to be to herself. And now, she must lose him—had lost him. Whether he did or did not marry Merryl, he did not want her. She would not even be his chum any longer. When Merryl should be his wife, how could she any more confide in him, as she had been wont? How tell him her thoughts, her aims, her troubles? It was very very hard!

Then a gentle voice within, a voice to which she was learning to give attention, said—

"Another opportunity!"

Was it that? Was this the next opportunity, which she had known must some day come? Not like the one in which she had so signally failed; for here lay no possibilities of grand action in the eyes of men, or of praise and admiration to follow. No one would know; no one might know. She had to keep to herself all that it meant; had to hide from Ned all she might feel or suffer. Yet the test was no less severe, the chance for self-sacrifice no less genuine, than last time. Perhaps, even more severe, even more genuine, while hidden from those around.

And the question was—would she be beaten anew? She had been so often defeated in the past. Would she refuse to do what Ned asked? It was a request not easy to face. She was to help him to gain his heart's desire; to try to persuade Merryl; to efface herself; to retreat willingly into the background, that he might have her younger sister!

She could not escape from the trouble itself. It had to be endured. But was it to be a sorrow taken sullenly and despairingly, taken only because it could not be avoided? Or should it be a test met bravely, an unselfish action embraced, a victory won in the face of odds? Was she going to think only of herself, and of what she had lost? Or would she do her utmost for the happiness of her sister and her friend?

The choice had to be made quickly. Ned was speaking still; but he would soon pause, and then she must say something. What should she—what could she say? And with the sense of helplessness, a passionate appeal went up for help; such an appeal, such a prayer, as never can be made in vain. A sudden calm came.

The pause occurred; and she heard herself saying—

"I'll do what I can for you."

"If you could just make her understand that it is all a mistake—that she never can be in the way—in anybody's way."

"Why don't you speak out yourself?"

"I'm afraid to risk it too soon. I did try a word or two this afternoon; and she simply would not listen. She seems to think it is disloyal to you. I shall be in Burwood now for a fortnight; and I want a clear field. You see?"

Magda did see. "I'll do my best," she repeated.

They were close to a little summer-house. Ned halted.

"I don't want to lose to-day," he said. "Magda—could you—wait here, and let me send her to you? I know where she is."

"Yes. And then you can come for her."

"Thanks—a thousand times. You are a friend worth having."

He sped away; and Magda sat down, gazing into the blue distance with eyes that saw little. It was hard! But the calm overshadowed her still; and she knew that in this fight at least she had come off victor; not in her own strength.

She found herself facing steadily the fact that, for the present, her life was clearly marked out. She would be the one efficient home-daughter. Her parents in their advancing years would depend mainly upon her for cheer and sunshine. The quiet daily round would be her portion. And if she were called to this—if this were the Will of her Master!—What mattered its insignificance, its dulness, or even her own loneliness?

"I've got to be brave about it—that's all!" she murmured. "I've just got to do it; and to do it well! Nothing grand about it. A plain little square of weaving! Sort of ground-work to the pattern, perhaps," and she laughed softly. "Not pretty, but useful. Well, I've had other chances, and I've missed them. I'll try hard now, with this. Life is worth living; when one sees what it means!"

Sooner than she would have thought possible, Merryl came in, looking puzzled.

"You want me!" she said.

"Come and sit down here. I've something to say. Merryl, what makes you run away from Ned as you do? Especially the moment I turn up!"

Merryl flushed and seemed embarrassed. "Has he told you—about this afternoon?"

"What happened?"

"Oh, nothing much. Only, he said something—I didn't quite understand. And I wouldn't let him go on. It didn't seem fair; and I told him so. He has always been your friend."

"You don't suppose I want to shut him up in a box for my own use! Was it that you were crying about?"

"I wasn't crying—really. Only—I was afraid I had hurt him—and I couldn't bear—"

"Don't cry now. There's no need. You like Ned?"

"Why—everybody likes him."

"Well, you've got to get it into your head that there is no question of unfairness, or of Ned belonging to me. He is free to choose for himself. And if he chooses to go after you, don't run away. Unless you really want to drive him off, and to make him miserable. Do you?"

Merryl shook her head.

"Then it is all right. Don't you suppose I want my old friend to be happy? So when he comes back in a few minutes—you had better go with him."

"Magda, you are a dear!" murmured Merryl, clinging to her.